The Fall

and

the Lift of Love

Debby L Wynkoop

A father of the fatherless,
and a judge of the widows,
is God in his holy habitation.
God setteth the solitary in families:
he bringeth out those which are bound with chains:
but the rebellious dwell in a dry land.
Psalm 68:5-6

ISBN: 978-1-734-7755-8-7
LLCN: 2023922128

DEDICATION

In memory of
Bertie Lee and Vera Lorene,
grandmother and mother.
Your stories, music, ways,
and manner of speech,
I continue to treasure.
Love always.

ACKNOWLEDGMENTS

This story was birthed with a writing prompt given by our teacher, Dave Larsen, one month before our class was cancelled due to the Covid Pandemic. While Dave would not live to see the completion of this story, I am forever grateful for that moment in time and the role he played.

I am thankful for the many writing buddies who have read snippets and listened to portions—who asked questions, discussed ideas, and encouraged me all along the way. I appreciate The Idaho Creative Authors' Network, whose good work in the author community has been a constant help.

Years ago, I recorded my grandmother and mother in conversation. That old cassette tape was invaluable in reminding me how those East Texan gals spoke.

To my husband, Dave Johnson—thank you for understanding the artistic process and for making the space in our lives for me to pursue writing.

CONTENTS

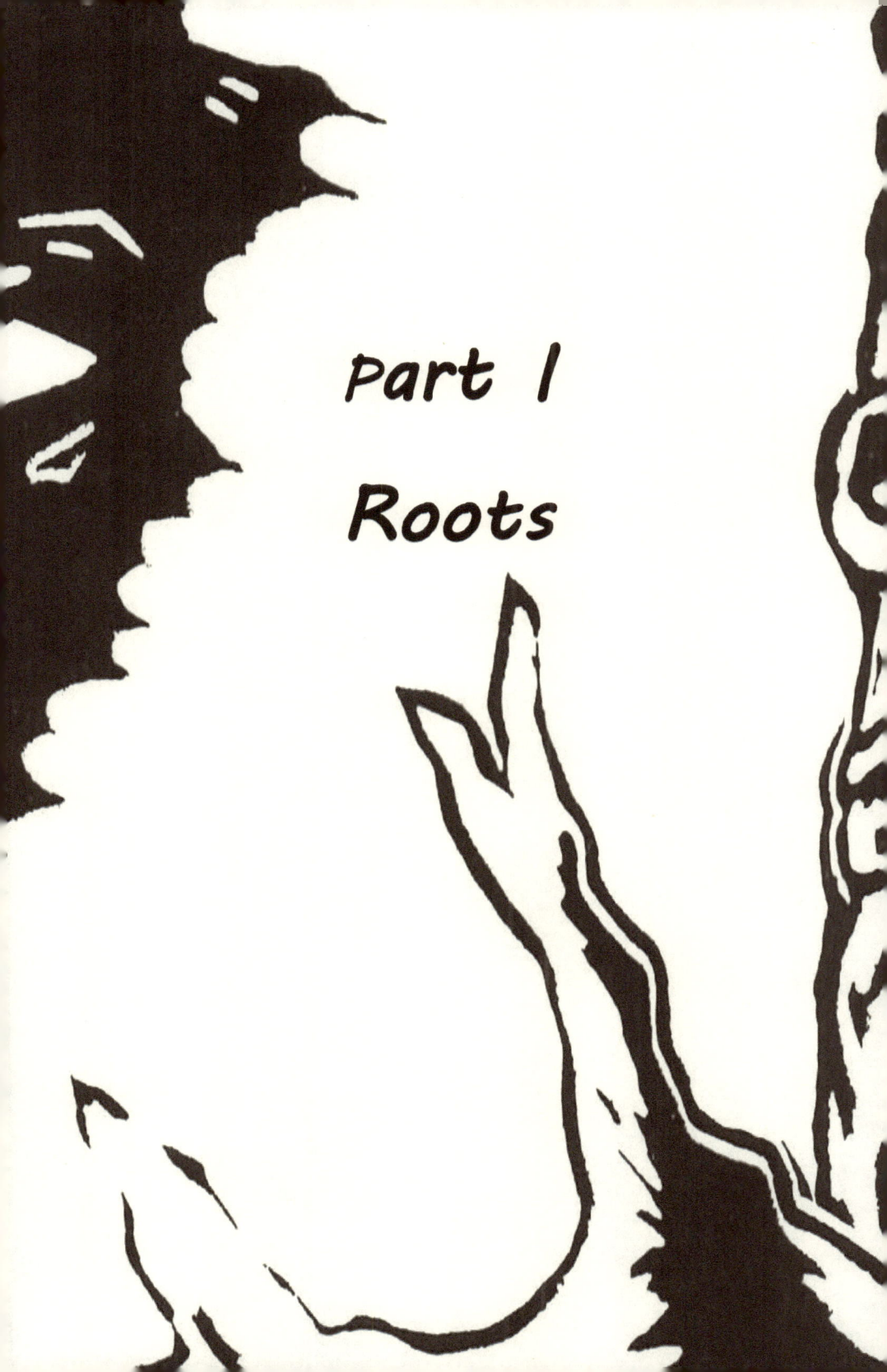

Part 1

Roots

Debby L Wynkoop

CHAPTER ONE

The day the tree fell was especially humid. It crashed through the undergrowth and landed with a thud. The old vine that made its twisted existence around Big Tree's body shattered. The water's edge splashed upon impact, washing green scum onto the bank. The frogs stopped their songs.

Betty Jo also stopped. Startled, she looked down the path, mud rising between her toes. Tentatively she moved again along the trail, her mind racing with explanations as to what had just occurred.

She had to get home with the basket of crawdads in time to get them boiled for supper. She didn't want Papa hungry. Hungry made him awful mean.

The bend in the trail led her to the river. Big Tree lay prone across the path, its uppermost branches extending into the water. Her eyes went upward with realization. The sky was missing its giant companion.

Betty Jo knew the tragedy of the fallen. She wished for a moment to grieve, but she could not linger. Too big to go over, she would fight the brush and go around the trunk.

Watch out for water moccasins, she warned herself.

She tried to find patches of sparseness to walk through. Avoiding chigger bites was a habit, but it was taking too long. She gave up and began bushwhacking a more direct route. When she reached the giant hole of upturned roots and mud, she paused. Nothing about that scene seemed right.

Hurrying on through the thick brush she intersected with the trail again. Tiny dribbles of red trickled down her legs and arms. She ran toward home, allowing splatters of mud to coat the bites and cuts.

She arrived at the clearing just before the county road, stopping to take some deep breaths. *Why you out in the heat of day?* She heard the scolding in her head. Sometimes she just couldn't help but get lost in her world of imaginings. Adjusting the basket and tightening the lid, she sprinted the rest of the way; her toughened feet gliding over the gravel.

Relieved that Papa's Model T was not parked out front, Betty Jo ran to stir up the coals of the cook fire. Once she had continuous flame, she hurried to the pump. Setting the bucket in the trough, she filled it and used what splattered to rinse her arms and legs. With the water

3

poured into the cast iron kettle, Betty Jo began to relax. If Papa came straight home from the oil fields, she was sure she would be ready. Of course, he sometimes made a stop before coming home. If he did that, then supper wouldn't matter anyway.

*****

Henri looked down at his hands. The stain of black never went away, no matter how much he scrubbed. At least the sticky was mostly gone. He hated when the steering wheel got gummy. He started up the Ford and headed on his way. Supper would satisfy. If he hurried, maybe this time he could make it home.

It had been a long hot day, but he didn't mind so much. Physical discomfort was his medicine, and the end of the work week ushered in gratification. Fresh bills were in his pocket.

He made good time traveling the state highway. The truck was running well, and he took pleasure in the movement of air through the cab. He approached Joaquin and slowed down. He didn't want to garner the attention of the sheriff should he be lurking in the east side of the county. The slow, however, gave him too much time to think.

He came to the Thorpe's farm and the turn-off to home, but the truck continued straight ahead. Half a mile before the bridge crossing into Louisiana, he looked in the rear-view mirror. No traffic coming or going. His hands tightened on the wheel as his resolve dissipated.

You had to be looking for it to know it was there. They did a real good job of tucking it away. Sighing, he checked again for any signs of unwelcomed eyes, then made the left turn. He drove back into the woods, avoiding the bigger puddles. There were tire tracks in the mud. Tonight, he wouldn't be the first person there. The two-track road tapered off and he parked. He got out of the truck and walked a faint trail to the shack. Scraping his boots off on the edge of the single step, he reached for the rusty handle and opened the door.

God help me, he thought.

*****

The cicadas had turned their music-making over to the katydids and crickets. Betty Jo knew by evenfall that she was in for a lonesome night. She had eaten as many crawdads as she could to take up time, but she could no longer avoid the decision. Should she stay home or go to Aunt Beu's? If she stayed and Papa showed up, it would likely be unpleasant. If she went to Great Aunt Beulah's, she'd surely pay the price tomorrow. *Safety now, or peace later?*

She stood in front of the house and closed her eyes for a moment. Hearing nothing but evening sounds, she walked up the porch steps, opened the screen door and entered the plank house. The slap of the door reverberated with unsettling familiarity. She navigated through the dark, crossing the crude wood floor to the tiny room in the back corner. Opening the cypress trunk, she reached under the old quilt and pulled out the autoharp. She returned to the porch and sat on the three-legged stool.

Cradling the instrument in her lap, she imagined her mother's face. Sometimes she would sneak a peek at the old photograph in Papa's chest of drawers, but somehow the autoharp provided a better picture. Long ago, Betty Jo had decided upon the sound of Mama's voice. Now she strummed and sang a duet with the mother she never met.

> *Roses love sunshine,*
> *violets love dew,*
> *Angels in heaven know I love you.*

Clarity came. She would stay home and hope that music would bring calm.

"That sure is pretty," a voice called from the road, piercing Betty Jo's solitude. "I know it's late, but I was wondering if you all could spare some food."

Alarmed that she could not recognize the voice nor the manner of speaking, she strained through the shadows to make out a man-shape. It eased her mind to see that the shape did not move.

"I was on my way to Logansport, but the day got away from me. My name is Philip," he continued.

Philip. Only one name. Certainly not of Granma's kin. Yet somehow knowing the name brought light to the shadows. "We ain't got much, but I'll carry a bit out."

Betty Jo carefully set the autoharp down. She took time to light the lantern and then went to work transferring the remaining crawdads into a kitchen bucket. She stepped off the porch, lantern in one hand and bucket in the other. She walked across the yard to where the manfolk stood on the side of the road, making sure to hold the lantern out in front and keep her distance.

He was taller than Papa and he stood straight. His shirt and trousers were store bought. A carpet bag sat on the ground near his feet. She had heard stories of this kind before. *Yankee*, she thought.

"Here's a few crawdads," she said, "to help on yer way."

She set the bucket down and backed up a couple of steps. It dawned on her that a Yankee might not know what to do with them, but Philip reached down into the bucket and stacked them comfortably in his large hand.

"Thank you, kindly," he said looking at her directly. She was surprised to see a smooth face unmarred by trouble.

A wave of shame washed over her. What must this man think, her in the dirty bib overalls cut off at the knees and all? She wondered what her hair looked like after the sweat of the July day.

"Help yerself to the pump before y'all go." Betty Jo pointed in its direction. She knew that hospitality required more, so she added, "Down this road a ways is a farmhouse. Mister and Miz Thorpe kin be of help."

"Thank you," he said again with a nod.

Betty Jo returned to the porch, setting the bucket down quietly. She held the lantern and waited, a silent battle on her insides. She hoped the Yankee would be on his way and not linger to eat while on their property. Yet she really didn't want him to leave. It would be so nice to keep company on the porch. But she knew it could not be. She understood propriety.

Mr. Philip made his way to the pump, just out of view. The handle squeaked and the water flowed. Then all was quiet, except the katydids and the crickets—and the sound of a strummed autoharp.

*****

Henri woke up with the light of the morning. His mouth felt like it was full of cotton balls. He raised his head from off his arms to find that he was pressed against the steering wheel of his truck. Blinking his eyes, he fought to focus, but the fuzziness was in more than just his eyes. Mud was splattered on the windshield—the broken windshield.

Slowly he turned his head, trying to orient himself. Green was all he could see—scrubby branches, leaves and moss. Bolts of pain shot through his temples, and his head dropped back onto his arms. Nausea came with the swaying motion of the truck. Closing his eyes, he sunk away, losing the fight to generate conscious thought.

*****

The morning light made its way through the window in the little room at the back of the house. Betty Jo rolled over onto her side and watched the dust motes dance in the sunlight. What would it be like to float around and not fall? The night had pinned her down in depths of uncertainty. Papa had not come home.

Now with the awakening sun, she would wait no more. Still in yesterday's t-shirt and overalls, she sat up and made the trip to the privy. She tidied the inside of the house and then grabbed the wash bucket and headed out to the pump. Returning to the house, she bathed and fixed her dark brown hair with Granma's silver comb. She would wear the old flour sack dress, even though the bodice had become a bit tight. She would not waste the use of shoes on this summer day.

Shutting the front door, she looked around the property. Satisfied that everything was in order, she took off walking the county road. Her eyes strained through the morning light, fixed ahead. She listened intently. If she heard the truck, she would hide in the woods until it passed. With resentment fully steeped, she no longer cared to see Papa.

She turned the final bend before the cotton field. The foursquare two-story farmhouse, dressed in yellow, stood as an oasis. She hurried the rest of the way, stopping to rinse her feet at the pump before running up the porch steps. She wiped her feet on the rug and then opened the screen door.

"Aunt Beu!" Betty Jo called as she walked across the front room to the kitchen. She did not need a response. She knew where to find her.

Aunt Beulah looked up from the kitchen sink. "Well, mornin', Sugar." She shook the water off her hands, dried them with a towel, then placed a quick kiss on the cheek before enveloping Betty Jo in a massive hug. "Where's yer grandpa?" she inquired after pulling away.

"Papa didn't come home," Betty Jo answered.

Aunt Beulah sighed. "Oh, goodness gracious. Probably sleepin' it off somewhere. I told y'all to come up to the house next time it happened. No sense y'all bein' alone at night."

"He be mad if I were gone," Betty Jo whispered as if trying to keep a secret.

"Oh, Sugar, he just plain be mad." Beulah turned back to scrubbing the pot. "So, y'all were home alone when the Yankee come by?" Beulah chided as she asked.

"Yes, ma'am." Betty Jo cast her eyes to the floor. No matter where she was, shame was always nearby.

"Well, y'all done right sendin' 'im on to us." Beulah took a heavy breath. "He left after an early breakfast. Said he come up from south and was on his way to Logansport. By the 'scenic route,' he said. Said he would be helpin' out the deacon at that upstart church. Handsome young fella." Then Beulah added, "Oh goodness, listen to me carry on. You'd think we never had passers-by."

Finished at the sink, Beulah turned to face Betty Jo. "Let's get y'all a bite to eat. Then we'll go out to the garden. If yer papa comes a lookin', I'll say I fetched y'all to work fer the day."

Betty Jo stayed in her Aunt Beulah's shadow for most of the morning. As they worked, the elder gave explanations and commands with hoe in hand. The younger stooped to the ground to do tasks that her great aunt's self-proclaimed raggety bones no longer allowed.

Uncle Jack Lee and the hired man were in the barn tinkering with something. She knew her uncle wouldn't make an appearance until noon meal. The lull of field activity in midsummer was the time to set things in order. Cotton harvest was coming.

Betty Jo cut back a patch of clover that had invaded the vegetable garden. When Aunt Beu went inside to prepare the noon meal, she promised to get the rest of the rows ready for second planting.

Alone in the garden, her mind began to drift. She couldn't for the life of her understand why Papa was so bitter against Granma's sister. Beulah lived in a real nice house, and her husband had good cotton fields. They were always willing to help the kinfolk and the stranger. Was Papa jealous? Or was it just because these weren't his people? She would like to ask him, but it would get her face slapped. Beulah and Jack Lee had been especially kind to her since Granma passed. Maybe she could figure a way to talk to them about it without being disrespectful.

Metal clanging rang through the air. "Come 'n' git it!" Beulah hollered from the back porch. In one hand she held a plate of food. The hired man emerged from the barn, took the plate with a nod of thanks, and retreated to a patch of shade.

Betty Jo and Uncle Jack met up at the water pump.

"Lookie who's here. Glad to see y'all, Betty Jo." Uncle Jack smiled and took the handle to pump. "Been here a while?"

"All mornin'. Got the rows done for the new plantin'." Betty Jo grabbed the lye soap and immersed her hands in the metal trough to begin scrubbing.

"Yer granpa not come home?" he asked.

"No, sir," she replied, embarrassed.

"That rascal." Jack Lee shook his head. "Stay with us 'til he come to fetch y'all."

With the residue of morning chores washed away, they walked toward the back porch.

"Uncle Jack, why is Papa mad?" Betty Jo asked.

Jack Lee stopped with the abrupt question. He looked at his wife's great niece. Betty Jo also stopped. "Not my place to say. Sometime, when it's the right time, ask yer Aunt Beulah . . . but mind yer manners when y'all do."

The sound of a car turning onto the gravel drive drew their attention. They stood together warily watching as it pulled up to the house and stopped. The driver got out and slammed the door shut.

"Afternoon, Sheriff," Jack greeted formally.

"Jack Lee," he acknowledged with a tip of his hat. He did not look Betty Jo's direction. With discomfort she lowered her eyes and edged back.

"A report come in of a vehicle run-off. It was seen down the river bank near the bridge. Deputy's on another call, so I come over. Hope y'all might ride with me."

"Yes, sir," Jack answered. "Lemme get out of these greasy overalls and I'll be right with y'all. Help yerself to the pump."

Jack Lee and Betty Jo turned to walk to the back porch. Betty Jo felt eyes boring into her back. She quickened her steps until she passed through the threshold into the safety of Beulah's kitchen.

"Y'all goin' with that man?" Beulah questioned incredulously.

"He's the sheriff, and he asked fer help." Jack turned and placed a hand on each of her shoulders.

Looking into his eyes, Beulah replied, "Well mebbe some of yer goodness will rub off on 'im." She pulled away to hand him cheese sandwiches wrapped in a kerchief. "There's an extry one fer James Roy."

"Yer a good woman, Beulah May," Jack said and then placed a kiss on her cheek.

"Y'all take care," she called as he pushed the screen door out of the way.

Betty Jo stood quietly watching the exchange. She wondered if what she saw was how married people were supposed to be.

The screen door slammed. Beulah motioned to Betty Jo to sit down at the kitchen table. "Just you 'n' me, Sugar."

*****

As clearly as if she were right in front of him, Henri could see his daughter standing on the horizon. The sky was opaque above her bright image. The green of the woods was all around. He focused his mind upon her face. At first, she moved slowly toward him, but then her pace crescendoed until it became a run. Soon she would be where she belonged.

Inexplicably, she stopped and turned her head to the right. She stood as if in a trance. Approaching her from the shadows was a dark-headed man. His face chiseled with menace. His eyes narrow like beads. He motioned for her to join him, but she did not move. Angry, he bent down and scooped up two fistfuls of mud. He threw them, soiling her beautiful white dress. The force of impact rocked her body and into her arms appeared a bundle covered in red.

Terror replaced her blank expression. She ran toward her father once again. Just before she was near enough to jump into his outstretched arms, she threw him the bundle. He looked down, alarmed at the softness and warmth inside.

He heard a thunderous sound and the earth beneath him shook. Steadying himself, he lifted his gaze to a crevasse opening in the ground between them. He called out, but there was nothing he could do to save her. She stepped into space and disappeared from view.

His beautiful daughter, Charlene, was gone forever.

Henri awakened, drenched in sweat. It was the same dream that had haunted him for 15 years. This time, though, he sensed that he was the one in danger of falling.

*****

The heat began its afternoon swell. Betty Jo picked out a *Life* magazine from the rack and leaned back into Uncle Jack's chair. She studied the picture on the cover. A bald-headed man in fancy clothes was dumping clubs out of a big bag. She smiled to see a mouse jumping through the air to make its escape. It must have surprised the old man because his cigarette fell out of his wide-open mouth. While she knew nothing about the sport of golf, she did know a lot about mice. Betty Jo smiled as she made up a story to match what she saw. She was good at reading pictures. Opening the cover, she thumbed through the pages. She picked out a few words here and there but wondered what they had to say.

Aunt Beulah sat in the chair next to her, crocheting. As her hands kept busy, she hummed, calm and steady-like.

Betty Jo thought it was the right time. "Aunt Beu?"

Beulah's hum stopped. "Yes, Sugar?"

"Why is Papa just plain mad?" After considering all afternoon if she'd know the right time, the words were out. Relief came—like finally convincing herself to let go of the rope swing and jump into the swimming hole.

Beulah's hands stopped. Resting them in her lap, she turned to look Betty Jo in the eyes. "How many years are y'all, Betty Jo?" she asked.

"Fifteen, ma'am." Betty Jo's hands began to fidget.

"My goodness gracious. Where does the time go? Y'all're 'most grown now." Beulah set her handcraft on the end table and stood up. She walked across the room and down the hallway.

Betty Jo was uncertain whether or not to follow. Being as Aunt Beu gave no instructions, she decided to sit still. Waiting was something she knew well to do. After a while, Beulah returned holding a letter. Sitting down, she pulled the pages out of the envelope. They were yellowed and crinkled.

"This letter was yer granma's. Our daddy, yer Great Grandpa Morris, wrote it many years ago. Leona threw it to the side after she read it. It made her so angry. While it was none of my bus'ness, somethin' told me I should rescue the letter and keep it. I thought 'bout throwin' it away—water under the bridge and all—but I just never could."

Beulah hesitated and gazed across the room before finishing. "Yer papa has faced many a hardship in life. They left 'im bitter. But I think this'll tell y'all where his mad began."

14

Betty Jo looked at the letter and then at her aunt. Aunt Beulah began to read it aloud.

May 12, 1896

Dearest Daughter, Leona;

With this letter, I send my greeting to you and the family. I am sorry to be away in Austin at this time, but my responsibilities to Texas depend upon it. I should return by cotton harvest.

By the time you receive this letter, high school graduation will have already taken place. I am so proud of you for being the first daughter among our kinfolk to hold a diploma! Your mother and I talked before I left, and we would like for you to continue with your studies. I am making arrangements here in Austin for you to be enrolled as a freshman this fall. You have many skills and talents, and we believe you are the one in our family to go to college.

Beulah looked up from her reading. "Yer granma was very good with the books and learnin'. Growin' up, I always knew she was different. There was no question what I would do fer my life—marry me a good worker, raise a couple kids, and care fer the folks. But yer granma, she was destined fer bigger thangs. Special thangs."

Granma graduated from high school? Betty Jo knew she could read, but she never knew she was book smart.

Beulah continued, her tone lower and tempo slower:

This brings me to the main issue of the letter. That boy you've been palling around with, Henri—he's not our kind. Break off all association with him. You may think this harsh, but I know boys like him. He's not going anywhere in life, and a future with him will be hard on you. Prepare to attend college this fall. God will bring you the right husband in time. Henri Landry is not him.

Give my love to your mother and sister, and know what I say is for your best.

Love,
Daddy

Beulah sighed. "Daddy stood 'gainst yer papa, but yer Granma Leet was stubborn. She loved 'im and chose 'im over college and Daddy's favor. Shortly after she got this letter, she and Henri ran off to Center and got married by the Justice of the Peace. It like to broke

15

Daddy and Mother's heart. Henri knew he wasn't wanted in this family. He also lived up to what Daddy thought of 'im. No matter how hard anyone tried to bond us together, forgiveness was always in short supply."

Betty Jo did not speak. Her mind raced to fill in pieces of the family puzzle that she never before could make fit.

"The Good Book tells us that a *soft answer turneth away wrath*. That's what I try'n remember ev'ry time yer papa come 'round—but he just remembers the words our daddy wrote those many years ago, and his mad keeps on a goin'."

*****

"Henri! Henri Landry, kin y'all hear me?"

The call brought Henri to reality. He groaned.

"Yer caught up in the truck, and the only thang keepin' the truck from fallin' to the river is this tree. Don't be movin' any, y'all hear me now?"

"Yessir." Henri managed to respond beyond the pain in his gut and the rising surge of panic. Never in his life had he stayed so still. He thought of how his wife, Leet, would scold him for his lack of patience. He no longer had her voice to ignore but now instinctively knew he must obey this one. Stillness would be his salvation.

With a rustling of branches, a form appeared. "Henri, I'm gonna try 'n' git this door open," said Jack Lee. The rope around his waist was tethered from the top of the embankment where Sheriff Davis stood watching. "Just hold on."

Using a crowbar, Jack Lee tried to pry the door open. The truck rocked forward and then back again. Henri felt his stomach in his throat but swallowed hard and held his breath.

"Lord Jesus, help us!" Jack exclaimed. When the truck stopped moving, he put the crowbar back into the bent jam. "Hold on now. Almost got it. One more time."

A popping sound followed the screech of metal. The door flew open and the truck lurched precariously. Yellow bile mixed with blood soaked into Henri's shirt. In that moment, he was only aware of his brother-in-law's prayers.

"Henri, I gotta pull y'all outta here. I could use yer help."

The two men played a dire tug-of-war game with the wreckage. Endowed with strength beyond his sixty years, Jack Lee pulled with his upper body. Henri pushed with the muscles least bound by metal. The truck hobbled back and forth. Once he was in Jack Lee's bear hug, fire shot through his body and brain. With nothing to extinguish it, Henri Landry passed out.

*****

Suppertime was nearing, and Betty Jo began to worry. Papa hadn't showed up and Uncle Jack was still gone. Like the cypress tree falling yesterday for no apparent reason, things just didn't seem right.

With the passing of the afternoon, she had plenty of time to think. She thought about her mother and wondered why Papa never talked about her. Sometimes Granma would whisper things like how she had her mother's brown eyes or how her singing was just the same. Her thoughts of Granma were enfolded in sorrow—not that Granma was in Glory, but that she had known her mostly in sickness. Then her mind turned to her missing grandfather. No matter what she did, she always felt his disapproval. Sometimes he was just plain mean. She thought Papa might love her, but she knew he didn't like her.

The sun was at its setting. Beulah and Betty Jo moved to the porch.

"There's nothin' to do, but wait," Beulah said as she sat in the swing next to Betty Jo. Slowly they began to rock together. Beulah's humming was accompanied by an occasional squeak of the metal chain.

The tune was familiar, but Betty Jo could not think of words to match. "Aunt Beu, what are you humming?"

"Oh, it's a song about love, Sugar."

"A love song?" Betty Jo asked.

"Well, not between a man and woman kind of love—the kind of love God has fer us. Beulah sang into the evening air, chin tilted to the sky.

> *Love lifted me,*
> *love lifted me,*
> *when nothing else could help,*
> *love lifted me.*

As she began to sing the refrain again, lights shone on the porch. The swing stopped, and Beulah and Betty Jo stood up. As the lights grew brighter, they moved to the edge of the steps.

James Roy Davis idled the car while Jack Lee got out of the passenger side. As soon as the door was shut, the car quickly backed away. Jack stood for a moment running his hand across his thinning gray hair. Then he made a tired walk toward the porch. Dark splotches had soaked into the fabric of his clothes. The cuffs of his pants were caked with dried mud and a shirtsleeve was torn.

"Oh, Good Lord, Jack Lee!" Beulah exclaimed as she hurried down the steps to him. Jack Lee looked at his wife and let out a slow breath. He turned his eyes to Betty Jo standing at the top of the steps.

"The truck that run off the road was yer grandpa's," Jack Lee began.

"Oh goodness," Aunt Beulah murmured.

"Don't know when it happened—mebbe early mornin'. He musta been goin' real fast. Took a while to git 'im up outta there. Decided it best to git 'im to the hospital, so we laid 'im out in the back seat and drove as fast as we could to Center. He was barely breathin' when we got there."

Betty Jo closed her eyes.

"Doc says he has broken bones and a concussion. The worst is the bleedin' on the inside. If he makes it through the night, his odds of pullin' through will be better."

She was surprised they came—the tears that slowly made their way down her cheeks. And with their appearance a revelation settled into her soul. Though she hated Papa, she surely did love him.

Debby L Wynkoop

CHAPTER TWO

Betty Jo looked down at the Sabine River as the car crossed the bridge. It seemed so different when viewed from above, like a picture postcard. She could see the lumber mill and the railroad bridge and where the boats docked. When they got to the other side, Uncle Jack Lee pulled off the road and got out. Aunt Beulah followed him. Betty Jo sat still in the back seat. From the time Uncle Jack suggested he would drive them by the site of the accident before heading to church, she was apprehensive. She wasn't sure she wanted to see.

"Come on, Sugar," Aunt Beulah coaxed through the window opening. "It's never good to ignore truth."

Betty Jo complied and joined the pair. Uncle Jack pointed to the wreckage on the other side. Twisted, broken, and precariously perched in a sea of green, the truck was barely recognizable.

"Thanks be to Jesus fer sparin' his life," Aunt Beu whispered, breaking the somber silence.

"There's no savin' that truck," Jack Lee said, "but Lord Jesus, we ask that'd Ya'll save Henri."

Betty Jo squirmed in the wooden pew as heat pressed in on her. Dressed in Sunday clothes borrowed from the wardrobe in the guest room and shoes that pinched her toes, she was confined inside this building full of folks.

She did not look directly at anyone, but she knew they looked at her. She was the reason heads leaned together and whispers were exchanged. In the course of her everyday life, she could push away the knowledge that she was an orphaned bastard. In here it could not be escaped. Aunt Beu said these were her people, but she knew the truth. She belonged to no one, and her existence was a provocation.

Granma's funeral was the only other time she'd been in Joaquin Baptist Church. She wasn't exactly sure how to act at Sunday service so she took her cues from Aunt Beu and Uncle Jack. Sitting between them was like leaning against the old oak tree on the farmhouse grounds. She was at rest in its shade while observing the world beyond.

With the singing and the speaking done, Brother Tucker began to pray. "Oh, God, Thou art our help and rescue in these hard times. Help us put our faith and trust in You. We pray today for Henri Landry and ask fer healin' in his life. In Jesus' name, amen."

Congregants chimed their agreement.

Betty Jo used the prayer time to look around. Bowed heads nodded and lips moved, it seemed, with their own words. She puzzled at this world. Papa always refused Aunt Beulah's request to carry her to church. *Bunch of busybody hypocrites*, he would say. She wasn't sure what a hypocrite was, but she did understand about busybodies. She felt she was a traitor for going against Papa's wishes today. Maybe being here made her a hypocrite, too.

Sometimes on a good day, Granma Leet would softly tell her stories from the Bible and talk about Jesus. In primary school, it seemed everyone knew about these things, but she had to drop out to tend to Granma when she was just eight years old. After Granma passed, she didn't return to school. By then she knew who she was. Besides, she was too far behind.

Not going to church or school made her world small, but her own world was comfortable. She had divided it in two. There was the world that was like the water's surface, full of light and freedom. Then there was the murky world of the dregs, bogged down in sorrow and the puzzlement of Papa. She learned long ago to keep them separate.

Sister Tucker began to play a hand-clapper tune as the church goers made their way out onto the grounds.

"Oh, Beulah May, we are so sorry to hear of Henri's tragic accident!" a woman in a catalogue dress said as she came in to hug Beulah's neck. Pulling back, she looked long at Betty Jo, her eyes landing on her chest. "This must be yer dear departed sister's grandbaby . . . all growed up I see." Then looking back at Beulah, "Now tell me, however did he end up with the truck over the edge?"

"Thank y'all kindly fer the condolence. We do ask fer yer prayers," Beulah responded. Then turning to her great niece, "Betty Jo, we best be gettin' along. There's Jack Lee now. Goodbye, Miz Westly."

Betty Jo knew that the abruptness was rude, yet she marveled how stealthily Aunt Beu untangled the vine that sought to wrap itself around them.

The car pulled up. Beulah got into the front seat, and Betty Jo scrambled into the back, forgetting for the moment that she was wearing a Sunday dress.

"Bless y'all, Jack Lee," Beulah said under her breath as she shut the door.

"It look like y'all needed a rescue," he said, pulling out onto the highway, leaving Mrs. Westly standing with her hands on her hips.

"Mercy, yes!" Beulah turned her head toward the back seat and added, "We'll hurry Sunday dinner and then carry y'all to yer papa."

*****

The smell of disinfectant greeted Henri as he came out of the morphine stupor. Willing his eyelids to lift, he struggled to focus. He knew this place by the smell. He must be in a bad way. Turning his gaze to the right, the frame of James Roy Davis filled his view. He was slouched in a chair with his white hat pulled down to the bridge of his nose.

What had happened and why was that ne'er-do-well here? Henri closed his eyes again. He could play possum with the best of 'em.

Soft-soled footsteps entered the room, followed by a tense whisper. "Sheriff, the doctor told y'all that there'd be no visitors."

A rustling sound was followed by two pronounced bootsteps on the tile floor. "Well, he ain't here now, is he?" snarled Sheriff Davis. "I'll be stayin' 'til I have a little talk with Mr. Landry. Y'all just go on yer way and mind yer bus'ness."

The soft-soled footsteps quickly faded away.

"Landry, wake up!" Sheriff's booming voice jolted through his head. "I ain't messin' around now," he added while shaking Henri by the arm.

Henri let out a reflexive groan. Possum game up.

"Well, lookie here . . . decided to join the land of the livin', now did y'all?" The voice lowered. "I have a few questions needin' some answers." The sheriff pulled the chair he had brought in from the waiting room over to the side of the bed. He sat down and leaned over the rail. "Y'all drinkin' at yer Blind Pig 'fore runnin' yer truck off the road last night?"

Henri pondered the notion that he'd crashed his truck. He sure did love that truck and couldn't bear the thought that it'd been wrecked. For the life of him, though, he couldn't recall what had happened.

"I dunno," Henri managed to whisper.

"Think real hard now." Sheriff tilted his hat off his forehead, revealing the untanned skin of a receded hairline. "Y'all drinkin' yer bootleg? Keepin' company with the wrong folks?" Sheriff Davis fired off his questions.

Henri moaned.

Sheriff Davis leaned forward. "Where's the still, Landry?"

"I dunno," Henri began to whimper. His head throbbed.

Sheriff Davis pushed the chair back and stood. He stared down at his long-time rival, surprised at the pathetic response. "Well, y'all need to figure it out." Disgust tinged his voice. "Looks like yer not goin' anywhere anytime soon. I'll be back."

As the sheriff's bootsteps echoed down the hall, Henri Landry gave way to sobs.

*****

Debby L Wynkoop

Betty Jo had only been to Center one time before. She remembered the stately courthouse occupying the middle of the spacious town square. Store front businesses and restaurants lined up on all four sides. She imagined that on a weekday, a mix of wagons and automobiles with folks in town clothes would be scurrying about; but on this Lord's Day, all was quiet. Just like the previous time she'd been here, today would have no sightseeing. The square would be bypassed as the car headed to the hospital.

"Betty Jo," Uncle Jack Lee began after parking the car, "I wanted y'all to see the wreckage of the truck, so y'all'd know how bad yer grandpa's accident was. Not shore we'll git to see 'im today, but be prepared—he won't be lookin' good."

In silence, the three exited the car and made their way to the entry. Beulah held Betty Jo's hand. The main door abruptly opened as Sheriff Davis made his way outside.

"Afternoon, Sheriff," Jack Lee said.

"Jack Lee," Sheriff Davis nodded, not bothering to tip his hat or slow his gait.

"Sheriff," Jack Lee called as he turned and followed after him. "Sheriff, thank y'all fer brangin' Henri in yesterday."

James Ray faced Jack Lee. "Well, he shorely did mess up the back of the car . . . take a while to clean up," he complained. He tilted his hat back off his forehead and exhaled.

"How is he?" Jack Lee asked.

"He's gonna pull through." Sheriff Davis began to fidget with the belt buckle lodged under his belly.

Jack Lee ventured one more question. "Talkin' yet?"

"Not much. Don't know if he cain't or if he's just bein' his ol' stubborn self. But we know what happened, Jack Lee. No sense pretendin'." Sheriff Davis readjusted his hat, then turned and walked to the patrol car in long strides.

As Betty Jo watched the exchange, she stole a glimpse at the Sheriff's face—long nose, beady eyes, and pursed lips. His manner and appearance were somehow familiar. She tried to dismiss it, but a strange feeling settled inside her.

"Oh, that man!" Aunt Beu exclaimed as Jack Lee returned to where he'd left them standing.

"Now, Beulah May, he did brang Henri all the way here yesterday. We need to return kindness with kindness," Jack Lee said.

26

"Kindness? My foot! I'm glad y'all got 'im to the hospital, but y'all know James Roy was workin' for his own self." Beulah's exasperation left nothing more to be said, so the three made their way through the entrance of the hospital.

Henri was in a deep sleep—deeper than any of his alcoholic slumbers. It had taken quite a while for Aunt Beulah to convince the nurse to allow Betty Jo into the room to sit with her grandfather.

"Be quiet and don't disturb 'im. His body needs rest," the nurse had said.

Betty Jo had nothing to say to Papa anyway. She sat still and considered his form in the hospital bed. He was not the same man she remembered as a child. He was less than he once was.

It was time to leave him be.

As she stood to go, a moan reached her ears. She paused and looked his direction with pity. "Goodbye, Papa," Betty Jo said. Then she left the room.

The seventeen-mile drive home was quiet, except for the noise of the car on the road. Jack Lee Thorpe was problem solving as he drove. *How can we support Betty Jo without appearing to interfere?* She was almost a woman, but she lacked so many things—a normal childhood, kinfolk, an education, and religion. Could he and Beulah help fill in the blaring gaps in her life? He sure didn't know what tomorrow held, but it was becoming clear that he was called to protect and guide. His wife's great niece should come to live in his house much the same way her mama once did.

Beulah May Thorpe was lost in the Spirit. The burden for Henri was heavier than she could bear alone, and urgency compelled her to prayer. She thought it best for him to die. It would be easier for all involved, but she knew God appointed a man once to die, and that He alone knew when that would be. So, she prayed, not knowing how to pray.

Betty Jo Landry sat in the back seat, looking out the window to the patches of cotton farms surrounded by the dense woods. Her mind was made up. She formulated a plan. She revised it. She rehearsed it until she was ready.

Betty Jo set out the forks and plates for a Sunday evening bite to eat. Aunt Beu arranged leftovers on the kitchen table: slices of cold fried chicken, hush puppies, honey, and sweet tea. Jack Lee had made the rare decision to skip evening service. There had been no time for a nap and tomorrow was shaping up to be a busy day. Now gathered around the table, the time for talking had come.

Uncle Jack sat tall in his chair and cleared his throat. "Betty Jo, yer aunt and I would like fer y'all to stay at the farmhouse with us."

"We're yer nearest kinfolk, and we'd be plumb glad to have y'all," Aunt Beulah interjected.

"We'll take y'all over in the mornin' to pack thangs up and move 'em here. Y'all kin take Ruth Ann's old room fer yer own," Jack Lee added.

"Y'all will like that now, won't ya, Sugar?" Beulah asked.

Betty Jo kept her face from expression. "Yes, ma'am."

Jack continued. "Beulah May will teach y'all yer letters and readin'. I'll help with the numbers and 'rithmetic. We also 'spect y'all to go to church with us as a member of our household. And help out with the chores, of course."

"But y'all're always good 'bout that," Beulah added with a smile.

Betty Jo softened her face. She must look agreeable.

Uncle Jack asked, "Does that sound acceptable?"

"Yes, sir," Betty Jo replied, eliciting a joyful sound and hug from Aunt Beu.

"Good!" Jack Lee said with a clap of his hands. "It's settled then. We'll move y'all first thang in the mornin'."

As Betty Jo helped her aunt clean up the kitchen, she noted carefully where things were placed.

"Aunt Beu, I shore am tired," she said. "I'd like to go upstairs now."

"Bless yer heart, of course," Beulah said meeting Betty Jo's eyes. "This is a bad thang that's happened, but it'll be good to have y'all here."

Betty Jo worried that her smile looked fake, so she quickly turned to go, heading upstairs to get rest while she could.

Barefoot and in her own dress, Betty Jo tiptoed down the hall and descended the stairs. She was quite sure that the floorboard creaks would not be heard over the snoring duet coming from the big bedroom on the ground level.

She went to the kitchen and quickly packed the portions of food she'd eyed earlier—foods that would travel well—into the large folded bandana. She felt a bit of remorse for taking the food and the bandana she'd found in the spare closet, but she needed this supply to get her start. Double-checking that the pantry and icebox doors were closed, she slowly opened the screen door and slipped out, mindful to cradle it shut.

Walking at night was usually something she avoided, but she knew this road well and there was a slice of moonlight to help. She went to the plank house, filled the rest of her supplies and changed into cut-off overalls. She did not worry about her footprints on the county road. They would know to look at Papa's place anyway. She knew all the secret places of the Pineys. She was sure she would not be found as long as she covered her tracks well after leaving the little house.

When everything was ready, Betty Jo took the time to say farewell. She opened the lid of the cypress chest and pulled out the autoharp. Sitting on the edge of the bed, she strummed and sang. Her mind heard Granma's voice, and she wondered if she'd sung it the same way to Mama when she was little.

Sleep, sleep, my little one
Listen to the river running

Before returning the harp to its place, she dug down to the bottom of the chest. After a moment of rustling, she found what she was looking for and carefully put it in her back pocket. There would be time to study it later. Now she must hurry. She let the crickets and frogs hear the screen door slam. She knew Beulah wasn't her nearest kin. She intended to find the man who was. She needed to belong to someone.

By the time Betty Jo arrived at the fallen Big Tree, a hazy light in the east made its appearance. Covering tracks took far longer than she had anticipated. She had carefully picked her way through brush, away from the river and the path. Arriving at the rooty gnarl of the toppled tree, she set down her load. She cleaned her hands as best she could before pulling the envelope out of her back pocket. She sat down. The dampness of the soil seeped into the bottom of her britches. Weariness made its way to her soul. The events and revelations of the past few days had begun to take its toll.

Carefully, she took the letter out and glanced at the first page of handwritten words. What it said would have to wait. Gently, she placed the second page on top. She studied the sketch of a young man leaning against the trunk of the upright Big Tree, his hat tilted back. She looked closely at the facial features—the shape of the nose, the squint of the eyes and the straight line of the mouth. He was the spittin' image of Sheriff Davis.

After a short rest in the morning, Betty Jo cached her supplies and began the walk upstream, traveling the river trail farther than she'd ever gone before. She suspected that Papa's Blind Pig was on the other side of the highway.

The new bridge came into view. Betty Jo crouched behind a bush at the edge of the clearing, forcing herself to avoid looking at the wreckage of Papa's truck. Sweat dampened her hair behind her ears and along her neckline. She listened to the hollow sound of a truck's tires as it crossed over the Sabine on the way to Logansport. When the coast was clear, she scurried under the bridge. Once back into the cover of vegetation and out of view of the mill, she ascended the steep slope away from the river. Her search had begun.

After exploring the woods north of the highway for three days, Betty Jo was sure she'd found the place where Papa spent so much of his time. The shack looked very similar to the plank house. The differences were that there was no porch and only a single step up to a screenless door. It was not visible from any road or established path. She figured the joint would not be active until Friday evening, but someone had to get things ready, and that someone likely knew her papa quite well.

She moved her things and nestled in a little arbor. She had not wanted to leave the familiar, but the risk of crossing the highway or scrambling under the bridge each day was too great to continue. From her new location, she could spy on the shack. Her stash of food was wearing thin, and she had begun to feel the creeping pangs of hunger. Hopefully she would find answers soon.

Friday morning, she heard a clattering in the pines. It was punctuated by rippling clanks. Betty Jo swiftly moved into position just outside the safety of her little arbor. The clatter and clanks grew louder until they stopped with the whinny of a horse. She shrunk down a bit lower and calmed her breathing. Hushed voices were followed by a tinkling sound.

A man in overalls and a floppy-brimmed hat emerged from the green cover. He moved along the path, carrying a crate of assorted bottles and jugs. A woman followed behind. She wasn't old. She wasn't young. Her strawberry hair was swept up in a braided bun. When they arrived at the single-step entry of the shack, the woman pulled out a key from her apron pocket, unlocked the latch, and propped open the door. The woman went inside. The man shuttled crates one at a time from the wagon to the shack while the woman remained inside. Finally, the clattering wheels resumed and faded away.

Wait, Betty Jo told herself.

She returned to her camp in the arbor and took a spit bath using the water she'd retrieved from a nearby spring. She was dismayed at the prevalence of bug bites and scrapes on her limbs, but there was nothing she could do about it. She put on her too-tight dress and brushed her hair. She was ready. She walked through the bramble to the shack below.

Betty Jo paused and listened. Cautiously, she stepped to the threshold and peered through the doorframe. The natural light from the entrance provided the only illumination. Planks supported by sawhorses filled the space of the single room. Three-legged stools lined each side. Against the far wall, the woman was working—cleaning mason jars and setting them out in rows on a long, crude table.

"Excuse me, ma'am," Betty Jo said.

The woman spun around.

"I shorely am sorry to trouble y'all," Betty Jo replied, thinking that good manners might serve her well.

"Girl, what're y'all doin' here?"

"I come to see where my papa fellowships," Betty Jo answered.

"Oh me, oh my . . . Y'all must be Henri's Betty Jo." The woman's face changed from quizzical to sympathetic.

"Yes, ma'am." Betty Jo had never thought she was Papa's property, but perhaps that was a good way to say it. "May I ask yer name?"

"They call me Dot. Dottie Sue fer actual."

31

"Pleased to meet y'all, Miz Dottie Sue." Betty Jo began to take comfort. She did not have a lot of experience swapping howdies with strangers, but a warmth radiated from this woman.

Dot set down the jar in her hand and walked through the maze of stools toward Betty Jo. She gestured for her to step outside and to the ground. She pulled the door closed behind them.

"We heard of yer papa's accident. Had to be bad, drivin' plumb over the edge and all. I'm so sorry." Dottie Sue shook her head. "This isn't the place fer y'all to be, Betty Jo. Y'all need to go on and git to yer folks. They be missin' y'all."

Dot turned to look Betty Jo in the eyes. "Good Lord, y'all shorely look like yer mama."

"You knew my mama?" Betty Jo asked.

"Why ev'rybody knows ev'rybody 'round here, Girl. Shoot, most ev'rybody be kin—but now y'all need be off." Dot's voice bore anxiousness.

Betty Jo wanted desperately to ask about her mother, but she forced herself to keep to the business at hand. She held out the envelope she carried. "I found this with Mama's thangs." She removed the papers and unfolded the one on top.

"Would y'all read this, Miz Dottie Sue?" she asked, handing it to Dot. "Please?"

Dot recognized the handwriting from her school days. She had never seen the girl up close. Her being here and talking would only pile on complication. Yet, the bonds of friendship with sweet Charlene demanded care for her offspring.

Before Dot could take a closer look, Betty Jo revealed the drawing on the second page. "And I want to know who this man is."

Dot gasped.

"Miz Dottie Sue, who is he?" Betty Jo implored.

Dot sighed. "Girl, this is Jimmy. There be more to know, but we cain't chat now. Come to my place in Logansport tomorrow at lunch time. Not before, mind you."

Dottie gave Betty Jo the directions and waited for her to repeat them. "Now scat. Don't be comin' back here."

Betty Jo wanted to linger, but an approaching clatter told her to head quickly through the bramble and disappear. With an empty stomach, Betty Jo sat in her little arbor camp. As night fell, she listened to the muffled sounds from the shack below and pretended that Papa was inside having a good ol' time. At home, he always had fun with the first couple drinks, but then it would get ugly. *Were the sounds of folks having a good time, or had they crossed into the ugly?* Eager for the light of a new day, she gave way to restless sleep.

Debby L Wynkoop

CHAPTER THREE

The house was small and tidy. Made out of milled lumber, it fit perfectly at the end of the town street. Betty Jo guessed by the sun and wafting heat that it was noon. Anxious, she steadied herself and knocked on the screen door with her right hand. In her left she clutched the treasured envelope.

"Hello, Girl. Come on in," Dot said as she pushed the door open.

"Thank y'all kindly, ma'am," Betty Jo acknowledged as she followed Dottie Sue to the kitchen.

"Sit here." Dot gestured to a chair at the small square table. "Help yerself. I reckon y'all might be hungry."

Betty Jo's heart filled with gratitude to see a spread of food before her. She tried not to eat too fast.

Dot waited for the chewing to slow. "Before I tell y'all 'bout the picture, I wanna know some thangs. Where y'all bin stayin'?"

"Camped in the woods north of the highway," Betty Jo answered.

"Y'all should be with yer folks. Why y'all leave 'em?" Dot asked.

"They're kind and all, but they won't tell me what I need to know." Betty Jo lowered her voice. "Aunt Beu said they were my nearest kin, but that isn't so, is it? I'm weary of not knowin'."

"I see. Y'all think answers will be found at yer papa's Blind Pig? Girl, that's no kind of place to be lookin'."

"I found y'all there," Betty Jo replied.

The pause in their exchange was interrupted by the pound of boots on the floor boards. The screen door in back slammed.

"Dot! We gotta git!" the man with the floppy-brimmed hat stormed in.

"Denny Ron?" Dot stood up and stepped toward the man.

"I hear tell that Davis and his ilk are gonna search the woods. We gotta hide . . . " Denny's voice trailed off with the realization that they were not alone. "Good Lord, Woman!"

"This is Henri Landry's Betty Jo—she come fer a visit." Dot surprised herself. She sounded like any other woman in town entertaining a social call.

"Fool thang to do, Dot!" Denny glared. "I told y'all, no complications. We gotta git." He left the house the same way he entered it.

"Betty Jo, it might be gettin' pretty busy in the north woods. Why don't y'all stay here and finish lunch? Don't answer should anyone come by. I'll be back in a few hours." Dot hurried out to join Denny.

Betty Jo snooped around. It was a woman's house—pretties and flowers on display. No photographs that she could find, but on the bedroom wall above a bureau was an ink drawing that had been framed—a landscape of a river flowing through the woods. A tall cypress ladened with vines was in the background. *Oh, please Miz Dottie Sue, come back soon. There's so much to know.*

With a belly full, and the heat funneling into the house, Betty Jo lay down on the braided rug to take a nap.

The rustle and rattle of dishes shook Betty Jo awake.

"Seen y'all got some good rest. Glad y'all weren't bothered none," Dot's voice ushered her into reality. "Come help yerself to a bite to eat."

The light was dimming outside the window. Betty Jo was surprised that she had slept the entire afternoon. She made her way once again to the little table and looked at Dottie Sue before pulling out a chair to sit. Dot's hair was disheveled, and the wrinkle between her brows had deepened.

Dot sat and folded her hands and closed her eyes. "Thank Y'all, Lord, for this food we are about to receive. Forgive us our sins of this day. In Jesus' name, amen."

Betty Jo was taken aback. She did not think a woman who worked in a business against the law could be a praying woman.

Dottie passed the bowl of red beans and rice. "I sent a message to yer Aunt Beulah this afternoon," she said.

Betty Jo looked up from her food, startled.

"I wanted yer kin to know yer safe. They be worried sick, no doubt."

Betty Jo scooted her chair back and jumped up.

"Now, Girl, calm down. Lemme finish." Dot raised her hand up as if to stop Betty Jo from moving. "In the message, I let them know yer gonna to stay with me fer a while."

Betty Jo stood still, uncertain if she should sit back down or make a run for it. All she knew is she wanted a mother. She wanted a father. This woman seemed to know them both.

"Mister and Miz Thorpe are patient, godly people. They just wanna know yer safe. Besides, yer pert near a grown woman. They'll trust me and leave y'all be fer a while," Dot reasoned. "Runnin' all the time leads nowhere fast. All it makes fer is tired."

Dottie Sue began to eat her supper. Hesitantly, Betty Jo sat back down.

Dot said, "After supper, we'll have ourselves a little talk."

Betty Jo nodded, and began to eat.

With the table cleared and dishes washed, Dottie Sue and Betty Jo moved into the sitting area.

"Y'all saw the picture over the bureau?" Dot asked, offering a lopsided grin.

Betty Jo nodded sheepishly.

"Yer mama made it—gave it to me. She was expectin' y'all at the time. She had to move outta yer papa's house, and yer Uncle Jack and Aunt Beulah took her in. It was a tough time, but the picture reminds me of the good with Charlene. She was my very best friend."

"Why did Mama have to move?" Betty Jo inquired.

Dottie Sue sighed. "I think y'all know why."

Betty Jo lowered her head. There it was again—that guilty feeling for just being.

"Y'all know yer Papa to be a harsh man," Dot continued. "He disowned yer mama when he discovered she was in the family way. She weren't a married woman. Folks not harsh by nature would do the same. She had to drop out of school, too.

"The Thorpes were kind to yer mama. They'd let me come to visit. I kin tell y'all that Charlene shorely did love y'all. She wanted nothin' more than to give y'all a healthy and happy life. She was fixin' to make the greatest sacrifice a mama could ever make. She planned to give y'all birth and then adopt y'all out to a lovin' family. All the arrangements had been made."

"But I grew up in Papa's house. What happened?" Betty Jo asked.

Dottie Sue rubbed her right temple then drew a deep breath. "I heard tell that the night of yer birth, Uncle Jack fetched yer papa and carried 'im to Charlene's side. As she held y'all in her arms, she looked at yer papa and said, 'Please love her.' Then she passed."

Dot's eyes filled with water. She blinked hard and a tear escaped, pooling in a little reservoir on her chin.

Betty Jo sat numb. She knew about her mother's passing, but this was the first she'd heard the story. *My life cost Mama's life.*

"Yer Granma Leet and Great Aunt Beulah cared fer y'all. Found y'all a wet nurse. They laid yer mama to rest in the family cemetery at the edge of the Pineys. It was a small funeral.

"Yer papa had run off. Got hisself good and drunk. After a couple weeks, he showed back up at the Thorpes. Told yer granma it was time to go home . . . and to brang the baby. So Leet took y'all with Henri. Y'all were his granddaughter, and nobody else was gonna raise you. Nobody was gonna interfere."

After a lifetime of silence, the floodgates had opened on the circumstances of her birth. It threatened to wash her away. They sat quietly until Betty Jo's original question floated to the surface. "Miz Dottie Sue, what 'bout the picture?" she asked.

"Oh, Girl." Dottie looked Betty Jo square in the eye. "Yer Mama was in love with Jimmy Davis—Sheriff Davis' son."

Betty Jo began to understand why her mama's people had sheltered her from knowing too much. The truth was painful and complicated; yet she was confused by Aunt Beulah's words a few days ago. *It's never good to ignore truth.* Aunt Beulah knew the truth but hid it from her. Did that make her a hypocrite?

The cot Betty Jo laid on was creaky and hard. She would have preferred the braided rug or the mossy bed of her camp, but manners dictated she take what was offered with gratitude. A new day would arrive soon. Dottie Sue had informed her last evening that they would be going to church in the morning. When Betty Jo showed surprise that Dot attended church, Dot had said, "Ev'rybody goes to church, Girl." Again, Betty Jo knew she'd been told something that wasn't completely right. Not everybody attended church. Papa never went to church, and until the last two Sundays she hadn't either.

When Dottie rose, motion was set in order to establish a morning routine. Dottie Sue showed Betty Jo how to use the tiny, pink-tiled bathroom—pedestal sink, tub, and even a toilet. She loaned her a comb to fix her hair and clothes to wear for church. They would fetch her belongings from the woods in the afternoon.

Meeting at the table for a breakfast of grits, Betty Jo ventured another question. "Do y'all know Jimmy Davis's whereabouts?"

Dottie threw the question back. "If'n I tell y'all what I know, will y'all be runnin' off on me, too?"

Betty Jo didn't answer. She didn't know what she would do with the information.

"I kin tell y'all that he's not 'round here. I do know we be needin' to think through thangs 'fore we act," Dot concluded.

We. Betty Jo was not sure what to make of the use of that word, but what Dot said rang true.

Betty Jo cleaned the breakfast items while Dottie finished up in the bathroom. Dot emerged with hair swooped up and red lipstick. The final adornment was a hat with a trace of lace in the front. She took the *Holy Bible* off the end table, and they began the six-block walk to church.

They passed through the doorway of the brick store-front, under the sign that said *Gospel Tabernacle*. The pews were simple wooden benches, remarkably resembling the furniture inside the Blind Pig. Betty Jo wondered if Dottie Sue ever noted the similarities. After a few, "Mornin', Sisters" and "Beautiful Lord's Day, aint it?" the pair sat down next to the aisle halfway back. Guitar strumming and a fiddle greeted the congregants, who enthusiastically contributed their hand clapping.

A small platform of plywood rested on cinder blocks at the front of the long room. A wooden pulpit was centered on it, and on the back wall a banner declared *Jesus Saves*. Betty Jo surveyed the congregation. There were fewer folks than last week's church. She turned her head and was shocked to see a family of Coloreds sitting off to the side. She looked at Dottie Sue to see her reaction, but Dot was smiling as she clapped her hands and tapped her foot.

Then she saw the man-shape, sitting in the front row. She couldn't be sure, but the clothes he wore stood out from the others. He sat straight and tall and still. *I was on my way to Logansport, but the day got away from me,* she remembered. Betty Jo battled to keep her eyes from being fixed on the back of his head. She was relieved when a middle-aged man stepped up behind the pulpit to begin the service.

"Welcome, y'all, this mornin'. Let's join together in worship." The man raised his voice above the whistle of a passing train. "Like the psalmist said, 'I was glad when they said unto me, Let us go into the house of the LORD!' " He gestured his hands upward, and the people stood. The instruments and hand-clapping resumed, and voices belted out songs Betty Jo did not know. In the pauses between songs, the Gathered spoke prayers of praise. Some even shouted. The longer the music played, the more movement filled the room. One man ran up and down the aisle, startling Betty Jo. Most people danced in place. Ladies furiously waved fans in front of their faces. Dottie Sue participated in full. Only Betty Jo and the man-shape kept their reserve.

Then the music slowed. The voices swelled one more time and then died down. A hush fell over the room. In the quiet, a compelling warmth bubbled up inside Betty Jo. Then the Colored man, off to the side, began to quietly sing. This song she recognized. With each pitch, fervent sincerity built.

> *Love lifted me,*
> *love lifted me,*
> *when nothing else could help,*
> *love lifted me.*

In Betty Jo's fifteen years, she'd never heard anything more glorious. When Granma sang, it was with a gentle caress. She imagined her mama's voice being beautiful. This voice, though, was something far more. It spoke to her very soul.

One by one voices joined, mixing harmonies until all were singing the rich song of the redeemed.

The warmth made its way to Betty Jo's closed eyes. Without understanding why, she began to cry.

Betty Jo felt a gentle pressure on her shoulder. She opened her eyes to the realization that the rest of the congregation had been seated. Together, she and Dot sat down. The man who had begun the service was speaking from the pulpit. *How long had she stood there crying?* Disoriented, she tried to focus on his words.

"The Lord has shorely answered our prayers by brangin' Reverend Philip Harris here to preach God's Word fer a season. We welcome y'all, Brother Philip, to the pulpit. Please do as the Holy Spirit would lead."

The man-shape stood and stepped onto the platform. Having removed his suit jacket, sweat stains under his arms and at his lower back became visible. After getting his neck hugged and a pat on the back, he turned to face the worshipers. He tugged at his collar while he surveyed the room. His eyes locked on Betty Jo's and recognition flicked across his face.

He began to speak. His words were quick.

"Thank you, Brother Delbert and each of you for the gracious welcome. I am humbled to be with you in God's Presence this morning. Let's open our Bibles to First John chapter four, beginning with verse seven. You'll find this book near the end of your Bible. If you get to Revelation, you've gone too far."

Dottie Sue turned to the scripture without hesitation. She held her Bible out and pointed to the location of chapter four verse seven, while pages rustled throughout the room. Focused on the sound of Preacher Philip's voice, Betty Jo pretended to follow the text with her eyes. When he finished, Dot pulled her Bible back onto her lap.

"Let's pray," Philip Harris said before beginning a lengthy prayer. Betty Jo's mind traveled to the night Papa didn't come home. She recalled how Philip had spoken to her in the dark of that night—the kindness in his tone. She pictured the fluid movement he made when reaching for the crawdads—the gentleness in his hands.

When the prayer was finished, he began speaking. He used words that were often strange. As he preached, his eyes swept across the congregation, examining each person. Whenever they approached her, Betty Jo lowered her own. When his gaze moved away, she made a study of his face: blue-eyes, clean-shaven, and no wrinkles or shadows. He was the same as ten days ago, but standing on the platform with a Bible in his hand, she knew there was much to know about Philip Harris. She began imagining.

Betty Jo was unsure how long Preacher Philip spoke. Before she was finished creating his story, the music began again. People stood and sang. Some hurried to the front to kneel in prayer. Finally, an amen was sounded, and the folks made their way out into the fresh air.

Dottie Sue led Betty Jo back through the doorway. Once outside on the boardwalk, they were greeted by Brother Delbert.

"Sister Dottie, how y'all doin'?" he asked, extending his hand.

Dottie Sue shook his hand and replied, "Days have been difficult, Brother."

"Keep puttin' yer trust in the Lord, Dot. He'll show the way." Then turning his head toward Betty Jo, "Young lady, so good to have y'all in church today."

"Brother Delbert, this is Betty Jo, the daughter of my dearest friend."

Betty Jo straightened her shoulders a bit as she reached to shake the church man's hand.

"She's visitin' me a while," Dot concluded.

"Well, Betty Jo, yer welcome to fellowship with us anytime." Delbert smiled.

Betty Jo was contemplating the welcome of this stranger, but remembered her manners just in time. "Thank y'all, sir," she replied.

Dottie Sue and Betty Jo walked down Main Street, chattering small talk as they went. The heaviness of the day before had lifted.

Preacher Philip joined Brother Delbert outside the store-front church. They exchanged quiet words as they watched the pair of women turn onto a side street.

After Sunday dinner, Dottie Sue and Betty Jo sat in the small sitting room. Dot was faithful to the Lord's Day of Rest, even though her mind was busy working.

"Betty Jo, y'all shorely do have yer mother's eyes," Dot spoke into the quiet.

Betty Jo looked at Dottie. "Granma told me so when I was little." Hungry to hear more, she added, "What was she like, Miz Dottie?"

"It's not exaggeratin' to say she was a beauty—the pertiest girl in school, though some paid her no nevermind on account of her being poor and all. I always thought she was as perty on the inside as she was on the out. Yer mama was a kind soul.

"She was smart, too. She knew more'n anyone 'bout subjects. Yer granma saw to that. I think what I loved most was her music. She could play the autoharp and sing so beautiful. She was good at drawin'. Y'all've seen that fer yerself."

Betty Jo smiled to think of the picture of Big Tree in Dot's room.

"Charlene was ev'rythang a family could hope fer in a daughter. She was ev'rythang I needed in a friend," Dottie added.

Betty Jo considered Dottie Sue's description. She didn't want Dot to continue. She wanted to dwell on the good.

"Where's that picture? Might I take another look?" Dot asked.

Betty Jo walked to the cot and retrieved the envelope from under the pillow. She returned with it to the living room. Carefully opening the contents, she handed the picture to Dottie Sue.

"I cain't believe how perfect yer mama captured Jimmy Davis!" Dot exclaimed. "He always got what he wanted. It weren't beyond 'im to use his daddy's name to do so. Sometimes he used his daddy to git hisself out of trouble.

"Yer mama was starry eyed 'bout 'im. He was a big flirt, but he never intended to take up with Charlene. After all, she was the Cajun's daughter."

Betty Jo lowered her head in shame—her spirit pushed into the muck.

"Lemme take a look at the other page."

Betty Jo handed the page of writing to Dottie Sue. "What does it say, Miz Dottie?" she asked.

Dot looked at her. "Girl, you never read it before?"

"No, ma'am." Betty Jo whispered in reply.

"All right, then. Let's see here." Dot cleared her throat. "It's a poem."

> *You just came to visit*
> *And give yourself a rest*
> *Frivolously playing*
> *Were you hoping for conquest?*
>
> *Take me far away from here*
> *Past the shadow of Big Tree*
> *Make the choice to love*
> *And that would set me free*

Dottie hesitated, looking up from the page to empty space.

Betty Jo waited intently for Dottie to resume reading. She sensed that there were more words to come.

For I would fall helpless
Into your hot embrace
If only you would save me
From this wooded place

Let's drift out to the ocean
A better world to find
And build a life together
Where a true home could be mine

This was not the mama Betty Jo had imagined.

"Well, if that don't beat all," Dottie whispered.

Dottie stood to hand the poem back to Betty Jo. "I think it's time fer a little Sunday nap. Make yerself comfortable, Betty Jo."

As Dot walked toward the bedroom, the neigh of a mare came through the back screen. Heavy footfall thumped up the steps, and the screen door suddenly opened.

"Woman, we need to have ourselves an understandin'!"

Dot faced the intrusion, head-on. "Denny Ron, I told y'all not to come bargin' in here ever agin! Git out, now!" She pointed emphatically to the yard.

Denny looked beyond Dot to see Betty Jo now standing on her feet. His cheeks reddened underneath the floppy hat.

"Git out, I said!" Dottie's eyes steeled against Denny's anger.

Denny Ron hesitated, but then made his way outside. Dottie Sue followed, letting the screen door slam.

Betty Jo's instincts and experience called out to her. *Hide!* She resisted the command and moved to the back entrance. Keeping to the side of the doorway, she listened. At first the two voices strained in their hush, but then the dam broke into a flood of hollering. Betty Jo did not understand the meaning of what she was hearing, but she felt each phrase inside her stomach's pit. Fearing for Dottie Sue, she began to think about what she should do when the angry words gave way to violence.

Then she heard the sharp, percussiveness of an open hand hurled at a face. The undeniable sound was seared in her memory.

Betty Jo pushed the screen open and ran out into the back yard, coming to a sudden stop next to Dottie, bent-over with her hand blanketing the side of her face. Betty Jo braved a look at the man. Shock was in his eyes.

"Oh, Dot, I . . . I didn't mean," Denny stammered as he stepped back. Moving his hat into his hands, he looked at the ground.

Dottie Sue straightened to her full height. Her words came slowly as each syllable pressed through gritted teeth. "No more. I'm done. With ev'rythang. Don't y'all ever brang yer sorry self here agin."

Denny raised his eyes and looked at Dottie Sue. His mouth opened. Then he closed it with a heavy sigh. Turning, he replaced his hat and walked away.

Betty Jo slipped her arm around the waist of her new friend. Together they stood—tears streaming down Dot's bruising face.

Betty Jo sat with Dottie Sue on her front porch as the sun began to lower. The afternoon's confrontation had delayed retrieving Betty Jo's possessions from the woods. It also made attending evening church not possible.

"He won't be back—least fer a while," Dottie assured Betty Jo. "He's ashamed of hisself. Fer all his faults, he's a decent man. We just got ourselves carried away."

Betty Jo reached over to take the pink washcloth from Dot, and looked at the purple cheek and blackening eye. She walked inside the house to rinse the cloth in cool water. She returned and Dot reapplied it to her face.

"When Papa got mean, sometimes he be sorry. But he'd just get mean agin, 'specially after the spirits," Betty Jo said.

Dottie looked at Betty Jo with her good eye. "Oh, Girl, I'm terrible sorry."

As the fireflies began their show, silence stepped onto the porch and took a seat between them.

*****

Even though it was Monday, Dottie Sue dressed in her Sunday clothes. Logansport was not a big town, but she would start looking for a job in the grid of streets where businesses were found. Times were hard. Family men had it tough holding work, so she knew a single washed-up woman like herself had little chance. She was willing to work as a domestic, but the few rich folk around had their Coloreds.

Dot had applied extra make-up to paint over the bruise and soften the black of her eye. Still, she knew that her face belied what had happened. Tilting the hat to the left was like an arrow pointing it out. She had no choice, though. In spite of the shame, she must find work.

Over a sunny side up breakfast of eggs, Dot discussed the situation with Betty Jo. "I have a bit of money saved, but it won't be lastin' long. Most my money come from the Blind Pig. I fell into the bus'ness with yer Papa and Denny Ron years ago. At first it was easy, but it's become a heavy burden. I figure I need to be brangin' in money by next week," she concluded.

Dottie Sue gave Betty Jo instructions for chores to be done while she was gone. In her head, Betty Jo heard Aunt Beulah. *Idle hands are the devil's workshop.* She'd had way too much time to think lately, so she set herself to keep the day busy.

In her own too-tight dress, Betty Jo left Dot's house, praying she'd go unnoticed. She crossed the bridge, this time braving a glance at the wreckage of Papa's truck. Her mind pictured the Model T catapulting over the edge. She shuddered and quickly looked over the other side. The lumber mill was busy with activity. People in boats moved up and down the river. Only one truck crossed the bridge, slowing down as it went by. Her heart sped up, and she lowered her gaze as her steps quickened.

Making it across, she entered the dense woods, retracing her way to the little arbor camp she'd made. Once she had her supplies, she would go fishing in the Sabine.

After an hour of fishing, Betty Jo ascended the bank with two catfish in her basket. She cautiously crossed the bridge back into Logansport, turned onto Dot's street, and walked to the lumber house at the end. The day was getting hot quickly, so she passed on eating lunch. Now in her cut-off overalls she went outside to put the small garden in order. She harvested the mature okra and green beans. She cut the biggest zucchini off the vine and then squashed the pesky bugs between her fingers. Before sheltering in the house, she fileted the fish.

The first task inside was to clean and organize her things neatly under the cot. She tidied up the house and then prepared the fish and vegetables for the fry pan. Finally, she washed herself, fixed her hair, and donned the dress Dot had loaned her. She smoothed yesterday's wrinkles out of it while enjoying the feel of the fabric. It was so different than the flour sacks.

Dottie returned late afternoon, dress damp with sweat and hair falling out of its swoop. Kicking her shoes off at the front door, she flopped onto the floral settee. Betty Jo greeted her with a glass of sweet tea.

"No jobs today," she said. "I tried the stores, the bank, the mill. Talked to ev'ryone l could. Nothin'. Not even a suggestion." Dot sighed.

"Miz Dottie, rest now. Supper be ready in a bit," Betty Jo said.

"Oh, Girl, that sounds lovely," Dottie said.

Before Betty Jo had even turned eight, she knew how to manage a cast iron skillet. As she began to fry up dinner on Dot's modern stove, she remembered Granma's saying. *A good fry can satisfy.* Later, she would understand that Papa fed was better than Papa hungry. She was thankful Granma taught her house skills before going to Glory.

When they sat down to supper, Dottie offered the blessing. "Thank Y'all, Jesus, fer this food and fer the hands that prepared it. Amen."

Betty Jo was glad, for of all the meals she'd fixed before, this one yielded appreciation.

The heat from the stove added to the heat of the day. Betty Jo and Dottie made their way to the small porch earlier than yesterday and sat down to watch as the evening made its appearance. Two men in collared shirts and trousers came walking down the street. The only folks to come this far were intending to get to Dottie Sue's house.

"Evenin', Sister," Brother Delbert greeted with a head nod as the pair approached the yard. Preacher Philip tipped his hat.

Dottie returned greetings. Betty Jo looked at Philip before lowering her eyes. She was relieved to have taken the time to clean up properly after the chores.

"May we sit and visit with y'all a bit?" drawled Delbert.

Dot stood and replied, "We'd be pleased." She turned to go into the house and Betty Jo followed. The women retrieved the chairs from the kitchen table and walked back outside, joining the men in the middle of the yard.

Betty Jo set down the chair and headed back to the house.

"I'll get the chairs from the porch," Philip said, walking in long strides to catch up with Betty Jo.

"It was good to see you at church yesterday. I thought you lived on the other side of the river," Philip ventured.

"I did," Betty Jo responded. With nothing more to offer, she entered the house leaving Philip to ponder the bang of the screen door.

Philip took the porch chairs down into the yard. With the four chairs arranged in a spacious circle, the men and Dottie sat down to the task of small talk. It was mutually agreed upon that the day had been hot but not quite as humid as it could be.

Betty Jo returned with a tray bearing four mason jars of sweet tea. She offered the first glass to the eldest, Brother Delbert. Next glass to the visitor, Philip. Then to Dottie Sue. Setting the tray on the porch step, she took the last one for herself and sat down next to Dot, proud to have heard the thank y'all kindlies.

With the small talk spent, Delbert broached the intended topic. "Dottie Sue, y'all were sore on my heart today, 'specially with yer days bein' so hard and all."

Dottie reached her left hand up to her face, fingertips resting gently above the eyebrow.

"We are prayin', but is there any other way we might be of help?" Delbert continued.

Dottie lowered her hand, tired of the futility of trying to cover her shame. "Brother, I really do need work. Went ev'rywhere I could think, but no luck."

"Sister, we don't be needin' luck. We be needin' to pray fer God's answer." Delbert said.

"Let's ask right now," Preacher Philip said. "He's able to do more than we can even ask or think."

As the cicadas sang praise, Philip led the four in a succinct prayer. "We agree together in Jesus' name, amen."

The four kept company in the stillness of the evening until Betty Jo broke the silence. "A week ago, Saturday, Uncle Jack was gettin' thangs ready on the farm fer cotton harvest. Bet it's time now, Dottie Sue, fer a visit to Aunt Beulah's."

Debby L Wynkoop

CHAPTER FOUR

Tuesday mid-morning, Betty Jo found herself sitting next to Dottie Sue in the back seat of Brother Delbert's car. She looked out over the Sabine as they crossed into Texas. Her mind rapidly jumped from one question to the next, much like the pounding of the pistons in the old Chevrolet.

Was Papa dead? When she left him a week ago Sunday, she was sure he wouldn't last long. Why hadn't Aunt Beulah sent word? Maybe her granma's people just decided to let her be. After all, she did run away from them. If Papa were gone, what would that mean for her? Would she get the plank house to herself? Would it be proper for her to live there alone with the ghost of Henri? She knew the land belonged to Uncle Jack. Maybe he'd take it back. What would she do with Papa's things? What would she do to make a living? Would Dottie Sue want to keep her around? Goodness knows, she had plenty of troubles herself. If Uncle Jack and Aunt Beulah took her back, how would she ever find her daddy? She needed Dot's help for that, but it seemed likely her new friend would forget about it with all the upset.

Of all the questions hammering inside Betty Jo's head, the most urgent was what in the world was she going to say for herself? She was sorry for stealing food and supplies and for leaving Aunt Beu and Uncle Jack with nary a warning. She was sad to know she'd caused them angst. Yet she had no regrets for seeing Papa's Blind Pig and for meeting Dottie. She was thankful to learn about her mother. Still, she knew her actions heaped disrespect on her kinfolk.

Have I fallen from favor?

Before she could figure out what to say, the yellow foursquare house appeared. Delbert turned the car off the highway and pulled into the long driveway. The crunch of the tires over gravel could be felt until the wheels of the Chevy came to a stop.

"Betty Jo," Delbert spoke above the idle of the car. "We'll leave y'all to business with yer kin. We're headin' on to Joaquin. Our meetin' with Brother Tucker probably be 'bouts an hour. We'll come by to check on y'all afterwards."

"Thank y'all, sir," Betty Jo replied.

"We are praying," Preacher Philip added, "for wisdom and for work."

Dottie Sue and Betty Jo got out of the back seat. Before Delbert had the car positioned to turn onto the highway, a buxomous figure appeared on the front porch. Beulah May Thorpe stood, unmoving. Dottie Sue and Betty Jo slowly walked the stone path, stopping at the base of the porch. Betty Jo focused on the first step.

"Good mornin', Miz Thorpe," Dot began. "Betty Jo and I come fer a visit, if'n that be acceptable."

Beulah descended the steps and wrapped Betty Jo in an unrelenting embrace.

Betty Jo melted into her Aunt's warmth. Relief soothed the throb of her questions.

"Oh, Sugar!" Beulah pulled away, holding Betty Jo by the shoulders. She examined her great niece and then brought her hand up to touch her cheek. Abruptly lowering it, she glanced over at Dottie. Beulah's eye twitched to see the greenish-yellow bruise on the woman's face. "Dottie, thank y'all fer takin' care of our Betty Jo."

To Betty Jo's surprise, Aunt Beulah hugged Dottie's neck.

"Let's sit on the porch." Beulah led the way.

Betty Jo's heart sank. The rising heat was a reminder that this was not porch time. Aunt Beulah wanted only a short visit.

The two younger women moved to the porch swing while Beulah May sat in the chair nearest the front door.

"I want to thank y'all fer allowin' me Betty Jo's company," Dottie Sue said as she positioned herself in the swing. "I must say fer actual we bin takin' care of each other." Dottie looked at Betty Jo before returning her focus to Beulah. "Miz Thorpe, is Henri Landry still living?"

Beulah answered, "The Good Lord was kind."

"Thank Y'all, Jesus!" Dottie exclaimed.

Betty Jo offered no expression.

"He's out of the hospital," Beulah continued, "but it will be a long row back to health. The accident will leave 'im marred, I'm afeared."

Betty Jo was perplexed. It had been easy these past few days to think him dead.

"Is Papa at the house?" Betty Jo asked.

"No, Sugar," Beulah answered. "He cain't care for hisself. He's here with us. In the front room."

Papa is inside this house? Betty Jo's head spun. She did not want to see him. She'd already said her goodbye.

"Beulah May, I'll talk freely," Dottie Sue lowered her voice. "Henri's Blind Pig got shut down by yer sheriff, right after the accident. It's time fer me to get free of it, once'n fer all. Time fer a new start."

"Glory be—so glad to hear it!" Beulah made no attempt to quiet her voice.

"Honest work would shorely be a big help. Harvest is comin'. Would Jack Lee consider hirin' me fer the fields?" Dottie asked.

Beulah hesitated before answering. "There be plenty of men needin' work, but I'll talk to Jack Lee at suppertime. I'll send word of his answer."

Dottie Sue nodded. "Thank y'all fer the consideration.

"Could we see Henri?" Dot requested.

"I think it best fer there to be no visitors," Beulah replied quickly.

Betty Jo silently let out the breath she'd been holding. Her relief mixed with curiosity. Why was she being denied a visit? It was Aunt Beu who arranged for her to see Papa in the hospital. It was Aunt Beu who said ignoring truth was never good.

Dottie Sue picked up conversation with Beulah May. The women shared the latest news of people they had in common and the happenings on either side of the bridge.

Then Dot stood to her feet. Betty Jo followed suit.

"We should be goin'. Miz Thorpe, I'd love to have Betty Jo's company fer a bit longer—if'n that's acceptable with y'all."

"Yes, I think that'll be fine fer the time bein'," Beulah affirmed, looking Dot straight in the eye. "Take good care, Dottie Sue."

Dottie stepped off the porch and into the sun. She moved along the stone walk to a respectable distance away.

Beulah turned to her great niece. "Uncle Jack and I are so glad to know yer whereabouts. We were scared fer y'all!"

"I'm sorry to have bin a worry," was all Betty Jo could muster.

"Why, Sugar? Why y'all run away like that?" Beulah's question was laced with frustration.

"I . . . dunno, Aunt Beu," Betty Jo stammered. "I 'spect I wanted answers to questions."

"What questions, Betty Jo?" Beulah's voice turned stern. "Think real hard now. Was there ever a question y'all asked I didn't answer?" Beulah waited for a reply that didn't come.

"Be careful where y'all ask yer questions and of whom." Beulah May turned and entered the house.

Betty Jo watched as the screen door closed, absorbing the chastisement. The guilt inside her grew. Maybe this was what it was like to have a falling out.

Aunt Beulah had called her *our Betty Jo,* but she didn't belong to the Thorpes. Dottie Sue had called her *Henri's Betty Jo*, but she didn't want to belong to him. She once asked Granma who she was named after, but Granma said her mama thought her up a special name. Seems she wasn't named after any kin. She was just plain ol' Betty Jo—who wasn't anyone's at all.

*****

The sound of a piston-thumping car coming down the drive roused Henri from his fitful sleep. Unable to sit upright on his own, he lay on the makeshift bed in the front room focusing on the beadboard above him. That Beulah May always did go for fancy. Never was fair that the Thorpes had everything and he and Leet had to scrounge around for leftovers.

Right now, he'd like to scrounge around for a drop of some good stuff. He sure was thirsty.

He settled his churned-up anger and focused on the sounds from the porch. He drew blanks on the voice that played off of Beulah's big mouth. He was sure he recognized it, but couldn't put a face to its sound. Then he heard the timorous sound of a third voice, and it jarred his memory. Until this moment, he'd forgotten all about Charlene's baby girl.

The screen door banged shut, and Beulah's heavy steps approached.

"Let's get y'all a drink of water," she said.

"Water's not what I be needin'," Henri replied.

"Well, it's what y'all be gettin'," came her retort.

The pair worked together to raise Henri up enough to take a few sips. Then he lay his head back on the pillow, closing his eyes for a moment. Beulah hovered over the bed, assessing the needs for his care.

"Who was visitin' on the porch?" Henri asked.

"Why y'all be askin'?" Beulah returned sharply.

"I thought I knew the voices, but my mind ain't clear since the accident. Jesus, Beulah May, don't shoot the man fer askin' a question." Henri turned his hands over in an I-give-up gesture.

Beulah looked down at her brother-in-law, cringing at the Lord's name being taken in vain. She'd been fit to be tied all morning. It was well past time for politeness to excuse itself.

"Seems to me, Henri Landry, y'all ain't bin thinkin' clear fer a *real* long time now. Y'all been makin' a habit of carin' only 'bout yerself. Since we carried y'all home from the hospital, y'all made not one mention of yer charge. Never asked where she was. Never asked how she was. Nothin'.

"That was yer granddaughter, Betty Jo, and her guardian on the porch just now. They asked to see y'all, Henri. But yer not ready yet.

The Good Lord has given y'all another chance at life. Git yerself well—all of yerself. Then git thangs set right.

"I ain't gonna allow Betty Jo to be hurt by y'all anymore." Beulah walked away leaving Henri before he could formulate a reply.

*****

Resigned for the long, hot walk home, Betty Jo and Dottie Sue headed down the highway toward Logansport. Their strides matched, but their thoughts were kept separate. Two miles before the bridge, the piston-thumping Chevrolet caught up to them. Brother Delbert pulled the car to the side of the road.

"Hop in. We'll git y'all the rest of the way," he called out.

"Thank y'all," Dottie replied over the noise. She and Betty Jo opened the door and settled into the back seat.

"Sorry we didn't catch up sooner." Delbert accelerated the car.

Thankful for salvation from the day's heat, Betty Jo tried to put her mind at rest. She looked at the patches of fields and the swaths of woods as they passed by. She imagined herself exploring the banks of the Sabine and resting near Big Tree. The Pineys were her comfort.

Brother Delbert turned onto Dottie's street and brought them all the way to her house. "I trust the visit went well. Lemme know if y'all be in need of anythang."

"Thank y'all fer carryin' us home," Dottie Sue called out.

"Thank y'all, sir," Betty Jo echoed.

Preacher Philip got out of the car with the two women and walked them to the porch. "Ma'am, I was wondering if I might make a social call later this week? Say Friday evening?" He turned his gaze to Betty Jo.

Dottie Sue was startled by her new role. She sized up the Reverend Philip Harris. His face was boyish as he shifted weight from one foot to the next. He could not be long into his twenties. She was pretty sure Henri would not be pleased for his granddaughter to be courting. He'd prefer to keep her close so as to have someone to keep his house. Beulah May would be reluctant because she wouldn't want to admit that Betty Jo was entering marriageable age. Yet, it seemed the decision was hers to make. It also occurred to her that having trustworthy manfolk around on a Friday night might be a good thing.

"That depends if'n Betty Jo is agreeable," Dottie said.

"Is it, Betty Jo? Would it be agreeable to keep company this Friday?" Philip appealed with a smile.

Betty Jo remembered the evening Philip happened by the plank house. She had longed to talk with this stranger then. She was eager to know his real story. Now she had the opportunity to do so with propriety. "Yes, Preacher Philip, that would be agreeable."

"Until Friday, then." Philip tipped his hat and hurried to the car.

Dottie Sue stood looking at the cupboard. The bareness kept growing. She needed to save every penny, and she knew it unlikely to receive grace at the general store for credit. There were only two eggs left. She sighed. If only she had laying hens and a means to feed them.

She reached up for a can of last year's fruit and the flour. Supper would be peaches over pancakes. They would save the remaining milk for more grits in the morning.

Dot recalled the story of a woman in the Old Testament who, in the middle of a famine, took the last of her supplies to feed the prophet Elijah. From that point on, her supply of flour and oil never ran out. Dottie hoped for a similar miracle.

Betty Jo came in from tending the garden, a crookneck squash in her hand. The women sat down to supper. Dottie blessed the food, thankful that for now they had what was needed.

Before Dot took her first bite she said, "Betty Jo, if'n I don't hear word about workin' fer Jack Lee, I think tomorrow mornin' be a good time fer fishin'."

Betty Jo answered with a smile.

Betty Jo led Dottie Sue along the fisherman's trail heading downstream—away from the noise of the lumber mill and railroad, and out of view of the bridge. She wished she were in her stomping grounds, but the walk to Big Tree was way too far. Sometimes the path petered out, but would pick up again. She enjoyed the challenge of locating a good place to fish, but was grateful they didn't have to go through thick brush. Dot was having a hard enough time navigating the hike as it was, and she surely did hate the chiggers.

Oddly, there'd been no rain since Papa's accident so the water wasn't horribly muddy. Betty Jo spotted a patch of sand along the bank. They wouldn't be the first to fish there. Lending Dottie a hand periodically, the two women descended the slope.

Betty Jo prepared her line. She turned to see if Dot needed help, but she was ready to fish.

"Did y'all and my mama go fishin' together, Miz Dottie?" Betty Jo asked.

"Oh me, oh my, Girl. That was a long time ago. I 'member we went a couple times just the two of us. Then Jimmy come along with some other pals. I liked the fishin', but yer mama preferred the company. Sometimes, we all'd split up and go our own ways. Yer mama would stay by herself, drawin' and writin' and I suppose thinkin' 'bout the future." Sadness shaded Dot's eyes. "Cain't tell y'all how much I've regretted leavin' her alone."

Dottie Sue moved down to the end of the sandbar and cast her line.

Betty Jo began to fish, chewing on Dot's words.

Dottie pulled out the first one, laughing. "Cain't believe I kin still do this!" she exclaimed, studying her catch. "Fried up, yer goin' to be real good!"

Betty Jo glanced at the squirming creature in Dot's hand. Then she examined the place her fishing line entered the water, and moved to the other end of the sandbar.

Dot brought in another catfish for the basket—this time with a lack of fanfare. Shortly after, with solemn face, Betty Jo caught the prize of the morning—a respectable sized bass.

With the three fish in the basket and the gear packed up, the two women sat in the cool sand watching the river roll by.

"Betty Jo, y'all're like that calm water over there. I cain't tell on the surface what's going on underneath," Dot ventured.

Betty Jo sat looking at the water.

"I know y'all made yerself quiet in Henri's house. But now yer with me. It's okay to talk."

Betty Jo looked at her new friend. "Dottie, do y'all think I come to be on one of Mama's fishin' trips?"

"Why, Girl, I'm shore it was so," Dot quietly responded.

"And y'all regretted leavin' Mama alone?"

Dot sat silent.

"Dottie Sue, do ya'll regret me, too?"

"Oh, heavens, Girl!" Dottie gasped.

"Seems like ev'rybody regrets me." Betty Jo stood to her feet. "Sometimes I regret me, too." She picked up her pole and the basket and turned to ascend the river bank.

By the time Dottie Sue arrived back home, Betty Jo had fileted the fish and was in the garden harvesting vegetables.

Dot entered the house and fried up the crookneck squash and catfish. It was no matter that it'd heat the house up early. The afternoon was devoted to canning the vegetables of the first summer harvest. Once a certain temperature inside was reached, hot was just hot.

The skillet was ready before the sun was straight up in the sky. Dot stuck her head out the back door to call Betty Jo in from the garden.

They sat down in their places at the small table—a routine now established. Dot prayed, "Thank Y'all, Lord fer a river with fish and a garden with vegetables. Amen."

Betty Jo and Dottie ate, relishing the rest as much as the food.

Braving her first words since the river, Betty Jo attempted small talk. "Yer fry is real good, Miz Dottie."

"Y'all have yer papa to thank fer it. He was the one to show me how to season Cajun style," Dot replied.

"My papa?" Betty Jo wondered how this could be.

Dottie reached for another helping of squash. "Shorely, Girl. When y'all were real little, Henri hired me and Denny Ron to help . . . well, distribute his products. Some of our hours were long, so we'd fix food on a camp stove so's we could keep on workin'. He didn't care fer my fry—said it was plain. So, he showed me how to spice it up to his likin'. I done it this way ever since."

"Was I there?" Betty Jo asked.

"No, y'all were with yer Granma Leet. Henri never mixed his bus'ness with home life." Dot set her fork down and leaned back in the chair.

Betty Jo chewed slowly as she considered what Dot disclosed.

Dottie changed the subject. "This morning y'all made big talk sayin' ev'rybody regrets y'all comin' to be. I can see why y'all might think that."

Betty Jo swallowed hard. She had feared that her words at the river would come back.

Dot continued. "The truth is that the circumstance of how y'all came to be was regretful. It brang upheaval and pain.

"But there be a big diff'rence 'tween regrettin' circumstance and regrettin' a person. Y'all're Charlene's daughter. Yer the Landry's legacy. Like a beautiful gift of silver that gets tarnished—when all the thangs that don't matter are polished away, the true treasure shines.

"Betty Jo, yer the treasure.

"And to answer the question—no, Betty Jo, I don't regret y'all. Not one bit." Dottie Sue pushed away from the table and began preparing the vegetables.

Betty Jo finished her food, then joined her mama's best friend in the kitchen.

*****

"Henri, y'all have a visitor," Beulah May said, walking across the front room.

"Mebbe I don't want one," Henri grumbled.

"Let's get y'all sat up now." Beulah reached her hand behind his neck and prompted him to lift his head. She pulled the pillows up for him to lean against the old wooden door cut to serve as the headboard.

"Push yerself up now," she commanded.

Seeing no options, Henri complied.

Beulah adjusted the bed sheet. "Behave yerself," she said before pulling a chair over to his side and exiting.

After the dizziness settled, it felt good to be upright. It was more normal.

Brother Tucker, with his genial countenance, filled Henri's view. *Good mercy—a hypocrite come to visit.*

Things had been getting boring just lying there, and he couldn't stop thinking about the one thing he really needed. Perhaps this distraction wouldn't be so bad.

"Afternoon, Mr. Landry. May I call y'all by yer given name?" Brother Tucker asked.

Henri shrugged. "Suit yerself."

"How y'all feelin' today, Henri?" Brother Tucker asked as he sat down in the wooden chair.

Henri, shrugged again.

"Is there anythang I kin do fer y'all?" the Baptist preacher asked.

"I shore could use a drink," Henri said.

Right away the preacher leaned forward and located the pitcher and a glass; but before he could act on it, Henri said, "Not water, Tucker. I need some good stuff."

Brother Tucker settled back in the chair. "Seems that kind of stuff has only brought y'all trouble."

"Don't be preachin' at me, Tucker." Henri said with disgust. "Y'all know most the menfolk in yer congregation make a habit of the hooch."

The two men listened for a while as the Thorpe's living room clock ticked out time.

"Well, Henri, I do believe the Good Lord has given y'all a new chance at life," Brother Tucker resumed.

"So, I bin told," Henri mumbled.

"Make good use of this opportunity. 'Today's the day of salvation,' the Good Book says. I'll come agin end of the week, Lord willin'."

Brother Tucker stood. He closed his eyes and moved his mouth with inaudible words before turning and walking away.

Henri could hear whispering between Tucker and Beulah May at the front door. He was sure they were discussing what a lost cause he was.

*****

The low rumble of a truck caught Dottie's attention. Wiping her hands on a towel, she hurried out to the porch. A farm truck laden with supplies pulled up in front of the house. Leaving it to idle, the driver quick-stepped up the walk.

"Afternoon, Miz Dottie. Mr. Thorpe said to get this to y'all 'fore headin' back." He handed her the note and with a nod of the head turned to go. As the truck disappeared down the block, she read.

> *Meet at the big barn tomorrow,*
> *just before sun-up.*
> *Bring Betty Jo.*
> > *Jack Lee*

"Thank Y'all, Jesus! Hallelujah!" Dottie exclaimed, drawing Betty Jo out of the house. "We have work—least ways for a day." Dottie Sue held the note out for Betty Jo to see.

Betty Jo recognized her name. "Me, too?" she asked astonished. Dottie Sue began to sing.

> *Oh, glory be to Jesus let the hallelujahs roll.*
> *Help me ring the Savior's praises far and wide.*

Her bliss blossomed into a jig. Betty Jo backed up to the limit of the porch and clapped the heavy beat.

> *For I've opened up tow'rd heaven*
> *all the windows of my soul*
> *And I'm living on the hallelujah side*

The third time through the refrain, Betty Jo contributed her voice to the last line. Laughing, the women pulled back from their felicity.

"Oh me, oh my, Girl!" Dottie caught her breath. "We best git to work. I'd like to give testimony to answered prayer tonight, but first we be needin' ev'rythang ready fer the mornin'. I 'spect it be well over 'n hour walk to Jack Lee's barn."

After the kitchen was set in order, food prepared for the next day, and work clothes laid out, Dottie Sue and Betty Jo walked to the little store-front church. They slipped into a bench at the back just as Brother

Delbert opened in prayer. After a song was sung, the sparse congregation was cued to sit down.

"Would any of y'all like to stand and testify of the Lord's goodness?" Brother Delbert asked.

Betty Jo looked around the long, narrow room. Like Dottie Sue and herself, folks were in their everyday clothes this Wednesday evening. Men wore bib overalls. Their white foreheads contrasted with tanned faces. Women wore flour sack dresses with hair pulled into tight buns—hair intended for chores rather than beauty. The Coloreds sat off to the side, their children barefoot.

Her eyes lingered on the back of Preacher Philip as he sat in the front row. No suit coat was in sight, and he had rolled up the sleeves of his button-down shirt. Someone in the middle stood to give praise. The others listened intently, nodding heads in agreement. The pattern repeated itself. Philip turned all the way around and made eye contact with each person who spoke. Betty Jo prepared to avert her eyes should he glance her way, but he looked directly at those giving testimony—even when the Colored man spoke. Betty Jo was troubled by the boldness of this behavior. The odd ways of Philip Harris betrayed the fact that he was not from around here.

The testimonies came to a halt. Brother Delbert tarried. "Anyone else?"

Dottie Sue rose to her feet. "Brother, I'd like to give thanks tonight fer answered prayer."

All the heads turned their way, except for the Coloreds who kept their heads forward. Betty Jo felt heat flush her face.

"The Lord is supplyin' all our needs according to His riches in glory," Dot continued.

Amens echoed through the room.

Riches? Betty Jo knew there weren't a single rich folk in that place. *Shoot, if the Lord was so rich, why were His people so poor?*

"Preacher Philip, please come and open God's Word to us." Delbert stepped aside as the young reverend positioned himself at the pulpit.

This time, in spite of his quick and fancy words, Betty Jo listened intently to what the handsome Yank had to say.

With the closing prayer completed, Delbert made his way to the back. "Thank y'all fer the testimony tonight," he said to Dottie Sue. "Did y'all find work at the Thorpe's then?"

"Yessir, he sent a message fer us to come tomorrow, first thang," Dottie answered.

"Well, praise the Lord!" Delbert exclaimed. "I'll drive y'all over."

"Oh, no, Brother," Dot shook her head. I don't wanna put y'all out any. We kin walk."

"No good y'all walkin' that highway in the dark. I'll pick up 'bout an hour 'fore sunrise. That'll leave plenty of time." He stepped aside to unclog the only aisle, then walked away.

Betty Jo looked across the room. Philip was up front talking earnestly with a young man.

"Ready to go?" Dot asked with a smile.

Betty Jo's face reddened. Her stare had been found out.

"Big day tomorrow. Let's git home fer a good rest," Dot said.

They walked home in silence. Then before entering the house Dottie Sue shared what troubled her mind. "If Jack Lee keeps us on fer the whole harvest, we be needin' to figure a way to stay near the fields. It's too far to walk, and we cain't be beholden to anyone fer a ride."

Betty Jo mused. It seemed that one answered prayer just led to needing to pray about something else.

CHAPTER FIVE

Henri's nerves were frayed. The airiness and brightness of the Thorpe's house threatened to erase the last piece of his sanity. He had to get out and back to his way of life. He'd done it before—stormed in and took what was his and left. The problem was twofold. What was his was now in the form of a young woman who'd clearly gained independence. The second problem was that his body was broke.

Two days ago, in spite of a surge of motivation, he couldn't get himself to even sit up, much less walk to the window to see who was on the porch visiting. Then yesterday the Thorpes had trapsed off to Bible Study, leaving him alone in the house. Listening to the steady tick-tock of the clock did nothing to alleviate the urge. The thought of the bed pan disgusted him, so he lifted the sheet away and pushed himself up in bed. He inched his legs over the edge and forced himself to sit up. The swooning throughout his body should have been his warning, but he lowered his feet to the floor and attempted to stand. Pain surged and mixed with intense dizziness. He lost the contents of his supper, and in the strain of gagging wetted and soiled himself. He collapsed back onto the bed in a puddle of despair.

When Jack Lee and Beulah May returned home, they spoke and moved with gentleness as they cleaned him up. They replaced the soiled clothing and bedding. Beulah set herself to the chore of laundry. Jack Lee stood next to his bedside.

"Lemme be," Henri said softly, as he leaned against the headboard looking toward the window.

Pulling up the chair to the side of the bed, his brother-in-law by marriage began with the small talk. "Early mornin' tomorrow, harvest starts. We're blessed that cotton's brangin' a respectable price. Oil's doin' good, too," he added

"I s'pose my job in the oil field is long give 'way by now." Henri turned his head to see Jack Lee's reaction.

Jack nodded. "S'pose so. Henri, y'all should know that Sheriff Davis located yer Blind Pig and shut it down the weekend after yer accident. Took advantage of the situation, he did."

"He come and harassed me at the hospital." Henri frowned. "Lost my truck, lost my job, lost my bus'ness. Guess I lost it all." He tried to shift his weight, seeking some kind of comfort.

"Not quite. Yer forgettin' somethin'—or rather someone." Jack Lee paused before continuing. "Betty Jo's comin' tomorrow to work harvest. Would y'all like to see her?"

Henry moved his narrowed eyes back to the window.

"I be lettin' y'all think 'bout it some," Jack Lee said. "Time to turn in fer the night." He slowly stood up. "I thank the Lord fer His kindness to y'all. He is the God of second chances."

"So, I keep hearin'," Henri muttered.

Anger had been boiling inside Henri since that conversation. There'd been many times in his life he'd faced humiliation—the day his momma cried as his father stormed out of the house, the times he was taunted at the schoolyard by chants of "Ragin' Cajun," when Leet's daddy refused to acknowledge their marriage, and the moment last night when Beulah May Thorpe walked into the house to his vile smells. To all of it now was added the indignity of his granddaughter being a common laborer for the man who'd had it all handed to him.

*****

Betty Jo stretched her frame upright. She rubbed her lower back with her left hand. Her eyes under the wide brim of a straw hat winced as she inspected the fingers of her right hand. Already red and jabbed by the pricks of cotton husks, she pondered what condition they'd be in by day's end.

Never before had she helped Uncle Jack with harvest. Papa wouldn't allow it—something about the Thorpes having everything given to them, and that no Landy should ever humble themselves by working for them. A couple summers ago, when Papa was on a spirit's binge, Betty Jo asked Uncle Jack and Aunt Beu if she could work the fields.

"Heavens no, Sugar!" Aunt Beulah blurted. Then composing herself, she explained that it wasn't proper for a young lady to work shoulder to shoulder with vagrants. Instead, Aunt Beu arranged for Betty Jo to work the vegetable garden near the house for a small allowance that would be kept secret from Papa.

Now that Betty Jo was experiencing harvest first-hand, she was thankful for her kinfolk's stance back then. Uncle Jack Lee was continuing to be protective. He'd made it clear that morning that there'd be two groups of harvesters and those groups were not to mix. Anyone failing to honor the rule could find work elsewhere. So, Betty Jo and Dottie were in a small group of women and children picking at the field nearest the house. The larger group of menfolk were driven in the truck and dropped off elsewhere.

Betty Jo stooped over and resumed pulling the white bolls out of the husks. Money wouldn't be earned by just thinking.

By noon, the small group of harvesters moved back into the shade where the field and the Pineys met. An involuntary groan escaped from Dottie Sue as she slipped the sack of cotton off her shoulder. She sat gingerly on the ground next to Betty Jo. The women ate quietly and slowly, taking turns relieving themselves in the cover of the woods. After a short rest they continued their work.

Betty Jo had started working quickly that morning, but as the day wore on and her sack became heavier, she found herself slowing down. Wiping sweat off her face with the back of a sleeve, she glanced at the row next to her. Dottie Sue had kept the same pace all day long— neither slow nor fast.

Music rose up from the group, as with the rising heat.

"Oh, I went down south for to see my Sal," one of the women called out in song.

"Sing Polly Wolly Doodle all the day," answered the experienced workers.

"My Sally is a spunky gal," sang the leader.

"Sing Polly Wolly Doodle all the day," the group responded.

As the singing continued, Betty Jo found herself able to keep a steady pace. Her mind went to the musical interactions and away from the pain of repetition.

Finally, the sun dipped past the tree line and the farm truck arrived with the water barrel and instructions.

"Boss says that's a day," Eddie, the hired man said. "Let's figure the pay. Come back tomorrow at the Big Barn, same time."

The women fell into line with their cotton sacks to conclude the day's business. When Dottie Sue and Betty Jo got to the front, Eddie instructed them to step to the side. They exchanged puzzled looks but followed the directions. As they waited, Betty Jo watched the proceedings. Bags of cotton were weighed and coins were placed into open palms. Momentary relief would appear in the eyes of her co-workers, but it was not enough to erase the despondence etched in their faces.

When the laborers had dispersed, Eddie said, "Miz Thorpe says to carry y'all to the house. Boss will square up with y'all there." He gestured to the truck bed. Betty Jo stepped up and lifted their precious bags onto the bed of the truck. Then she held out her hand to assist Dottie Sue. They brushed past the water barrel and through the sacks of cotton to sit on the wood bench along the side. Holding the railing, they braced for the bumpy ride to the big yellow house.

Beulah May walked down the drive to meet the truck. Eddie idled it and hurried to the back, lending a hand as the women disembarked.

"Mr. Thorpe will be here soon," he said.

"But y'all need to weigh our bags." Dottie Sue's voice held urgency.

"He'll be here shortly," the man repeated. Dottie Sue and Betty Jo numbly stood watching the truck pull out.

"Come y'all. I fixed a bite to eat," Beulah gestured to the oak tree with a table underneath. Hunger overtook their puzzlement as the women looked at the spread of food.

"We'll tarry for Jack Lee. Y'all kin wash at the pump and then pull up a chair and rest," Beulah instructed.

At the washing trough, Dottie Sue and Betty Jo whispered their suppositions to one another. It had been a harsh day of work. Now they were wary at this unusual treatment.

"Thangs will come to light soon 'nough," Dottie whispered.

Uncle Jack Lee pulled up in his Dodge Brothers pick-up truck. He'd bought it in Shreveport three years ago before the trouble with the banks. Betty Jo remembered well the day her Papa had seen the new truck parked out front of the Thorpes. He was mighty angry that night. She did her best to stay out of his way. Once the drink took hold, she snuck out of the house and into the shelter of the woods.

The women waited for Jack to wash up and come to the table. He greeted Beulah with a kiss on the cheek and an *evenin' ladies* to Dottie Sue and Betty Jo. He reached his hands out, and they joined in an unbroken circle.

He prayed. "Thank Ya'll, Lord, fer the blessin's of the field and the good work of harvest. Give us wisdom for our days. Bless this food. Amen."

The eating and the conversation commenced.

Betty Jo did not understand how small talk could go on for so long when there were important things to discuss. She knew, though, the politeness of attending to it.

With an empty plate, Jack Lee thanked his wife for the meal. Then he began. "Dottie Sue, Beulah tells me y'all are gettin' free of the bus'ness. Shorely glad to know it."

"Times bin hard, Mr. Thorpe. Bin tryin' fer a while now. Henri's accident and ev'rythang that's happened since is like God sayin' 'Get out now, Dottie!' "

"Yer folks would be proud," Jack added.

"I 'spect there hasn't been much I've done they'd be proud of," Dottie admitted. "I do so miss them ev'ry day."

"Their love fer y'all was strong," Beulah assured.

"Yes, ma'am. I'm grateful." Dottie Sue blinked, preventing water from escaping her eyes.

Dottie Sue had parents? Betty Jo had been thinking only about getting answers to her questions. She hadn't thought to ask any about Dottie.

"Thangs are a bit complicated right now, but we'd like to be of help. Dottie Sue, I'll speak blunt. Y'all need to keep clear of Henri. 'Specially now in his recovery."

Dottie nodded her understanding.

"This is difficult since Betty Jo is in yer care," Jack Lee said.

"Uncle Jack, I ain't in anyone's care." Betty Jo entered the conversation with veracity. "I bin on my own fer a long time now. Dottie and I are takin' care of each other."

"That be enough disrespect," Dottie interjected sharply.

Instantly, Betty Jo silenced her free talking.

"We know y'all grew up quick, Betty Jo." Jack Lee resumed, "Fact remains that the two of y'all're together and in need of a way to live. Henri is recuperatin' at our house and in need of stayin' plumb away from his old life.

"I'd like to keep y'all on at the farm least through harvest, pickin' cotton and other jobs needin' doin'." Jack reached into his pocket and pulled out some coins. "Here is yer pay fer today.

"Y'all be paid an allowance, enough to sustain and mebbe even some to save. Bein' Henri's here at the farmhouse, y'all could stay at the Landry's. This should give time to see a clearer picture of our circumstance. How does that arrangement sound?"

Dottie Sue and Betty Jo exchanged glances.

"It sounds real good. Thank y'all, sir," Dottie Sue said. "I agree that it'll be good fer me to break away from Henri Landry. I'll do my level best to stay clear."

"Good. Then it's settled," Beulah concluded.

"Thank y'all, Uncle Jack and Aunt Beu," Betty Jo added.

She was happy that she was returning to the little plank house. She loved being near the river and Big Tree, but not too far from the yellow farmhouse. How much better would it be with the good company of Dottie and without the threat of Papa?

Jack Lee drove them to Logansport. When they arrived at Dot's house, Betty Jo gave him a hug of thanks. For the first time, she noticed the tired on his face.

"I'll fetch y'all 'morrow mornin' after I get the laborers started in the fields," he said.

Sore and exhausted, the women made their way inside. They would close up the house and pack their needed items after getting a night's rest. Betty Jo crawled onto her cot. Her final thoughts of the eventful day were of Preacher Philip. He was to come courting tomorrow evening and they wouldn't be there. Remorse drifted her into a deep sleep.

*****

Through the shadows of gray, Henri could see his granddaughter bending over a massive cotton plant. The bag around her shoulders weighed her down.

At first, she picked quickly, but then she slowed until she came to a stop. She looked at her surroundings—puzzlement on her face and questions in her eyes.

She sat down and lifted her head. She waited with eyes closed, as if in a dream of her own. Walking between the rows of cotton, a blonde-headed man approached. His smile filled his soft face. He motioned for her to stand up, but she did not move. Calmly, he sat down next to her. Taking her hands, he smoothed the fingertips until the cuts disappeared and torn skin returned to smoothness. Joy replaced her blank expression.

Together they stood.

Hesitating, she turned to look at her papa.

Henri crossed his arms. He looked back at his granddaughter, unblinking, and saw the sorrow in her eyes.

The couple began to walk out of the field, hand in hand. Dismay seized him, and he thrust out his arms in desperation. An amber beam of light enveloped her. He tried to call her name but no sound came out his mouth. It was too late. A black cloud descended, obscuring his view. Charlene's baby girl had disappeared from his sight.

Henri rustled in the bed. A new dream had unfolded in his mind, and he sensed that he was the now the one to be left behind and left alone.

*****

Betty Jo awoke to the sound of pounding rain. It did not come as a surprise. They were due for a soaker. No picking would be done this morning. She stretched, trying to alleviate the ache in her back. Dottie was in the kitchen, so now it was her turn in the bathroom.

When she emerged, Dottie Sue was sitting at the table with a rose-patterned china cup in her hand.

"Coffee?" she asked.

"Yes, ma'am," Betty Jo said as she sat down.

Dot took the second cup she'd placed on the table and filled it from the pot.

"Thank y'all. These shore are perty," Betty Jo said before taking a sip.

"They were my mother's pride and joy." Dot explained, "Ev'ry so often, I take them out of the hutch. I figured this mornin' was a good time to use 'em."

"Yer mama's gone?" Betty Jo asked, though she knew the answer.

"Both Mother and Daddy passed a while ago," Dot answered.

"Y'all have brothers and sisters?"

"I do. My sister, Suzanne, lives off in Houston with her husband. I don't see her very often. It's such a far piece. My brother, well . . . he has nothin' to do with me on account of the life I've lived." Dot reached for the pot and filled her cup.

"I'm thankful to have people, though. Yer Granma and Aunt Beulah were my mama's cousins. So, yer mama wasn't just my best friend. She was my second cousin." Dot giggled at Betty Jo's surprised expression.

"We're kinfolk?" Betty Jo asked.

"Shore 'nough. Twice removed." Dot laughed. "See, I told y'all that pert near ev'rybody is related 'round here."

"Well, I'm glad fer it." Betty Jo responded. Then she dared a bigger question. "Miz Dottie, you ever married?"

"Oh, Girl," Dot sighed. "Never married. Just entangled." She stared at the contents of her cup before taking a sip. Setting it down again, she changed the subject. "Don't know if Jack Lee will be comin' in the rain or not, but we be needin' to get ev'rythang ready fer when he does. So thankful we have work and a place to stay nearby."

Betty Jo's eyes studied the china in the hutch. "My house is shore not as fine as yers," she volunteered.

"Don't y'all worry none. It'll be just right fer us," Dot assured. "I know how to use a pump and an outhouse, Betty Jo." A broad smile crossed her face.

"Dottie Sue, what if Uncle Jack comes to fetch us today? What 'bout Preacher Philip?" Betty Jo wondered.

"That preacher man, he's smart. He'll figure where we be. And if he's serious about courtin' y'all, he'll make ev'ry effort." Dot finished her coffee and stood up slowly. "If y'all like, write 'im a letter explainin' our situation."

Betty Jo lowered her head. "Miz Dottie, I cain't write anymore'n I kin read."

Dot sat back down, chagrined at her verbal error. She looked her young friend in the eye. "At some point we be needin' to remedy that."

*****

Jack Lee called off the pickers on account of the rain. He was relieved in a way. Harvest had just begun, and he was already tired. He needed to regulate his energy in order to see it all the way through. A day of quiet would be good.

He'd told Dottie Sue and Betty Jo that he'd move them over today. Surely, they'd understand the postponement.

There'd been a lot of pressure lately to get things figured out. Too many people needed his help right now—folks desperate for work, the tragic circumstances of his wife's kin, and financial problems at Joaquin Baptist Church that was known only to the deacons. So much of what he could provide hinged on a good harvest this year.

Carry one another's burdens and so fulfill the law of Christ rolled through his thoughts. Well, he figured he had about all he could carry. Anymore and he wouldn't be able to breathe.

As he walked into the kitchen to get another round of coffee, sharpness stabbed him. He stopped and inhaled in a gasp of pain. One hand on the counter and the other clutching his chest, he forced himself to resume breathing. Fighting to stand aright, he got his bearings. He stutter-stepped toward the kitchen table, but before he reached his chair, Jack Lee Thorpe fell onto the floor.

*****

The humidity hung in clumps against the trees. Heat rose in the aftermath of the downpour. Uncle Jack did not come. With the packing done and the house prepared for vacancy, Dottie and Betty Jo took a quick walk to the general store and spent their hard-earned coins on food staples to add to the newly canned vegetables. Now they waited, welcoming the extra rest.

Betty Jo turned her thoughts to Philip's pending visit. She didn't know much about the menfolk. Papa and Jack Lee were the only ones she really knew. She wasn't sure how to act with a young one. Whatever would she find to say? Would he expect something she didn't want to give? Like most things, she was pretty sure she'd need to figure it out for herself.

Philip Harris, in church shoes, trousers, and collared shirt, strode down the walkway. He hesitated a moment before stepping onto Dottie Sue's little porch.

Dot met him at the screen door.

"Good evening, Miss Dottie Sue," he greeted. "Quite a storm we had earlier."

"Yes, indeed, Preacher Philip," she replied.

"Please, just call me Philip," he requested.

Dot smiled in acknowledgment. "Make yerself comfortable. I'll fetch Betty Jo."

"Thank you kindly," he said, removing his hat and smoothing back his blonde hair. He sat down in one of the two chairs. Looking around, he fumbled with the hat before resting it in his lap.

The screen door pushed open. Betty Jo appeared in the same dress she wore last Sunday, her dark hair styled neatly. A hint of rose wafted across the porch.

Philip stood. "Good evening, Betty Jo. You look lovely."

"Evenin', Preacher Philip," she returned, surprised at the quiver in her voice. Her plan had been to match the character of his speech tonight, but she did not know what to do about the compliment. She could not think of anything else to add.

"Please call me Philip," he said and gestured for her to sit down.

They sat looking out into the yard as the light dimmed. Betty Jo synchronized her breathing to the evening sounds.

"Does this remind you of the night we met?" Philip ventured. "The humidity after the rain. The cicadas and crickets. Everything except the beautiful singing."

"And the crawdads," Betty Jo added with a giggle.

Philip smiled. "A lot has happened in the days since then. How are you doing, Betty Jo?"

How am I doing? In her 15 years, this was the first she recalled being asked that question in a way that wished for an honest answer.

Dottie Sue pushed open the screen door, carrying a tray with two glasses from the hutch. She placed them on the little table between the two chairs then quickly returned inside the house to the duet of thankfulness.

Betty Jo reached for the glass nearest her. She sipped the sweet tea, collecting her thoughts.

"Y'all know when a real big fish is on the line and fightin' for all it's worth? Y'all kin think mebbe that fish is gonna win. I think thangs bein' as they are is like that. Lots of struggle and all goin' on and me just tryin' to hold the line." Betty Jo took another sip.

Philip sat quietly.

"Y'all need to know that Dottie Sue and me are gonna be on the other side at the plank house. We'll be workin' at Uncle Jack's place and be needin' to be near."

"Of course, that makes good sense. I'm so glad that the two of you have work." Philip turned to look at Betty Jo. For the first time, she met his blue eyes. "I must say, though, I'll miss you not being nearby. I would like for us to be better acquainted."

In Betty Jo's imaginings of what it would be like to keep company on the porch with a fellow, she could never have thought up a more perfect moment.

The clatter of a wagon announced an arrival. Dusk light revealed a floppy-brimmed hat sitting on top of a manfolk in overalls. The mare stopped with a jerk in front of the house. A slew of curse words ascended above the night sounds. The driver slipped off the seat and wobbled up the walk, yelling Dottie Sue's name.

Philip stood, set his hat on the chair, and stepped to the edge of the porch.

The man looked up at the towering figure before him. "Who in hell are y'all!"

Dot arrived at the screen door. "Denny Ron? What're y'all doin' here?"

"I come to make amends," he slurred.

"I told y'all not to be comin' here agin." Dot walked onto the porch and stood next to Philip. "I'm done with the bus'ness, and I'm done with y'all. Turn yer drunk self 'round and git on."

"Woman, I come to claim what's mine. Ain't leavin." Denny stepped up and attempted to push past Philip. He was met with two iron hands gripping his arms.

"The lady said she doesn't want you here. You need to leave."

"Lady? My word!" he scoffed.

"Leave now, sir." Philip tightened his hold.

"This ain't yer bus'ness, Yankee!" he exclaimed, twisting to get free. Philip used the drunken man's momentum to turn him around. He stumbled down the porch steps and landed in the yard.

Philip stepped down to the walk after him. Taking him by the arm, he helped him up. "Leave now, sir," he commanded.

Denny Ron hesitated. The fire in his eyes extinguished. He turned and swaggered toward his wagon.

Philip Harris quick-stepped to the porch and grabbed his hat. "I'll make sure he gets home. Blessings to you both." He hurried to the wagon and redirected the drunk man to the back. With the women watching the spectacle, Denny Ron was wrestled into the cargo bed before passing out.

Philip approached the mare, speaking gently to her. He looked toward the porch and tipped his hat. Climbing up to the seat with reins in hand, he gave soft commands. The wagon turned and disappeared down the street.

"It's good we won't be here fer a while," Dot said as the women sat down.

Betty Jo pondered the situation. Leaving might help Dottie get free of Denny, but leaving would keep her from Philip. She wasn't sure how she'd be able to keep that fish on the line.

The sound of a vehicle approached.

"What now?" Dottie Sue asked. "Too late for Mr. Thorpe to be fetchin' us."

They recognized the Dodge Brothers truck through the shadows as it came to a stop—its headlamps eerily illuminating the woods at the end of the street. It was not Jack Lee who got out from the driver's side. It was the hired man, Eddie.

He ran up the walk. Dottie and Betty Jo stood when they saw the tension in his face.

"Betty Jo, come quick! Miz Thorpe needs y'all."

*****

At long last, Beulah May Thorpe sat down. Still, she fought the inclination to cry. Trouble followed Henri around. He held it by a leash and wouldn't let go. But Jack Lee's trouble was just plain unfair. He was a good man, doing his best to live by The Word of Truth. Truly it does rain on the just and the unjust.

"We're in trouble. We need help," she prayed, losing the battle and giving into tears.

She thought through the events of the day. She had shared an early breakfast with Jack Lee, the rain sequestering them from the world. They exhausted their thoughts about all the problems surrounding them. Jack concluded the conversation by stating that God was faithful and would help them walk through the murky waters.

Beulah went in to tend to a surly Henri. Then she headed upstairs to tidy the rooms. It was a perfect chore for a rainy day. As she was tucking the clean sheet on the guest bed, she stopped. Her spirit knew.

"Oh, God, no!" Her feet thudded down the stairs.

In the troubles of life, Beulah May had prided herself on being steady and calm. She was a prayer warrior, not given to the winds of upset. But when she saw her sweet husband of 42 years fallen on the kitchen floor, angst erupted.

She screamed.

God sent Eddie to help. Uncharacteristically, he had come up to the house. It was her scream that set him into action. He helped Jack Lee to his chair and eventually to the bedroom. He fetched the doctor, sent word to their children, and drove to Logansport. He reminded her that it was Betty Jo's place to care for Henri. Indeed, he guided her through the flood waters of this turbulent day.

With a bag of clothes and personal items in her arms, Betty Jo entered through the back door of the Thorpe's farmhouse and into the kitchen. She noted the unwashed dishes and muddy boot tracks across the floor. She set her bag down on the table. She would go straight to the big bedroom, hoping Papa would not notice her as she passed through the front room.

Lightly knocking on the door, she pushed it open. Uncle Jack lay in bed asleep, bathed in pasty pale. Aunt Beulah looked up from her chair, red-eyed.

Betty Jo walked over, bent down, and hugged her great aunt.

"Oh, Sugar." Beulah let out a whisper.

Betty Jo rested her hand on her aunt's shoulder, thinking about what may have transpired in the Thorpe's house that day. Beulah pushed herself out of the chair and gestured toward the door. They moved out into the hallway.

"It was a heart attack. Doc says that if Jack Lee's gonna recover, he be needin' rest—and rest for a real long time. We sent word to the kids. Told Bernie not to come on account of his harvest. I expect Ruth Ann will come Sunday."

Beulah hesitated before getting to the main point. "Sugar, there are matters of bus'ness I be needin' to attend to. At the same time, it's my duty to give Jack Lee undivided attention. Now it's yers to care fer yer papa."

Betty Jo understood this to be the case from the moment Eddie fetched her. She wanted to leave behind her life with Papa. Now she would be stuck caring for him.

"Yer Papa is set fer now. Check on 'im a couple times through the night," Beulah instructed. "Take Ruth Ann's old room upstairs. Make use of anythang y'all need from the wardrobe and dresser."

"Yes, ma'am." Betty Jo added, "I shore am sorry 'bout Uncle Jack."

Betty Jo stepped lightly down the hall, fetched her bag from the kitchen, and walked upstairs to get organized. She recounted the events of the last two weeks and how she had returned to the upstairs bedroom of the Thorpes. *Full circle*, she thought.

Betty Jo awakened early. Her eyes traveled through the shadows of the room. She looked at the small dresser and its matching mirror. She pushed her feet against the patchwork quilt folded at the foot of the wrought-iron bed. Now she realized that this was where her mother stayed while she was pregnant. Some of the musty clothes in the closet fit her length, but were too big for her shape. *Were they my mother's?* If this was the room where she was birthed, then this was where her mother crossed River Jordan. The thought was somber, yet it seemed right for her to be here where her life began and where her mother's life ended. Somehow it connected her to her people and eased the dread of caring for Papa.

Twice in the night, she had checked on Papa. He groaned with restlessness but, to her relief, remained asleep. No doubt she would face him today.

Betty Jo quickly cleaned up and put on a dress from the closet. Descending the stairs, she walked to the kitchen. She looked in the pantry and icebox, marveling to find each one full—a contrast to Dot's house and her empty life with Papa.

She lit the wood in Aunt Beu's cast iron stove. She had never cooked for more than two people at a time. She pondered the amount needed for two women, two ailing men, and perhaps a hired man. She reached for the medium pot and measured out the water to heat, took a scoop of bacon grease out of the can, dropped it in the size 12 skillet, and assembled the ingredients for a breakfast of scrambled eggs with diced ham, grits, milk, and coffee.

Beulah May shuffled into the kitchen.

"Oh, bless yer heart, Sugar!" she exclaimed.

"Mornin', Aunt Beu. How's Uncle Jack?" Betty Jo asked.

"Peaceful. Lord blessed us each with good rest," Beulah answered.

"That's what y'all be needin' fer shore." Betty Jo examined the melting grease in the skillet and finished whisking the eggs. "It'll be ready in a bit."

*****

The misty light placed a halo around the roofline of Brother Delbert's house. Dottie Sue paused. What she was about to ask stepped beyond any reasonable request from the polite offer of help, but the sooner she moved across the river, the better. She strode up to the front door and knocked.

Delbert opened the door slightly. "Sister, ev'rythang all right?" he inquired. He stepped outside wearing a white tee and denims, his hair askew.

"So sorry to impose on y'all, 'specially early. Was wonderin' if'n y'all could help me move out to the Thorpe property today?"

"Mr. Thorpe keepin' y'all on, then?" he asked, smiling.

"He offered as much, but not shore what'll happen now. Seems Jack Lee had a spell yesterday." Dottie was aware of the impropriety of her presence on the deacon's doorstep. She must do her part to keep the exchange short.

"Oh, so sorry to hear," Delbert responded. "Pick y'all up, mebbe two hour or so. I kin make a couple visits while on that side."

"Thank y'all kindly," Dottie said as she turned to go.

"Betty Jo be with y'all?" Delbert asked casually, as if an afterthought.

"The hired man moved her over last evenin'." Dottie quickly added, "I didn't pack much. Should be room in the back seat fer me and my thangs."

Dottie shuttled the bags and boxes to the front yard. Closing up the house, she waited on the porch. She was reconciled to the idea of moving into the unknown. Lord knew what she had known wasn't so great. Nothing to lose, she figured. She did have to admit to herself, though, that she would miss the modern house and her mother's fineries.

Philip Harris walked up the road. "Good morning, Miss Dottie Sue," he said, his voice low.

"Mornin', Philip," she returned, surprised at his formal tone.

"Brother Delbert asked me to join him on his visits today," Philip added. "Said Betty Jo already moved over on account of her uncle falling ill."

"The hired man fetched her after y'all departed," Dottie said.

"Philip, I wanna thank y'all fer visitin' last evenin'. Grateful y'all were there to help out. Denny Ron's not a bad sort. It's just the drink." Dot repeated what she'd often told herself. She gestured for Philip to join her on the porch, but he remained standing on the walk.

"I got him home last night. To his wife." Philip looked Dottie in the eyes. "If you don't mind my saying so, wasn't he the reason for your black eye?"

Dottie's mouth opened and her eyebrows raised.

"Perhaps you should consider that he is a bad sort." Philip concluded.

Dot fumed. *How dare the Yankee say such things out loud!*

The piston thumps of Delbert's car punctuated the offense.

*****

After giving Betty Jo instructions on Papa's convalescence, Aunt Beu stepped outside to take Eddie a plate and discuss the harvest operation. With the kitchen clean, it could no longer be avoided. Betty Jo sighed. *Eggs or grits?* She would offer both. She loaded the tray and walked to the front room.

Henri lay on his back, staring at the ceiling.

"Mornin', Papa," she said simply as she set the tray down on the night stand.

His eyes shifted to the side and landed on her. They focused with recognition.

First things first she thought. She pulled back the sheet and removed the bedpan. Returning from emptying it, she said. "Let's sit y'all up a bit." She reached for the extra pillow and was surprised that Papa assisted by pushing with his good leg. Gently leaning him forward, she fluffed the pillows and positioned them before nudging him to lean back. She poured a glass of water two-thirds full and handed it to him.

"Where y'all bin, Child?" Henri asked.

"Take a drink, Papa. Y'all kin eat eggs or grits. Which one y'all like?" Betty Jo asked.

"I asked y'all a question. Where ya'll bin?" The water in Henri's glass quivered side to side.

"I'm here to tend to y'all, Papa. Eggs or grits?" she asked, punctuating the single syllable words.

"Listen. Git yerself to the house. The key to the cellar lock is in the top of my chest of drawers. Fetch me some drink." The movement of the water in the glass intensified.

Betty Jo stood, unmoving, looking down on her grandfather. "Eggs or grits?"

"Y'all hear me, Child? Fetch my drink!" A splatter of water landed on Henri's lap.

Betty Jo reached out and took the glass from his hand. "No, Papa." She picked up the tray. "When yer ready fer a bite to eat, lemme know." She took a couple steps away from the side of his bed.

Betty Jo had never balked at the terms folks used for her. Some of her earliest memories involved being called Sugar by Aunt Beulah. Dottie Sue called her Girl, and it felt right. Granma usually called her Sweetie. All three, though, used her given name, too. But Papa? He had always called her Child, as if he'd found her lost in the middle of the road. She wondered if Papa actually knew her name—or anything about her, for that matter.

She turned around to face Henri. "And use the name my mama gave me. It's Betty Jo, if'n y'all cain't remember."

Betty Jo slammed the tray down on the counter next to the sink just as Beulah returned to the kitchen.

"Didn't go too good, Sugar?" she inquired.

Betty Jo shrugged her shoulders.

"He's a stubborn sort," Beulah May sympathized. "Y'all just have to be persistent. He must take water and eat.

"Eddie's gettin' a crew to pick this afternoon now that it's dryin' up. Don't know 'bout our money situation, so it'll be work to eat today. I'll be tendin' Jack Lee and studyin' the books. Jack Lee always took care of the farmin' bus'ness. Now I gotta be learnin' fer myself."

Betty Jo moved to the outside kitchen. Cooking for the crew and household would lighten Aunt Beulah's load, and it would occupy her mind so Papa couldn't dominate it. As she pumped the water to quick-soak the beans, she recognized the distant thumping of the Chevrolet.

The drive across the river and toward Joaquin had been void of verbal exchange in spite of Brother Delbert's occasional small talk phrases. He slowed at the junction of the county road to make the left turn.

"Not the Thorpe's," Dottie Sue called over the sound of the motor. "Down the road 'bout a mile or so."

"Isn't that Betty Jo?" Philip said, pointing to the pump at the side of the house. "Let's stop."

Delbert nodded, and turned the car onto the Thorpe's drive. Philip was the first to exit the vehicle and cross the yard.

"Hello, Betty Jo. How is your Uncle Jack doing?" Philip asked as the group assembled at the pump.

Betty Jo worked to still her breathing. The surge of joy she felt was awkward. This was not a time to be happy. "He be weak and tired. Doc says he kin heal if he's shore to rest real good."

"We'll keep Brother Jack Lee in our prayers," Delbert stated.

Betty Jo nodded with a thank y'all kindly. The offer of prayer was always to be expected. Philip and Delbert had prayed that Dottie would find work. She'd thought God answered that prayer, but now everything was tossed up in the air. No telling where it all would land.

"And yer papa?" Dottie Sue ventured.

"Oh, Miz Dot. He's just plain difficult," Betty Jo said.

Dottie stifled a giggle. "Fer certain, Girl. But I know yer a blessin' to Beulah May." Dot looked at the large pot. "Cookin' fer the pickers?"

"Aunt Beu is busy tendin' Uncle Jack and studyin' up on the bus'ness. Eddie got some pickers willin' to work fer food." Betty Jo sighed. "I'm lettin' Papa be 'til later. Just too ornery at the present time."

"Lemme move into the place, then I'll be back to help with the fixin's," Dot said as she and Delbert returned to the car.

Betty Jo smiled. Dot's company would bring welcome relief. It had been less than a full day away from her new friend and already she missed her terribly.

"I'm so glad I was able to see you today, Betty Jo." Philip's eyes shone in the sun as it emerged from behind a cloud. "When things settle down, I'd like to reschedule our porch visit. Until then, the Lord bless you and keep you."

Betty Jo waved as the car pulled out and turned toward the plank house. As it disappeared down the road, she looked up at the Thorpe's old oak tree. A beam of light descended through the branches. She focused on the silhouette of a single green leaf as it shimmered, surrounded by a chorus of leaves. It was so different from Big Tree.

With the boxes stacked on the porch, the church men said goodbye and drove away to begin their visitation. Dottie Sue looked at the Landry house. She considered the man who built both this shack and the Blind Pig. Seems that Henri Landry lived under a dark cloud. It was not her place to study the mote in his eye when she had a beam protruding from her own. It did seem to her, though, that he just didn't want to rinse the ugliness out.

He was connected to so much good. His granddaughter was a special young lady, his in-laws were upstanding Christian folks, and he made more money than most. He was fortunate to get that job in the oil field and the business had been successful for years until Sheriff Davis's torment of late. For all that, though, it seemed Henri's preference to constantly squander it away. The only thing he treasured was that Model T. Mercy, he took such good care of it until the accident. If only he'd care for Betty Jo half as much as that ol' truck.

Dottie Sue pushed aside her thoughts and set to work unpacking and making herself at home. She remembered well growing up in a little house very similar, but she had never been in Charlene's house until now.

Whether she got pay or not, she would keep useful and busy. She had served up plenty of spirits in her day, but now it was time to serve the Lord. She'd walk in the humid heat to the Thorpe's to lend a hand any way she could. She'd be careful to stay clear of the farmhouse. Many bad things could be said of Miss Dottie Sue Dawson, but keeping her promises was something she could take pride in.

CHAPTER SIX

Through the shadows of the Pineys, Henri made out the image of the Model T. The crowd had drifted away and now it was time to get his tired self home. He walked through the darkness 'til he felt the handle. The driver's side door opened with a creak.

A shudder made its way from his skin to his gut. Henri sensed a presence behind him, lurking in the thicket. He fumbled with the ignition key in a prolonged battle for control. At last, with the engine started he began the turbulent drive out of the woods.

The presence followed him.

Disoriented, he turned left onto the highway—panic-seized as a bright light began to overtake him. He accelerated, pushing his truck to its limit.

In a blink of an eye, he was catapulting through the air, diving as one with his truck. Falling, falling, until he passed through the surface to worm into the depths.

Surrounded by water, time came to a stop. It was a peaceful moment. It would be so easy to die.

Though he was drowning, he was oh, so thirsty.

Henri awakened with a gasp.

"Henri, yer all right now," a deep voice soothed. "Musta bin a bad dream."

Brother Tucker sat quietly by the bedside while Henri grounded himself in reality.

"Would y'all like to talk 'bout it?" the reverend asked.

Henri turned his head to the side and focused his eyes. "Mind yer own bus'ness, Tucker," he whispered.

"The well-bein' of folks 'round here is my bus'ness," Brother Tucker replied, matter-of-factly. "And I'd say y'all aren't doin' so good."

Henri looked up at the ceiling. His eyes traced the grooves in the beadboard above his bed. Surely that Baptist preacher would leave him alone if he was quiet long enough. Pretty soon, though, the clean white ceiling faded as his mind began to replay the dark images of the latest dream. Henri turned his head to the side. Tucker still sat in the chair.

"Tell me, Preacher, why y'all 'spect I didn't die in the accident?" Henri finally asked.

Brother Tucker shifted his weight in the chair and leaned forward. "There's no doubt a miracle happened that night." He waited for the words to resonate before adding, "Henri, God's givin' y'all another opportunity. Y'all have a chance to redeem the time."

Henri closed his eyes. The preacher's words confirmed what the dream made clear. He should have plunged into the Sabine and drowned, but something, or Someone, prevented it.

It had been a busy afternoon. Aunt Beulah's pastor had come to visit each of the ailing men, offering a prayer of blessing before leaving. Now with Dot's help, the food was ready for the pickers. It was time to tend to her grandfather.

"Papa, y'all awake?" Betty Jo approached the bed in the living room.

Henri opened his eyes in response.

"Y'all wanna take water? Yer body sorely needs it."

Henri managed a nod.

"Let's get y'all sat upright now." Betty Jo had to do most of the work. Papa was weaker than in the morning. His eyes were dull, and the bedpan held little contents.

She filled the water glass two-thirds full. Placing it in her papa's hand, she did not let go. She guided his hand to his mouth. He took a sip and then another. When he was ready to lower the glass, she slipped it out of his hand and set it on the end table.

Encouraged, Betty Jo moved to the kitchen. Taking a piece of cornbread, she covered it with honey and milk, mixing it to a mush in a small bowl with a spoon. Figuring tea might help calm the jitters, she poured a small glass. Adding a napkin, she placed it all on a tray.

Returning to Papa's bedside, she detected a bit of light in his eyes.

"Would y'all like a bite to eat, Papa?" She placed the spoon in his right hand, supporting it with her left. With her right hand she held the bowl at his upper chest and under his chin. Henri ate on his own accord, with Betty Jo providing physical support. When he slowed to a stop, she pulled away.

"Wanna wash it down with some tea?" Betty Jo asked. Papa did not seem disagreeable to the idea, so again she helped him with the logistics.

Betty Jo wiped Henri's face with the napkin, cleaned up the area, picked up the tray, and turned to go.

"Thank y'all, Betty Jo," Papa whispered.

With wonder, Betty Jo walked to the kitchen and set the tray down. Her mind traveled back in time to the swimming hole. She was real little. She and Granma had gone on a picnic with Aunt Beu, Ruth Ann, and her brood of kids. Ruth Ann taught her how to float on the water's surface. At first, she struggled in the water, swallowing its muddy contents. But then she learned to cooperate with it. When she relaxed, she discovered that she could float. Funny how that memory just popped into her head.

The sun was disappearing. It was time to get outside and help serve the pickers. She hurried out to the grounds to work beside Dottie Sue.

*****

Beulah May Thorpe sat in her chair. The family Bible had been moved from the end table to her lap. The only work today would be tending to the two infirm menfolk. There'd be no cooking. There were leftovers from the weekend's meals.

This morning, Jack Lee was eager to get out of the bed and back to work. She reminded him what the doctor had said and that Ruth Ann would be fit to be tied if she found him not at rest. Besides, it was the Lord's Day. Beulah was tempted to discuss the finer points of their business but instead read a psalm and sang a hymn.

Henri was at rest on the other side of the living room. He was far less anxious today and his surliness had subsided. It seemed as if he'd made somewhat of a truce with his circumstance. She could see the Lord's hand at work. While she desired to protect Betty Jo, she also knew there were many things needing to be worked out between them. She'd keep her eye on him, though. Fifteen plus years of hurt was quite enough.

Betty Jo descended the stairs, hunger driving her out of the bedroom. She'd not eaten much breakfast. Beulah looked up from the Bible. "Help yerself to a bite to eat."

Betty Jo walked across the room. Her papa was resting peacefully. She was pleased that he took some water and scrambled eggs that morning. The next challenge would be to get him changing position and moving. Aunt Beu warned her about the bedsores.

After some cold beans and cornbread in the kitchen, she sat down next to Beulah. Betty Jo watched her great aunt, fascinated at how her eyes would glide over the words in the Bible.

She waited until Beulah looked up. "Aunt Beu, is it hard to read?" she ventured.

"Well, Sugar, it's just like anythang else," Beulah answered. "Not hard once y'all know how. I'm not a good teacher like yer granma was, but I'd be glad to show y'all what I know, soon as harvest is in."

The rattle of wagon wheels caught their attention.

"Must be Ruth Ann!" Beulah exclaimed, lumbering out of her chair. She made her way to the porch with Betty Jo close behind.

The driver hopped down and hurried around to offer Ruth Ann his hand as she stepped down. Mother and daughter met on the walk in an expansive embrace.

When they pulled back, Beulah said, "Ruthie, 'member Betty Jo? She was just a little one last y'all were together."

"Fer certain. How're y'all?" Ruth Ann offered the greeting but her eyes avoided Betty Jo. She turned to look at the man who followed her with a box.

"Afternoon, Mother Beu," he greeted, leaning over to kiss her cheek. "Here's the books, Ruthie," he said. "I'll set 'em on the porch."

"Thank y'all kindly, Walter," Ruth Ann replied. "Brought some good readin' to keep Daddy's mind busy as he recuperates."

"Be back 'bout an hour 'fore sunset. Have a good visit." Walter tipped his hat. "Please give my best to Jack Lee."

Before the wagon pulled away, Ruth Ann said, "Lemme see my Daddy."

Betty Jo watched as the two women, arms around each other, entered the house. It seemed the circle they enclosed did not include her. She thought it best to make herself scarce. Papa was set for a while. Though the heat of the day was on, she'd go to the plank house and keep company with Dot.

With a wooded cathedral as its backdrop, Betty Jo focused her eyes on the headstone. A branch from a rose bush in need of pruning reached out as if to caress the marker. Sweat trickled down Betty Jo's back. Early morning would be a better time for such a visit, but as Dot said, there was no time like the present.

"Oh, how hard it is to lose a mama," Dottie Sue whispered.

The older woman put her arm around the waist of the younger, and pulled her close. Betty Jo began to cry.

In her life, she'd often imagined her mother—the sound of her voice and her appearance. Stealing a look at Papa's old photograph, she had seen a teenage girl—but that image was akin to fantasy. Now at the graveside of her mother, Betty Jo stood in reality. She was a daughter and her mother had died.

Betty Jo bent down. Dot said the name of each letter as Betty Jo traced them with her finger, "C-H-A-R-L-E-N-E." Then Dot added, "Underneath it says, 'Love Always.'"

"And here's yer granma laid to rest next to her. And her Daddy and Mama Morris over there." Dottie Sue gestured to each grave.

Betty Jo stood up. "Why've I never bin here before?" she wondered aloud.

"Yer papa never come to Leet's graveside. I 'spect it due to this bein' the Morris private cemetery and all." Dottie hesitated before adding, "I also 'spect the Thorpes paid fer the burials and the headstones."

Wiping sweat and tears from her face, Betty Jo looked at Dottie. "Thank y'all fer carryin' me here."

Dot smiled. "What y'all say we git outta this heat?"

As they began the walk through the fields, a distinct rumble reached Dottie's ears. Perhaps a family was taking a pleasure drive on this late Sunday afternoon. When they reached the county road, the women said goodbye. Dottie Sue turned to the south and Betty Jo to the north.

After a long visit with her daddy, Ruth Ann was able to secure a promise from him. He would read at least five books before getting back to any business. Satisfied, she left him to rest with a kiss on the forehead, then joined Beulah at the kitchen table while waiting for Walter's return. They sat engaged in hushed conversation.

"It's a fine kettle of fish," Ruth Ann said. "If Uncle Henri hadn't bin so stubborn, Betty Jo would've bin much better off! She would've growed up with a normal family and had an education. I swear we would have loved her as our own. Now it's just all so hurtful to see."

The back screen door opened and fell shut. Daughter and mother turned to look at Betty Jo Landry.

"Oh, Sugar," Beulah murmured.

"Y'all're the one who wanted to adopt me?" Betty Jo asked as she walked toward the table.

Ruth Ann nodded. Her eyes traveled to her mother's and then back to Betty Jo. "The plans were made, but yer papa changed them."

"Yer mama's death hit 'im real hard," Beulah added. "Y'all were Charlene's little girl. Keeping y'all would be a way to hold onto her."

Betty Jo sat down in a vacant chair, stunned. "But I cain't recall Papa ever holdin' me, or huggin' me, or sayin' 'I love y'all'—never nothin' like that. If by keepin' me, he was tryin' to hold onto Mama, I reckon he dropped us both."

"Betty Jo, y'all mind yer . . . " Ruth Ann stopped the admonition when Beulah rested her hand on her arm.

"There's no end to these wounds," Beulah gently said. "There kin only be healin'. Someday, I think it'll be clear the good that comes. Time bein', there's reason to give thanks. Just think, Sugar, of all the kinfolk y'all have—yer mama and granma who loved y'all so, yer Uncle Jack and me who think the world of y'all, yer mama's cousin who'd've changed her whole life to raise y'all." Beulah reached out to take Ruth Ann's hand. "And even yer papa, though he never showed it, loves y'all."

Letting go of her hand, Beulah turned to face her daughter. "And Ruthie, it's time y'all move beyond the past. Stop lookin' through eyes of hurt, and start seein' with eyes of faith."

Beulah May Thorpe stood up, kissed her daughter on the cheek and then her great niece. She walked out of the kitchen and crossed the living room, glancing a moment at her sleeping brother-in-law. Then she made her way to the bedroom to sit beside her husband and spend time in prayer.

A car smothered in glossy black was parked directly in front of the plank house. Seeing it confirmed that she had, in fact, heard a vehicle pass on the road. *Shelby County Sheriff* was emblazed in gold letters on the door. It left no doubt as to who was inside Henri's house. Likely her belongings were being rifled through. Dottie Sue shrunk off the road and into the brush, her stomach in a sudden churn.

Oh, Lord what shall I do!

She prayed as she swallowed gulps of fear. Then Dottie Sue forced herself fully upright. She knew the truth, and the truth would bring freedom.

She walked the remainder of the way—past the pump, past the invading automobile, and up the three steps onto the porch.

"Sheriff, Sheriff Davis?" she called.

Boots pounded the floor planks. The screen door thrust open.

"What're y'all doin'?" Dottie Sue challenged.

"My, my, my, Miz Dawson," Davis drawled. "I'm the one who asks the questions 'round here. Why y'all here? Surprised yer not at a hide away somewhere with some poor woman's man." The sheriff stepped out onto the porch. "Come to think of it, this would make a perty good hideaway. What'd'y'all say, Dottie Sue?"

"Haven't y'all done enough damage?" Dot fixed her eyes on the sheriff's face. Davis stepped toward Dottie, his sneer giving passage to a burst of hot air.

Dot stood, feet apart. "It was you who run Henri Landry over the edge, wasn't it?"

Recoiling, the sheriff cocked his head.

"Ya ol' fool!" Dot exclaimed.

Sheriff Davis squinted as if to protect himself from excessive light.

"Betty Jo's lookin' fer her daddy," she pressed with a knowing look. "Just a matter of time 'til she finds out 'bout 'im."

"Wild claims! Y'all got no proof. No proof at all." Davis stepped off the porch, then turned back to the house. "Y'all best not be spreadin' yer lies 'round or I'll have y'all strung up. Mind yer bus'ness, Miz Dawson."

"It's the truth," Dot persisted. "Y'all're tryin' to destroy a man y'all have a lot more in common with than aginst. She's a Landry and a Davis."

"You filthy . . . " Davis pivoted and marched back up the steps. Percolated fury now erupted. The Sheriff of Shelby County charged Dottie Sue Dawson. He shoved her against the siding of the house and pinned her with his arms, pushing his elbow into her neck.

"No more, y'all hear!" He yelled with acrid breath into her face. "No more!" With a final shove, he left her to sink to the floor boards of the porch.

Crumpled and shaken, Dot rested her head in her hands as the black patrol car sped away. She was wrong. This truth only brought more bondage.

Dottie Sue slowly entered the shack. The dimming light did nothing to cover the violation. She went into the larger of the two back bedrooms and discovered all the drawers of the chest open and contents spilled out. Henri's room took the biggest hit.

She had hoped for respite away from her house in Logansport, thinking a temporary change would provide a degree of security. Now

she was sure there was no place she could really be safe.
She began moving about to set things in order. Raspily she sang.

O Lord, You know I have no friend like You,
If heaven's not my home then Lord what will I do;
The angels beckon me from heaven's open door,
And I can't feel at home in this world anymore.

*****

The warden stepped down the corridor between cells. The ring of keys hanging from his belt punctuated his approach.

"Well, Jimmy Boy!" he boomed out to the heap lying on the wood slat. "Looks like y'all have a friend in the gov'nor. Yer sentence bin commuted. Get yer bones up. Yer a free man!"

Jimmy Davis sat up, shaking off his lethargy. *Well, I'll be. Daddy come through after all.*

With wobbly stride, Jimmy Davis followed the warden down the long hall. A cacophony arose as tin mugs banged against iron bars. The pair made their way through the maze of the facility and arrived at the processing station. Jimmy was handed a set of street clothes and directed to a toilet room.

"Make yerself presentable," the clerk said.

He emerged in time to witness the signing and stamping of the final documents.

"Don't be a stranger now," smirked the warden as Jimmy passed through the metal door to the other side. The reverberation of the heavy clang behind him rattled his brains. He squinted against the light.

In a few paces he came face to face with James Roy Davis.

"Son," Sheriff Davis said with a nod. "We need to have ourselves a talk."

Part II

Trunk

Debby L Wynkoop

CHAPTER SEVEN

Big Tree lay silent across the path. Its upper branches, severed away, rested at the water's edge. Black slime coated the wooden tentacles. Fungus grew all around the tree's body. New vegetation covered the disrupted soil where it once stood. A fox squirrel barked out an alarm before running along the tree's length to disappear into the bramble. Decay and vitality cohabited.

With his strength spent, Henri leaned against the trunk of Big Tree. He had underestimated the physical abilities needed to walk the path to the Sabine. The muscles in his legs spasmed as he studied the landscape. What was once familiar appeared so different now. *When had the old cypress fallen?*

He had developed a schedule for living day to day: sleep as long as his bones would allow, prepare the coffee, stretch, walk, and pump a bucket of water. The rest of the day was spent in a battle to keep his mind off moonshine. Early on, once his energy began to return, he had searched the property for any spirits the do-gooders may not have discovered when they cleaned him out. They had been very thorough. He wondered where Denny Ron hid the still and how he might get a message to him. *Where in tarnation was that woman, Dottie Sue?*

More than his anger at the missing hooch was the discovery of the stocked cupboard: canned fruit, vegetables, corn meal, flour, lard, and coffee. Pragmatism now softened the humiliation of being the community's charity case. At first, he didn't care to eat at all, but now, oh, how wonderful a catfish would taste! If only he could get strong enough to climb down to the river. If only he could get brave enough. *Maybe tomorrow.*

Henri slowly returned to the plank house he'd built when he was a young man. This was the first time he lived there alone. He mused that he no longer could boss around anyone or anything—not even his legs. They cramped and twitched on the venture to Big Tree and back. A drink would really help the pain.

Damn Beulah May and her church folks!

*****

Beulah made the final curve of yellow icing to enclose the 6. *Sweet 16* was centered on the sheet cake, resting on a bed of chocolate butter frosting. Stepping back to observe her handiwork, she nodded her head in self-approval. Betty Jo was coming of age tomorrow and it was her intent to mark it well.

She wondered how much longer the young woman would be living with them. No question her great niece had caught young Preacher Philip's eye. She hoped they wouldn't tumble into a future together quite yet. There was much Betty Jo needed to learn first, and marriage could be difficult enough within your own kind. It was much more complicated when marrying an outsider. Family history made that clear.

After the storm of summer's events, a peace had settled over the Thorpe residence. The harvest was brought in with God's good grace and a bastion of teamwork. Eddie possessed the practical skills of the field. Dottie Sue quietly stepped in to do whatever tasks were needed, even working to keep the ledger updated. Betty Jo just plain worked hard, both in and out of the house.

Time for celebrating was overdue. Besides, a party might just fill the stark gap of Dottie Sue's absence.

"Afternoon, Aunt Beu," Betty Jo said as she entered the kitchen. Drawn to the birthday cake, she exclaimed, "Oh, it's lovely!"

"Someone has a big day tomorrow." Beulah grinned. "Glad y'all like it."

"Fer my birthday?" Betty Jo was dumbfounded.

"Well, fer certain, Sugar. It's a mighty important one at that!" Beulah turned to the sink to begin cleaning the baking dishes. "How were yer 'rithmetic lessons?"

"Uncle Jack says I be needin' to learn the times tables by heart." Betty Jo poured a glass of milk.

"Best set yer mind to it, then," Beulah said. "We'll do yer readin' work in an hour or so. That'll give y'all some time to study."

"Yes, ma'am." Betty Jo took a sip of milk and sat down at the kitchen table. She studied the paper Jack Lee gave her. Count-bys, he'd told her, were the way to learn. She began to recite the numbers, committing each column to memory, but before too long, her mind began to travel other places.

Philip was coming courting tonight. It'd been two Fridays since she'd last seen him. There was much to share, but she mostly wanted to surprise him with a commemoration of the night they first met, three months ago.

Aunt Beulah returned to the kitchen. "Sugar, what y'all like to work on today?"

Betty Jo was ready with an answer. "I was thinkin' to write to Miz Dottie Sue. Would y'all help me make my letters?"

"Why shorely, Sugar." Aunt Beulah gathered writing supplies and placed them on the table. She lowered her frame into the chair next to Betty Jo. "It'll take patience. Let's see how far 'long we all make it today."

Fallow cotton fields contrasted with the Piney green. Pockets of hardwoods wore fall colors. Betty Jo walked in steady strides, head up. Her eyes, wide-open, saw with clarity the beauty of the world around her.

She stopped at the pump for a drink of water, hoping to garner Papa's attention. An outside conversation, with the woods as witness, would be preferable.

Henri's skeletal figure, summoned by the squeaking, appeared on the porch.

"Betty Jo?" he called out.

"Hello, Papa. I come to check on y'all," Betty Jo returned.

Henri leaned against a porch post as Betty Jo approached the house.

"How y'all doin'?" Betty Jo ventured a look at her grandfather's face.

"Bin better. Bin worse." Henri pursed his lips together.

"Do y'all have ev'rythang yer needin'?" Betty Jo asked.

Henri scoffed.

"Enough food and supplies, Papa. Do y'all have enough to live on?"

Henri glared at his granddaughter. "Child, it be time to come back home."

Betty Jo sighed. "No, Papa."

"Y'all belong here—not with those highfalutins."

Betty Jo shook her head and lowered her eyes.

Henri sat down on the three-legged stool.

"Tomorrow's my big day," Betty Jo said. Henri looked away with a blank face. "I was hopin' to get Mama's autoharp to carry back. It'd sure be nice to play agin. That'd be all right, Papa?"

"Yer mama's harp stays here in her home—yer home. Want the harp? Y'all need to come back home." Henri crossed his arms.

"Yessir," Betty Jo said. Turning around, she walked back to the yellow farmhouse, her view obscured by the tears in her eyes.

The pleasant temperature that evening did not require porch sitting, but the privacy of courtship made it necessary. Wrapped in Mama's sweater she'd found in the closet, Betty Jo nestled into the porch swing awaiting Philip's arrival. She tried to shake off the disappointment that her plan to greet him tonight with song was thwarted by Papa's orneriness. Betty Jo began to rock, humming a tune she'd heard Granma sing when she was a young child. Music was inside of her. Maybe it didn't need an instrument.

The door opened and Beulah stepped out with a loaded serving tray.

"Here's coffee 'n' sweat bread, should y'all be inclined." Beulah set the tray down on the little table.

"Thank y'all kindly." Betty Jo smiled up at her great aunt.

"Oh, precious Sugar," Beulah said as she sat down in her chair. "Philip shorely fancies y'all. He's a good man, but there's much to know 'bout his ways and his folks." Beulah stopped her lecture and smiled. "I hope y'all have a real good visit."

"Tell me, however did it turn out at yer Papa's?"

Betty Jo hesitated. "Didn't go too good."

"He gettin' along all right?" Beulah tilted her head.

"Seems so. Wouldn't answer if he needed anythang." Betty Jo shifted her weight, hoping to not be captured further in conversation.

"He *is* a stubborn one," Beulah whispered, confirming yet again that it was so.

In spite of admonishing herself to keep the matter between herself and Papa, Betty Jo gave in to blabbing. "I asked if I could have Mama's autoharp. All the time settin' up the house before he moved in, I never thought to carry it back with me."

"I see," Beulah said.

Now a prisoner of her own words, Betty Jo continued. "But he said 'no'—said the harp was gonna stay put. He cain't play it, Aunt Beu. It just sits in the chest. Just mean. Just plain ol' mean!" Betty Jo lowered her head, surprised by her own blatant disrespect.

"Sugar, yer papa wants to cling to anythang that reminds 'im of his daughter." Beulah paused. "Kind of like y'all and that sweater. Wrappin' up tight in yer mama's sweater makes y'all feel close to her. That's just how God made us. We carry our missin' around with us."

Beulah May pushed up out of her chair. "Betty Jo, y'all're welcome to sit at the piano anytime y'all like." Beulah quietly made her way inside the house.

Betty Jo mused over their conversation—glad it'd been had. Some vines entangled, and a person needed to escape them. Other vines wrapped precious things together and kept them close. Seemed the secret was in knowing what kind of vine it was.

Her attention turned toward the slender manfolk walking up the gravel drive. Dressed in his Sunday suit and topped in his Yankee hat, she marveled that Philip Harris had walked so far just to see her.

Jack Lee and Beulah May met Betty Jo at the breakfast table with a package wrapped in newsprint and twine. A single orange ribbon was displayed on top.

"Happy Birthday!" they greeted gleefully.

"Oh, my goodness!" Betty Jo exclaimed.

"Go ahead, open it," Uncle Jack prompted.

Betty Jo carefully removed the ribbon and untied the twine. Folding away the newsprint, she separated the tissue paper to reveal a colorful autumn-print fabric.

"Hold it up. Let's see if'n it'll work," Beulah encouraged.

Betty Jo unfurled the new dress and held it up as Beulah made the final inspection.

"Yes, indeed, Shug! Looks like a good fit. And the colors are perfect fer yer dark hair."

"Do y'all like it, Betty Jo?" Jack Lee asked.

"It's beautiful," came Betty Jo's hushed response. "But . . . but it's too much."

"Nonsense," Jack Lee said. "It's yer special day. Besides y'all worked hard at harvest. Think of it as a bonus."

"And Miz Tucker needed some work to take in. Praise God! This dress is just a blessin' all the way 'round!"

Betty Jo marveled at how her great aunt turned every occasion into praise.

"Try it on, Sugar," Beulah urged.

Betty Jo ascended the stairs to her room. She took time to fix her hair with the orange ribbon before putting on the dress. The feel of the fabric was so fine! Looking in the mirror, she thought herself no longer just plain ol' Betty Jo.

Approval met her descent down to the living room.

"Thank y'all fer the dress." Betty Jo's eyes filled with tears.

Gathered under the oak tree in the sweet autumn air, the well-wishers sang and clapped out a happy birthday to the young woman come of age. Betty Jo, red-faced at center attention, made her wish and blew out the candles to the applause of the guests.

Her cousins came for the day—Ruth Ann, Walter, and their kids. A group of the Thorpe's friends, mostly church folk, came for the party. Brother Delbert and Philip stood together on the perimeter of the gathering, having arrived from Logansport just in time to join the happy birthday song.

Beulah served up cake, and Jack Lee scooped out the ice cream over which he'd meticulously labored. Bellies content, the elders sat to small-talk the afternoon away, while the youngers joined in organized games. The littles ran around, playing tag and acting out roles in their made-up world.

Brother Delbert sat down next to Reverend Tucker. Beginning with small talk, he stealthily began to deploy words of persuasion. The Grange Hall just outside of Haslam would be a good place, and Philip Harris, being a visiting preacher, would make a fine evangelist. There would be minimal costs, and spiritual renewal was sorely needed in these difficult times. Surely, they could work together for the Harvest.

Never having played horseshoes before, Betty Jo was first out of the tournament. She would have preferred the games of imagination the littles played, but she understood expectations. Besides, the one she most wanted to be with was at the horseshoe pit. She stepped back and watched the proceedings.

Philip was competent at pitching, but he stood out from the group. The jokes did not include him, and no one spoke with him. He served up words occasionally, only to have them die in the air.

As the horseshoe tournament wound down, Philip cast his eyes toward Betty Jo. She smiled and began walking toward the house. Instead of stepping up to the porch, she edged around to the blind side of the farmhouse.

Philip caught up to her. "A very happy birthday to you, Miss Landry," Philip said with a nod and bow.

"Why, thank y'all, Reverend Harris," she replied, curtsying. "It's shorely bin a lovely day."

Philip reached out his hands, the open palms slightly glistening. Betty Jo placed hers, quivering, into his. As his hands enfolded hers, nerves became irrelevant.

"The loveliness of this day is the way you look," he whispered. Philip nudged closer to Betty Jo, and she leaned in. Frozen in the moment, the world around them paused.

Two littles ran by them.

Abruptly, Philip stepped back.

He exhaled and let go of her hands. "I'm not sure when I'll see you next. I'll be in a time of fasting and prayer. We feel led to conduct revival meetings, and I will need to make preparations."

Betty Jo nodded, though she was not certain she understood. "I'll be thinkin' of y'all."

"Would you pray for me, too?" Philip appealed. "That my heart and mind will be open to God's will? That me being an outsider wouldn't hinder people from hearing God's Word and responding?"

"Yes," Betty Jo replied, "I'll pray."

"Thank you, Betty Jo." Philip looked her in the eyes. "That means so much to me."

Betty Jo watched as the young preacher turned to make his way around the corner of the house. Her eyes looked across the field and to the line of trees. She'd only known this place. Philip Harris was from a bigger world—a place called Rhode Island. He had so much that she didn't—an education, proper speech, parents. Beyond all that, there was something more he had. It wasn't just religion. Everybody around here had that. It was something much deeper, and she wanted to figure out what it was.

Betty Jo returned to visit with the guests and give her thank y'all kindlies as they left. She ended her first day as a woman helping Ruth Ann and Aunt Beulah clean up the kitchen and the grounds.

Wearing her new dress, Betty Jo sat on Aunt Beu's right side holding her half of the shared hymnal. While she struggled to identify all the words, she was learning to follow the lines with her eyes. She began to sing the part that repeated itself.

This is my story, this is my song.

Her eyes moved from the page to the piano. Sister Tucker's hands glided along the keys, putting on a show that gave Betty Jo a reason to be glad that they sat near the front. Uncle Jack was serving as usher. It was assuring to have an ally behind her.

Praising my Savior all the day long.

The deacon at the pulpit lowered the arm that had been moving to the music. Picking the hymnal up, he stepped down.

Brother Tucker stepped to the pulpit with Bible in hand. "How wonderful to live in that blessed assurance! Amen?" he began, eliciting a chorus of amens from the congregation.

"We're livin' in difficult days. The world is groanin' under the load of sin and care—but there is rest for the weary soul found in Jesus alone." Several believers voiced agreement to their pastor's sentiment. "Before we open the Word this mornin', I'd like to share with y'all that we'll be joinin' with other fellowships in our area fer revival meetin's."

"Glory to God," Beulah May whispered under her breath. Those perpetually at the amen-ready sat silent.

Brother Tucker looked over his parishioners. "The revival will be held the weekend of Thanksgiving over at the Grange Hall in Haslam in conjunction with our time of givin' thanks. Would y'all pray with me and prepare yer hearts?"

Brother Tucker preached his sermon to a silent audience.

Beulah May and Betty Jo expressed niceties as they made their way out of the church. "Let's wait fer Jack Lee in the car," Beulah said softly as she quickened her steps.

A triad of church ladies intercepted the pair.

"Oh, Miz Thorpe, however are y'all? Haven't had time to catch up lately. Seems y'all been real busy." Mrs. Westly looked past Betty Jo to search Beulah's face.

"God is good, and we're so thankful," Beulah replied with a smile.

"And it shorely is the season to give thanks," contributed the woman wearing a brown hat.

"We were a bit surprised to hear about the meetin's. Seems rather last minute," Mrs. Westly fished. "Whoever agreed to such a thang?"

"Why not have our own meetin's, with our own people?" brown-hat lady jumped in to say. "I heard tell there be a fellowship 'round here that allows Coloreds inside their church."

"Imagine that!" the third lady exclaimed.

"I cain't believe the deacons would be in agreement 'pon this," Mrs. Westly concluded.

Betty Jo stood a spectator as the vines braided themselves together. She knew that a cord of three strands was strong.

The wind blustered through the group of ladies, causing a rush of hands upward to secure head coverings.

"Brother Tucker asked the flock to be in prayer 'bout the meetin's, and that we prepare our hearts." Beulah looked at Betty Jo. "That's what we'll be doin' at the Thorpe house. Hope y'all will do the same. Lovely Lord's Day to y'all." Beulah smiled again and resumed the walk to the car with her great niece by her side.

Jack Lee, finished with ushering duties, met Beulah and Betty Jo at the sedan. Sighing, he smiled whimsically. "Guess I was too late fer a rescue."

With Sunday dinner dishes done, Betty Jo found her opportunity. She walked into the sitting room and sat down on the sofa nearest Beulah's chair. She pulled a magazine out of the rack to spend the time until her great aunt roused from the cat nap.

She could now identify key words in the headlines: bank, crash, work, poor. She opened the magazine to a photo of a city street lined with people waiting to be handed food. She recognized the word, hunger, in the text.

Aunt Beulah adjusted her weight and pushed herself up in the chair, looking around. "Oh, Sugar, guess I dozed off a bit. 'Spect I should git to the kitchen and finish up."

"All the work is done, Aunt Beu," Betty Jo said.

"Oh, that's real nice. Shore is lovely to havin' another woman in this household." Beulah smiled at her great niece.

"Aunt Beu, I was wonderin' if'n y'all could teach me somethin'," Betty Jo began.

"Shorely. What is it?"

"Philip asked me to pray fer 'im. I said I would, and that made 'im happy." Betty Jo looked down at her lap. "But I don't know how."

"Of course, I'd be plumb pleased to tell y'all what I've learned," Beulah said. "We should start with our Lord's answer to that very question."

Beulah May Thorpe reached for her Bible, and began her discourse long-prepared.

*****

Dottie Sue Dawson stirred the pot of soup. The broth was thin, but the line of bedraggled souls on the sidewalk was long. Back home, she had known a moment of despair when the cupboard was bare. She had witnessed the misery of the pickers at harvest. Still, the folks of her region had it better than most. Gardens, the woods, and the Sabine could yield sustenance for those willing to work and learn nature's ways. Here in the city, though, there was an utter lack of opportunity. Desperation was stamped onto the countenance of those waiting for a portion of thin soup and a slice of bread.

Dot arrived at her sister's house feeling quite sorry for herself. It was good to see Suzanne, but her brother-in-law did not seem too happy to see her. Dottie had not wanted to crowd in on them. It was humiliating to be dependent. The day after her arrival, her sister introduced her to the soup kitchen downtown. Seeing the suffering of others brought her self-pity to an abrupt halt.

Finished with her shift, she began the walk back to the bungalow. Her thoughts turned to her young friend in East Texas. Delighted that she had received a letter in the mail, she would reply this evening after supper chores were completed.

November 8, 1931

Dear Betty Jo,

Thank you for your letter. I was so glad to hear from you! Happy belated birthday! I am sorry that I missed your special day. I pray that 16 will be a wonderful year.

I am doing well. I fill my days working at the soup kitchen. We help feed people in the city who have no means. I attend church with my sister, and take care of chores around her house. I read the Bible and pray about what I should do next. For now, this is a good place and I am thankful to have all I need.

Keep working hard on your book learning. I am proud of what you have accomplished already! Give my love to the Thorpes.

Blessings,
Dottie Sue

Debby L Wynkoop

Dot sealed the letter inside the addressed envelope. It was heading where she knew she should be. Her heart longed for home.

Mr. Sam, the proprietor of the Joaquin Mercantile, set down the stack of mail he had been sorting. He studied the letter in his hand, turning it over several times. It was addressed to Miss Betty Jo Landry in care of Mrs. Jack Lee Thorpe. Observing the return address, he knew this was information to be passed on. He never liked himself for indulging the Sheriff of Shelby County, but staying on the lawman's good side was best for his business.

*****

Henri Landry lay on his side in bed, staring at the light entering through gaps in the wall planks. He probably should fill them. Winter was coming. What was the use, though? Nothing he did would ever keep the damp chill out of his bones. He closed his eyes. Maybe he would fall to sleep for good.

Before he could drift off, a renewed alertness overtook him. He opened his eyes. The sound of the Dodge Brothers truck was unmistakable. It dusted up resentment.

The engine cut. A door slammed. Footsteps approached and there was a knock at the front door.

"Henri, y'all in there?" The familiar voice waited for a response before resuming. "Henri?"

"Lemme be. Please just lemme be," Henri whispered through clenched teeth.

The door complained as it opened. Henri sat up. *Who does he think he is? He might own the land, but he has no right waltzing in here like he owns the place!*

"Henri?" Jack Lee Thorpe stood in the opening to his bedroom, surveying the scene. "Let's go fishin'."

Before the accident, the slope down to the river from Big Tree had been inconsequential. Now, broken and tottering, it seemed an insurmountable task to Henri. He looked at the dark water lapping at the edge of the Sabine and shuddered. He could never admit his fear.

Jack Lee carefully stepped down the bank—a walking stick in one hand and a pole in the other. His fishing basket was slung over his shoulder. Once his feet leveled at the bottom, he turned around and looked up. Henri took one step and then backed away. Jack Lee set down the pole and removed the basket, stashing them securely next to a bush. Then he anchored his feet and extended the walking stick toward Henri.

"Here, I'll toss it up," Jack Lee offered.

"Naw—y'all go on with the fishin'. I be needin' to catch my breath." Henri moved away from the slope and leaned against the spongy trunk of the decaying Big Tree. Seemed that he no longer could do anything he wanted.

After a while, Jack Lee returned to the trail—his fishing basket empty. "Nothin' lost. They're not bitin'," he said when he got within earshot. He struggled to steady himself. Absent-mindedly, his right hand stretched up to his chest. "Storm's comin'. Let's head back."

The pair walked to the shack as a cold rain began to fall.

Sitting at the small table he'd made many years ago, Henri considered the egg salad sandwich in his hand. Jack Lee had pulled it out of Beulah May's picnic basket and handed it to him. He was so tired of living in the strange land between loathing charity and accepting it. For years now, he'd resented the Thorpe's abundance while benefiting from it at the same time. He exhaled and took a bite. Beulah May's food was always real good.

Jack Lee ate slowly. He set down the half-eaten sandwich and took a swig of Henri's tepid coffee. "Y'all done a good job with the property," he commented.

Henri looked up and tilted his head. "What'd'y'all mean?"

"Well, y'all built yer house from scratch, put in the well, made the furniture—made the most of the land. Y'all made a place fer Leet and Charlene and fer Betty Jo."

Henri's eyes narrowed. "Shootin' sure, Jack Lee. This is Betty Jo's home. Y'all oughter not be interferin'."

Jack Lee's face paled. "She be a grown woman now—makin' her own choices."

"With yer persuasion!" Henri pushed back from the table. The chair's scraping sound served as the exclamation.

"Come now, Henri. Don't be offended," Jack Lee urged. "Yer her proper kin, but the accident brought diff'rent circumstances. Betty Jo's workin' on her book learnin' and socializin'. She's caught the eye of a young man."

Henri stood up, fists clenched.

"This house must feel empty, but time moves on and thangs change," Jack reasoned.

"Mind yer bus'ness, Jack Lee!" Henri glared at his dead wife's brother-in-law.

Jack Lee rose to his feet. "Even though Betty Jo doesn't live here, there's no need fer y'all to be alone. Yer part of a family if'n y'all choose to be."

"Y'all best move along now," Henri cautioned.

Jack Lee closed the lid to the basket and picked it up, leaving the remainder of his sandwich on the table. "We're goin' to revival meetin's in Haslam Thanksgiving weekend. Why don't y'all go with us?"

"Get outta my house," Henri growled.

"Think about it. Mebbe it'd be good to be with folks agin," Jack Lee chanced as he walked out the door. He stopped on the porch and took a deep breath. Dread invaded his head. The sharpness was undeniable. He needed to get in the truck and get home in a hurry.

Cold seeped through the layers of clothing and permeated every inch of Betty Jo's skin. She walked quickly down the county road, grateful that the pelting rain had passed. The extinguishing light laid down a heavy cloak of anxiousness.

Uncle Jack had not come home.

She had countered Aunt Beu's worry throughout the late afternoon, but could hold it off no longer. Now her mind created all manner of scenarios as to what may have happened.

Almost to the plank house, the mist parted to reveal the Dodge Brothers truck. It was parked neatly at the side of the road. Betty Jo ran, not stopping until her hands pressed against the driver's side window.

Slumped over the steering wheel was the lifeless form of Jack Lee Thorpe.

Betty Jo lifted her cry above the mist and to the heavens. "No, God, no!" She fumbled with the door handle until it opened with a jolt. "Jack, Uncle Jack! Y'all hear me?" She bent over, felt his cheek and knew for sure. He was gone.

Betty Jo sat in the mud and leaned against the inside of the truck's door. Even with the physical evidence right next to her, she could not comprehend the loss.

"Papa! Papa!" Betty Jo banged on the door of the plank house before barging in.

"What in thunder, Child?" Henri looked up from his chair.

"It's Jack Lee, Papa. He's . . . he's gone." Betty Jo choked out the words.

"What y'all mean he's gone?' " Henri asked.

"Dead, Papa. He's dead." Betty Jo blinked hard. "Found 'im in his truck just a piece down the road."

Henri examined his granddaughter's tear-streaked cheeks and hollow eyes.

"Need yer help, Papa, to drive the truck. Gots to carry 'im to Beulah May."

Betty Jo waited, leaning against the door while her grandfather put on his boots and coat. Tears streamed down her face.

CHAPTER EIGHT

Aunt Beulah sat in her chair with hands folded atop the skirt of her best dress. Her bosom waxed and waned in steady rhythm. Uncle Jack's body was next to her. He was dressed in his Sunday suit, and laid out on a door supported by two sawhorses and draped with their wedding quilt. Comfort was no matter to his old soulless shell. In helping to prepare the body of Uncle Jack for the wake, Betty Jo became certain of the simple fact that her great uncle was no longer in that shell of flesh.

Betty Jo did not know she had so many kinfolk, and she surely hadn't realized just how many people could fit inside the Thorpe's house. As word spread of Jack Lee's passing, folks came, crowding in and creating a hushed-buzz of activity. Platters of food and trays of beverages continually circulated.

The circles of fellowship were apparent. Aunt Beu and her two children and grandchildren were tight-knit. Around them were the people of the church they called Brother and Sister, as well as relations, and near neighbors. The outer wheel were acquaintances and town folks. In the center of these circles laid Jack Lee Thorpe. He was the hub.

Sometimes, those in the circles mixed; but it was clear that each person knew to which circle they belonged. *Everyone except me*, Betty Jo thought. Papa must not have thought he belonged in any of them. He hadn't come to the wake.

She thought back to when she was in school, before she had to drop out to tend to Granma and the house. Her class had put on a program. All the students were divided into Pilgrims and Indians and they acted out the first Thanksgiving following the teacher's directions. She remembered being so sad when the play was over. She hadn't wanted to stop pretending. Pretending was better than real life.

Betty Jo looked around the sitting room before returning to the kitchen with an empty tray. It all felt like pretend.

Brother Tucker kept himself near to the family, fielding the questions and comments of those coming to pay their respects. Earlier in the day, he'd managed to distract Mrs. Westly from consuming Beulah's attention. Ruth Ann sat near her mother, sprinkling her quiet cries between conversations. With a stoic face, Bernie Thorpe manned the front door. Sister Tucker maintained her post in the kitchen. Eddie had seen to the practical matters of readying the plot in the family cemetery. Everybody acted out their part, doing what was expected.

Tomorrow, mid-morning, they'd put Uncle Jack in the pine casket and carry him out to be buried.

When this play is over, what then? Betty Jo wondered. She approached the sink for another round of dish-washing.

A knock at the front door was met by Bernie Thorpe. James Roy Davis stood on the other side of the threshold. Maisie Davis stood next to him.

"Sheriff," Bernie nodded. "Miz Davis. Thank y'all fer comin'." Bernie opened the door wide. The couple walked into the house, escorted by a cold draft.

Conversations halted. The sympathizers parted like the waters of the Red Sea for the Sheriff of Shelby County. Beulah May pushed herself up from the chair. Ruth Ann stepped to her mother's side.

Maisie Davis took hold of the matriarch's hands. "So sorry fer yer loss, Dear," she whispered. James Roy looked down on the body of Jack Lee Thorpe and tipped the hat he seldom removed. Turning toward his wife, he grasped her elbow, and the pair made their way across the room and out the front door.

In the kitchen, Sister Tucker stepped beside Betty Jo to dry the dishes. They worked to the sound of the more unrestrained voices of those piled around the table.

Betty Jo longed for a friend. *I wish Dottie Sue were here.*

"Looks like you two ladies are doing an excellent job."

Betty Jo's heart warmed with the familiarity. She turned around, shaking the soap and water from her hands.

"Philip," she breathed out.

"We surely try our best." Sister Tucker smiled. "Good evenin', Reverend Harris."

"May I?" Philip took the towel out of the hand of the puzzled preacher's wife. "Please, sit for a while. I noticed there was an empty chair next to your husband."

Sister Tucker hesitated as she moved her eyes from Philip to Betty Jo. "Well, thank y'all." Placing her hand on the young woman's shoulder, she reached over and kissed her cheek.

Several young adults who'd been keeping company in the kitchen followed Sister Tucker into the sitting room.

"How are you doing, Betty Jo?" Philip asked.

"I be doin' fine," she replied. With no more words to add, she turned to finish the task.

"Brother Delbert and I have come to sit the night, so those needing rest can get it." Philip studied Betty Jo's profile. "I am so sorry for your loss. It must have been quite the shock. Mr. Thorpe was an admirable man. More importantly, he knew Jesus."

All day long Betty Jo had heard folks say similar things, but Philip was the first to say them to her.

*****

" 'Let not your heart be troubled: ye believe in God, believe also in me. In my Father's house are many mansions: if it were not so, I would have told you. I go to prepare a place for you. And if I go and prepare a place for you, I will come again, and receive you unto myself; that where I am, there ye may be also.' "

Brother Tucker closed his Bible.

The family of Jack Lee Thorpe stood next to the open grave and began singing.

> Sing the wond'rous love of Jesus;
> Sing His mercy and His grace;
> In the mansions, bright and blessed,
> He'll prepare for us a place.
> When we all get to heaven,
> what a day of rejoicing that will be!
> When we all see Jesus,
> we'll sing and shout the victory!

For the first time in Betty Jo's experience, her Aunt Beulah did not sing.

> While we walk the pilgrim pathway,
> Clouds will overspread the sky;

Betty Jo looked across the field to the edge of the Pineys. A slender form, hat in hand, leaned against a tree. She strained through the November light to focus on the details. His head was bowed, his gray hair askew; and to her great surprise, her Papa's shoulders heaved.

> But when trav'ling days are over,
> Not a shadow, not a sigh.

*****

In the pitch-black, Henri abruptly sat up. There were no images, no shapes, no shadows—nothing to gravitate toward. Yet compelled to move, he stood and began walking with heavy feet. He must find his way out of this darkness.

Disoriented, he lost his balance. It seemed he had fallen into thick mud. He pushed himself upright and moved his legs and feet once again—trudging on to where he did not know.

Exhausted, he despaired. His clothes were filthy. His efforts were wasted for he had no destination.

A flicker of light appeared behind a scrim. It grew into a beautiful circle of ambiance. From within it, he heard music. Encouraged, Henri fixed his eyes and moved closer.

The form of a man, dressed in clean overalls, came into focus. Jack Lee looked over his shoulder and smiled. He pushed back the scrim to allow Henri to step through. Standing side by side, the pair turned their attention to the source of the music.

The light broadened to reveal a youthful Leona dancing with her daddy. Sitting on a three-legged stool was their daughter, Charlene. Her face glowed as she strummed her autoharp and sang a song he did not know. His wife backed away from her father, and looked at him, her face rapturous. She reached out her hand.

Henri stood in indecision. His feet refused to step into the full light. Suddenly, a veil of utter blackness smothered him, tumbling him into mucky confusion. The music of angels gave way to shrieks of despair.

Henri fought to fill his lungs with air. He struggled to clear his thinking, trying to find the line between dreamworld and the real world. Then he heard the sound again and was settled in recognition. Someone was at the pump outside.

Henri dressed hurriedly and opened the door. An old mare was tethered to the dilapidated post. She wasn't about to make a fuss, and the post wasn't about to hold. Henri wondered why Denny Ron had even bothered.

The outhouse door slammed closed and his bootleg partner, floppy hat on head, made his way to the porch.

"Mornin', Henri," he said.

"Denny, what brangs y'all out here?" Henri asked.

"Just come to see how y'all're gittin' along," Denny returned to the older man's skeptical face.

"Come on in, then, and see fer yerself." Henri stepped back into the house. Denny Ron, in a cloud of earthy stench, followed.

"Pull up a chair."

Henri kindled a flame in the little cast iron stove and set about to ready the coffee pot. He pulled two mugs off the shelf and placed them on the table.

"Haven't seen y'all in a long while. Why y'all show up now?" Henri looked at his visitor as he sat down in the other chair.

"Was glad to hear y'all've recovered. Thought we might talk bus'ness," Denny answered.

"What bus'ness would that be? Davis shut it all down." Henri shifted his weight in the chair.

"He perty much destroyed it all, but he never found the still. We hid it real good." Denny Ron smirked. "Holidays are comin'. There's money to be made on the Lou'siana side."

"I dunno," Henri shook his head. "Got no truck. Barely got strength. Lost my appetite fer such."

"But y'all got the skill." Denny pressed. "And shorely y'all could use the money."

"We don't have Dottie Sue. She's gone missin'." Henri hesitated. "Y'all know what happened?"

"Ah, that Dottie Sue—she went and got religion. Says she's done with the bus'ness and all." Denny Ron fidgeted with an empty mug.

"And all?" Henri scrutinized the younger man's face. "Y'all run her off?"

"No, sir," Denny asserted. "She left after helpin' the Thorpes with harvest. I dunno where to. Honest to God, I dunno why."

Henri sighed. "Denny Ron, how'd we manage 'tween the two of us?"

"I have connections to help with the details."

"What about supplies?" Henri asked.

"Y'all heard me now, didn't ya? I have connections on the east side," Denny answered. "Just show me what y'all know."

Henri leaned back in his chair and crossed his arms. "What'd be my cut?"

"Twenty percent," Denny Ron was ready with his reply.

Henri slapped his hand down on the table causing his mug to jolt. "Good Lord, don't y'all be insultin', now! Without my recipe and know-how y'all'd have nothin' "

"Without workers willin' to risk, y'all'd have nothin'," Denny retorted.

Before the coffee had time to percolate, Denny Ron set down the empty mug and stood up to leave. "Think on it, Henri. I'll be back fer an answer in a few days."

Denny Ron left the plank house, but his odor lingered. Henri sat and mulled over the conversation. He walked to the stove and poured his first cup of coffee. For the first time in a long time, he craved something else to drink.

Betty Jo looked up from the book in her hands when her great aunt entered the sitting room. She was dressed in town clothes, with a hat pinned into her tight bun.

"Eddie's drivin' me over to Center today, Sugar. There's some matters need tendin'." Beulah May walked across the room and put on her coat. "Should be back by suppertime."

"Yes, ma'am," Betty Jo acknowledged as Beulah stepped outside.

Returning to her reading, Betty Jo labored at the words. Her mind wandered. The house was too quiet. She marked her place in the science book Jack Lee had loaned her. *Was that just a week ago?*

This morning she'd prayed for Philip and read some scripture best she could. She'd prepared breakfast and convinced Aunt Beu of the need to eat a few bites. She'd seen to the chores that needed done. She wanted to write a letter to Dottie Sue, but decided it would be best to wait until her aunt could assist her. It was a cool day, but maybe a walk this afternoon would do her good.

She stood up and stretched. The red-varnished piano met her eye. She walked over and sat down at the bench. Lifting the fallboard of the old upright, she pushed it back and studied the black and white keys. She curled her fingers as she'd seen Sister Tucker do at church. She placed them on the keys. Tentatively, she began to explore the sounds until she was able to pick out the melody of her childhood lullaby.

Sleep, sleep, my little one;
Listen to the river running

Satisfied, she returned the fallboard to its place and wondered why she hadn't acquainted herself sooner with the instrument.

A knock sounded. Betty Jo scooted off the piano bench and quickly crossed the room. She opened the door. "Papa?"

Henri swayed with fatigue. His arms clutched a black case.

"Papa, come inside."

Betty Jo drew him into the house and guided him to the nearest chair. She stepped quickly to the kitchen and returned with a glass.

"Y'all walked over?" Betty Jo asked as she handed him the glass. She stepped back and sat on the edge of the sofa. Her grandfather was clean-shaved and clean-clothed, and at his feet was mama's autoharp.

"I come'n brang y'all the harp," he said earnestly. "I figure yer mama would be pleased fer y'all to make music with it."

"Oh, Papa," Betty Jo whispered. She looked at her grandfather.

Henri bent over and nudged the instrument toward his granddaughter. "Go ahead, then."

Betty Jo walked over and knelt on the floor. Pulling the case toward her, she opened the lid and slid her fingers over the strings. She lifted the autoharp out, located the tuning wrench and set to work. Once it was returned to pitch, she began to play. After a time, she started singing the songs Granma had taught her. Then, at last, she strummed and sang the Cajun lullaby.

Dors, dors, mon p'tit bébé,
'coutes la rivière, 'coutes la rivière

Henri closed his eyes and leaned back, oriented in peace. His energy returned. He had not thought his feet would keep moving today, but to his surprise they had carried him to a perfect moment.

The afternoon passed in subdued pleasantness. Henri reminisced about life in the plank house before Leet became ill. He told his granddaughter stories from when she was a toddler. Betty Jo listened intently and asked an occasional question. Yet, neither mentioned Charlene, and they both kept silent about the dark days.

Betty Jo noted the length of her Papa's hair and offered to cut it. He accepted, and the two moved into the kitchen. When the task was complete, she stepped back for a final inspection. Henri ran his fingers through the gray crop, brushing away severed remnants. He nodded his thanks. Order was restored.

After the floor was swept clean, Betty Jo opened the pantry and brought out the pecan pie leftover from the wake. She sliced and served two pieces—a slender portion for herself and a generous one for Papa. She poured two glasses of milk. They ate, relishing the taste.

The pins and needles that often tormented her in Papa's presence left. He knew her better than she'd realized, and it seemed that at some point he'd even cared for her.

The back door opened and Beulah May stepped into the kitchen. Her right eyebrow slightly raised. "Henri," she greeted.

"Afternoon, Beulah May." Henri stood. "I come fer a visit with my granddaughter. Hope that be all right with y'all."

"Course, Henri. Yer welcome anytime." Beulah gestured to the chair he'd been sitting in. "Please." She set her purse down on the counter and unbuttoned her coat.

"Aunt Beu, would y'all like pie?" Betty Jo asked.

Beulah draped her coat on back of a kitchen chair and sat down. "No thank y'all."

Henri chased the last portion of his piece with the dessert fork. Finally, he set the fork down on the plate. "Jack Lee shorely is missed," he said, studying the scattered crumbs. "So sorry, Beulah, fer yer loss."

Beulah May looked at Henri. "It be difficult losin' a spouse. I 'spect y'all know that fer truth."

"We bin through plenty of loss," Henri replied. "Guess we're gettin' old."

"A person doesn't need be old to deal with such." Beulah met Betty Jo's eyes. "Loss is what this ol' world gives." She turned her head to focus on her brother-in-law. "But we all have a Heaven to gain."

"Now, Beulah May . . . " Henri began.

Betty Jo caught her breath. The pins and needles were returning.

"Listen, Jack Lee's not lost to me," Beulah asserted. "I know where he is. I know where Leet is, too." Beulah hesitated. "Question is, do y'all know where yer headin' when this life is o'er?"

Henri leaned forward in his chair. "Don't go tryin' to give me religion," he cautioned.

Beulah lowered her voice. "Not religion, Brother. Truth. And there's no use ignorin' it."

Henri sat back as if his sister-in-law's words had pushed him. In the hush that followed, Betty Jo thought to exhale. The pins and needles vanished.

"There'll be meetin's in Haslam this weekend," Beulah May said. "Jack Lee was so hopin' y'all might come. Why not join us?"

Henri shook his head. "I don't think passin' time with a bunch of hypocrites is somethin' I wanna be doin'."

"All of us are flawed. That's the point. We all need a Savior." Beulah May persisted. "Come at least once . . . to honor Jack Lee."

Henri sighed. "Damn, Beulah May. Y'all're persistent." The corner of his mouth lifted slightly upwards. "I'll think on it."

Beulah smiled. "Would y'all like to stay fer supper?

"Nah—best be gettin' home," he answered.

"Eddie's still 'round. He kin drive y'all back," Beulah suggested.

"No need to trouble the man." Henri pushed the chair back from the table.

Betty Jo stood and slipped out to the sitting room.

"Very well, then," Beulah replied. "So glad y'all come to visit."

Betty Jo returned to the kitchen with her Papa's coat in one hand, and the autoharp, inside its case, in the other. She held them out to him.

Beulah May opened her mouth, but closed it again quickly.

Henri took his coat from his granddaughter's hand and put it on. "Keep the harp here, Child. It'd please yer mama."

My mama? Betty Jo's eyes teared. *"Oh, thank y'all,"* she whispered, braving a quick one-arm hug.

Henri stepped away from his granddaughter and walked to the back door. Beulah May followed. "I was wonderin' if'n sometime y'all might teach Betty Jo to drive. Be a real help."

Henri turned around. "Got no truck."

"But we do," she replied.

Henri shook his head before jostling through the door and closing it soundly.

The day had been long. Too many events in too little time squeezed the strength out of her. She must complete one more task. Beulah May prayed, asking for guidance. She moved to the secretary in the corner of the bedroom. Pulling stationary out of the drawer, she began to write.

November 24, 1931

Dear Dottie Sue,

I trust this letter finds you well. Our world is in hard times, and I do fear they will continue. Through it all, we give thanks for the Blessed Hope!

As you may have heard from the kinfolk, Jack Lee has passed on. While we grieve, we also must make decisions for the future. We plan to keep the house and all the Morris property. You have proven yourself very capable. If it's acceptable, we would like to employ you to manage the farm and our business affairs.

I admit that I have slowed down considerably. Both Bernie and Ruth Ann are busy with their own endeavors. Betty Jo is occupied with study. This evening she said that she wanted to enroll in high school in January. This will take all of our effort. She will have many exams to pass, and I will have much persuading to do. Henri Landry has dried out and he has shown no intention of getting back into the business.

With all that said, please consider returning home. We need you and will compensate you well.

Give Suzanne my greetings.

Love,
Beulah May

Beulah proofread the letter. Satisfied, she laid it on the desk. In the morning, she would get it in the post. Now, she could rest.

Debby L Wynkoop

CHAPTER NINE

Wooden folding chairs were arranged in tight rows facing a two-step platform. Stuck in the corner, with her back to the chairs, Sister Tucker played the Grange Hall's old upright. Wincing, she abandoned the slow, melodic hymn of prayer and assumed a left-hand stride. *Boom-chick.* A rhythmic ragtime seemed more appropriate.

The musician from Gospel Tabernacle struggled to tune his guitar. He finally gave up and joined the gospel song being banged out on the egregious piano. Rhythm would save the day.

Betty Jo escorted Aunt Beulah into the building. Eddie had dropped them off at the front door, not being persuaded to join them. Beulah walked to a row in the middle. She settled herself into the chair, her girth expanding beyond its wooden boundaries and encroaching upon the next. Betty Jo inspected the wobbling legs and thought a quick prayer. *Oh, Lord, let them hold fast.* She squeezed in next to her great aunt. Beulah's eyes closed and her lips moved silently. Betty Jo's eyes watched the room and the handful of people who showed up for the first night of revival meetings in Haslam.

Philip sat behind the pulpit. From his perch on the platform, he surveyed the hall. He tugged at his tie. He fidgeted with the Bible in his lap. He shifted his weight in the folding chair. Then his eyes met Betty Jo's. He returned her smile and began to tap his toe to the prelude music.

The faces of the Gathered were familiar to Betty Jo. She'd seen them before when attending church on each side of the river. Several had visited during Uncle Jack's wake. While not surprised, she did note that the Coloreds from Logansport were not present.

She watched two young ladies from Joaquin and wondered if they were school girls. Their heads leaned together as they chatted quietly. One girl looked Philip's direction, then offered her friend a coy smile. Betty Jo's shoulders tensed, and she sat a bit taller in her chair.

Brother Tucker walked over to Brother Delbert. After examining his pocket watch and surveying the hall, they huddled together for a moment. Delbert nodded, and the pastor walked to the piano bench and whispered into his wife's ear.

The music continued, but no others passed through the door. Conversation lulled, and the people spread out among the chairs to await the start of the proceedings. The music's tempo slowed. Restlessness ensued.

At last, Brother Delbert stepped up to the platform to greet those attending and to open with a word of prayer. The song leader from the Baptist Church led three hymns to the accompaniment of the pitchy piano and guitar. Lackluster voices followed the tempo of the musicians. Periodically, the song leader cued words. No hymnals or convention books were to be found.

After another round of prayer, Brother Tucker hospitably introduced the young evangelist from Rhode Island. Reverend Philip Harris stepped to the pulpit, shook the Baptist preacher's hand and received a double pat on his right shoulder blade. He positioned his Bible and looked up.

" 'O give thanks unto the LORD,' " he boomed, " 'for He is good: for His mercy endureth for ever!' "

The Gathered steeled themselves for an amen-hallelujah exchange, yet no one ventured vocal agreement.

" 'Let the redeemed of the LORD say so, Whom He hath redeemed from the hand of the enemy,' " Reverend Harris continued quoting the Scripture.

A hush fell in an awkward place.

Philip hesitated, closing his eyes for a moment. He picked up his Bible and stepped down to the floor level.

"Tonight, we begin a special time of meetings for the Thanksgiving season. Let's do something different." Philip smiled broadly. "One of the wonderful things I've experienced since coming to your beautiful region has been the sweet fellowship found on the porch—just the chance to sit and rest and enjoy the company of the people dear to you.

"There aren't many here this evening, and we're all members of God's family—spiritual kin, you might say. Let's sit together a while. Would you all come closer?" Philip gestured to the stunned audience, motioning them forward. "Please, come on down and we'll talk."

Aunt Beulah stood. Betty Jo followed her lead. Together they moved down the aisle to the first row. Others soon straggled forward. A few stayed put.

Philip took a chair from the front row and turned it around. He sat down.

"You may be wondering how it is a skinny Yankee boy happened to come here tonight as your evangelist." With that introduction, Philip Harris told his story. He engaged the listeners with humor and intrigue, slowing his speech to counteract his accent.

Betty Jo was stirred with wonder. There were so many things she had not known about the real story of the man courting her.

"And so, I believe God has sent me here for such a time as this," Philip concluded.

Heads nodded and an elderly saint exclaimed, "Well, glory!"

" 'O, give thanks unto the LORD, for He is good: for His mercy endureth for ever,' " Philip quoted again. " 'Let the redeemed of the LORD say so.' " This time the words drew out thoughtful amens and hallelujah praise.

"Turn with me to the Book of Psalm, chapter 107." After the rustling of pages and a read-through, the young preacher began to speak. He set the context for the passage. Then he narrowed the topic to the mercy and goodness of God. He highlighted key verses for illustration, gently coaxing the Gathered to testify with examples from their lives. When he finished the lesson, he reread the ninth verse, " 'For He satisfieth the longing soul, and filleth the hungry soul with goodness.' " Then he closed with a simple prayer.

Betty Jo had not known what to expect at this first revival meeting. Observing the church men throughout the evening, she could tell that it did not go the way they had expected. All she knew was that her inside person had been wrapped in comfort and that no one seemed to be in a hurry to leave the sweetness that had fallen in the Grange Hall at Haslam.

*****

Henri stopped at the pump outside the Thorpe place. The walk had been easier today than Tuesday past, and for that he was grateful.

Every Thanksgiving since he'd built the plank house, there would be an invitation to dinner. Beulah May would send it, and he would ignore it. He felt shame for the times early on when he'd been in the spirits and beat Leet for sneaking off to join her kin on the holiday. Eventually, he gave in and didn't oppose her, though he easily found ways to punish her disloyalty. Even after Leet passed, the invitations continued—every year except for this one.

Henri walked to the front door of the house and knocked. After a moment, it opened.

"Mornin', Beulah May," he said. "Was thinkin' today be good fer the first lesson."

"Oh, shorely. Please come in." Beulah opened the door wide and waited for Henri to bristle off his boots and enter. "Betty Jo is studyin'. Why don't y'all come into the kitchen fer coffee, and I'll call her down?"

Henri made his way to the kitchen in the back of the house and sat down.

Soon Beulah ambled through the doorway and headed to the stove for the coffee pot. She filled a mug, and asked, "Y'all need a bite to eat?"

"No, thank y'all." Henri answered as his sister-in-law delivered the coffee.

"How many lessons y'all think to teach Betty Jo?" Beulah asked.

"I dunno—'spect not too many," he replied. "Probably kin tell y'all better after today."

Beulah sat down at the table. "Car or truck?"

Henri swallowed his envy with the first sip of coffee. "Truck's most useful. We'll start with it, and then we'll move to the car."

"Mornin', Papa," Betty Jo said as she entered the kitchen.

The heart of Henri traveled back in time. Standing before him, was his beautiful daughter, Charlene. Her dark hair framed a face lit with vitality—a visage ready to take on the world. *No*, he allowed reason in his head. *This is her baby girl.* How on earth had he allowed all those years to slip away from him?

"Mornin', Child . . . Betty Jo," he corrected with a nod. "Y'all ready fer yer first drivin' lesson?"

Redeem the time he remembered the preacher man telling him. Maybe he could.

*****

Singing greeted Beulah May's small contingent as she led the way to the back row. Betty Jo had never known her aunt to be late. She suspected that it was an accommodation for Papa's discomfort. The Gathered in the Grange Hall for the second meeting had increased in number. Tonight, the guitar player from Logansport led the songs. Sister Tucker sat dutifully at the piano. A tambourine-playing woman stood to her side. Many of the folks clapped their hands to the music as they raised their voices.

They situated themselves in a space of five chairs. Betty Jo was relieved that the back row had not been taken. While she was experiencing a different Papa whose face had softened, she did not want to sit close to him. She remembered the Papa with a snarled face. While he rested his hands in his lap during song service, she recalled the impact of his oil-stained hand on her face. She glanced sideways at his profile. His eyes were fixed on the song leader. Never could she have imagined her papa attending a church service. The world of the water's surface and the underworld of the dregs had merged.

Brother Delbert led in a time of prayer. Brother Tucker made the announcements and asked a blessing on the offering. Two deacons from Joaquin Baptist Church passed the plates that had been forgotten the previous evening. Papa fidgeted in his chair. When they reached the last row, Beulah May waved off the puzzled ushers.

Philip Harris stepped up to the pulpit and situated his Bible. After a short greeting, he quoted Scripture; " 'For He satisfieth the longing soul, and filleth the hungry soul with goodness.' "

Philip began, "Our God is loving and kind. No matter what we have done or how far away from Him we have run, He is ready to meet the need of our soul if we will but turn to Him."

As Philip preached, Betty Jo wondered what her Papa was thinking. She knew what Aunt Beu thought—her *amens* were well-placed and clear. Papa squirmed and lowered his head. She struggled to set her mind on the words of the message. By the end of the sermon, a thought rattled her. While she'd been doing churchy things lately, she really did not know this God of love who Philip preached.

The Reverend Harris concluded with an appeal to the Gathered to turn to the Lord in every part of life. The closing song was a hymn of consecration. No one seemed to notice the out-of-tune piano, for sincere prayer filled the hall.

With the final amen, Papa edged toward the door. Before the three could exit the building, the guitar player approached them from the aisle.

"Henri, Henri Landry!" He held out his hand. "Been a while. Glad to see y'all up and about."

Bewildered, Papa shook the man's hand.

"Glad y'all come tonight," he added, turning to smile at Beulah and Betty Jo. The man laughed. " 'Spose y'all're wonderin' what happened to ol' Jessie? Well, I got wonderfully saved. I'm a changed man—playin' music fer Jesus now!"

"That so?" Papa replied.

"Glory be," Beulah praised, covering over Papa's sarcasm. "Thank y'all fer leadin' song service."

Papa resumed his path to the exit. Without comment of the evening's events or the guitar player, Papa drove them to the foursquare farmhouse.

"It's late. Y'all take the car to yer house," Beulah May said before getting out of the passenger side. "Mebbe y'all kin carry us to meetin' in the mornin'?"

Not waiting for an answer, Beulah got out and walked up to the porch. Betty Jo followed, and turned to look back at Papa. He sat at the driver's wheel watching them. He shook his head slightly from side to side before a smile formed on his face. Betty Jo waved. Henri waved back.

Beulah May looked out the window as the morning rain began to fall. She dried her hands and untied her apron just as her surprisingly punctual brother-in-law pulled up in the car.

"Thank y'all, Sugar," Beulah said. "I shorely would not have bin ready in time without yer good help."

"Yer welcome, Aunt Beu," Betty Jo returned as they stepped out of the kitchen.

Beulah stopped and briefly inspected the dining nook. It was good to see her mama's china poised for service. The last time it had been out was Easter. With a bit of guidance, her great niece had set a lovely table.

Beulah grabbed her Bible, then the two women put on their coats at the front entry. They stepped into the cold air. After giving a simple greeting and settling in the car, Beulah turned her thoughts inward.

For the first time since being in the farmhouse, she had not entertained at Thanksgiving. It was too close to Jack's funeral. While proper, the lack of kin in the house these past few days amplified the emptiness. She was thankful for Betty Jo, who offered companionship and practical help. Without her, Beulah could not have hosted Sunday dinner. She had waited until yesterday before extending the invitation. The men of God should be provided for, especially on the Lord's Day. It was clear no one else was going to assume the honor. Just like in Bible times, it fell to the widow.

Widow. It was going to take time to get used to the idea. She always thought she'd go to Glory before Jack Lee. Until the heart attack, he appeared the picture of health. She would just have to accept by faith that everything would work out. *Not my will, but Thine*, she prayed.

They entered the Grange Hall in Haslam in plenty of time for a choice of seats, but Beulah May again led them to the back row. She hesitated and gestured for Betty Jo to move down the row first. After situating in a chair, she scanned the room. There were fewer folks than last evening. Mrs. Westly had been particularly offended that Pastor Tucker cancelled Sunday morning service to fellowship with those *Holy Rollers from the Lou'siana side.* She was none too pleased that the guest speaker was a *young know-it-all Yankee.* Mrs. Westly's offense did appear to be gaining momentum.

As for Beulah, the Word brought by the young reverend had come at just the right time. It was a Balm of Gilead.

The musical prelude prompted Beulah to count her blessings. She had been entrusted with land and enjoyed its bounty. She had known the affection of parents and her dear sister, Leona. She had precious memories of her life with Jack Lee. She was a mother of two wonderful children and was blessed to know their children. She took pleasure in laughter, the harmonies of music, and written words. She inhaled the rich fragrances of earth and delighted in tastes of food. Goodness was all around her.

Beulah's mind turned. Bad lurked in dark shadows. The needs of the poor were overwhelming. Bruised relationships and battered bodies burdened many a weary soul. The scourge of spirits and sexual misconduct exacted a great price on innocent ones. Power-loving men, in the world and even in their own county, would do anything to have their own way. Stubbornness, selfishness, pride—all sins handed down from generation to generation. Ultimately, there was death.

Beulah sighed. Good and bad lived together in this old, flawed world. Reverend Harris brought the simple truth. *On the cross, Jesus, the Perfect and only Good One, bore all the bad. He became the Good for us.* She would take her hope in the mercy and goodness of God.

The service began. Seated between her two relations, Beulah May Thorpe's song returned. She joined the Gathered as they sang.

> *Blessed assurance, Jesus is mine!*
> *O what a foretaste of glory divine!*
> *Heir of salvation, purchase of God,*
> *Born of His Spirit washed in His blood.*
> *This is my story, this is my song,*
> *Praising my Savior all the day long;*
> *This is my story, this is my song,*
> *Praising my Savior all the day long.*

*****

"Miz Thorpe, what a truly fine meal!" Brother Tucker declared as he pushed back from the dining table.

The other guests murmured agreement.

"It shorely is a blessin' to break bread with y'all," Beulah May returned. "It's a real comfort."

Betty Jo stood and began to clear dishes. Sister Tucker assisted.

"Keep yer forks," Beulah directed. "Hope y'all saved room. Betty Jo made a pumpkin pie fer dessert."

Betty Jo blushed as she left the dining nook with her arms full, followed by the pastor's wife. Once in the kitchen, she set about brewing a fresh pot of coffee.

"Yer aunt is quite the woman," Sister Tucker commented. "I cain't imagine hostin' Sunday dinner so soon after layin' a husband to rest."

"Been difficult days, fer sure," Betty Jo said. "But Aunt Beu always says that when the day is dark, we're to be the sunshine."

Sister Tucker nodded. "That's a good way to live. Beulah May has known her share of sorrow, but she keeps her light shinin'."

The serving of pie and coffee settled the company into deeper conversation.

"Hard to believe there be only one service left," Brother Delbert commented.

"I wasn't sure how it'd go. There's bin opposition to these meetin's, but they've been real good." Brother Tucker looked at Philip. "Thank y'all fer yer teachin'. I know we'll see fruit grow from this time."

"Amen," Delbert agreed. He hesitated before adding, "But it's disappointin' no one's got saved."

"Mebbe tonight," said Brother Tucker.

Philip Harris looked at the church men. "When I was preparing for the meetings, I sensed in my spirit that we should trust God to do a work in lives inwardly, even if outwardly we saw no results."

"We walk by faith and not by sight." Beulah's words came as a benediction.

As the company put on their coats and expressed their thank y'all kindlies at the front door, Philip stepped to Betty Jo's side and handed her a letter. Then he turned to Beulah May. "Mrs. Thorpe, may I come for a visit next week?" he asked.

Beulah nodded. "Thursday or Friday evenin' would be good.

"Thank you, ma'am." He smiled at Betty Jo and followed Delbert out the door.

In the Sunday afternoon quiet, Beulah May took rest. A restless Betty Jo went upstairs to the bedroom. She opened the wardrobe and found the dress with the expansive skirt. She stroked its fabric. Since she was old enough to understand such things, a haunting thought had whispered in her ear. Now it yelled at her. She was born out of sin, and she was captive to it. How could it ever be possible that her life would be right?

She closed the wardrobe. A wave of shame washed over her. Lying down on the bed, she turned Philip's letter over and over in her hands. It was addressed to her, Miss Betty Jo Landry, as if she were a lady in proper standing. She was not sure she could read it. She was not sure she should read it. Philip Harris was a man of God. He was light and air. She was a bastard child. She was dark and filth.

The Gathered sang. Their joy highlighted the shadows in Betty Jo's soul. She sought shelter next to her great aunt's side. She wanted to stay home this evening and wallow in emotional mud, but manners would not allow her to do so. Matters were made worse when Aunt Beulah chose seats nearer to the front.

Right before speaking, Philip requested one more song be sung. It was well-known. *A love song of another kind*, Aunt Beu once said. Betty Jo would never forget how the Colored man sang it that first Sunday in Logansport. Tonight, she listened as if hearing for the first time.

> *When nothing else could help,*
> *Love lifted me.*

Philip Harris stepped to the pulpit. "Our text tonight is Psalm 40." Aunt Beu opened her Bible and rested it on her lap. Pages rustled throughout the hall. "We have been considering the mercy and goodness of God, and how He satisfies the longing soul. Tonight, the psalmist gets very personal. Let's read the first four verses."

141

I waited patiently for the LORD; and He inclined unto me, and heard my cry. He brought me up also out of an horrible pit, out of the miry clay, and set my feet upon a rock, and established my goings. And He hath put a new song in my mouth, even praise unto our God: many shall see it, and fear, and shall trust in the LORD. Blessed is that man that maketh the LORD his trust, and respecteth not the proud, nor such as turn aside to lies.

Betty Jo followed the words with her eyes as Beulah pointed. *Horrible pit. Miry clay.* Written on the page, it looked as awful as it sounded. She knew those words described where she was trapped.

As Philip Harris preached, a revelation fell on Betty Jo. She wasn't stuck in the muck of someone else's sin. She was living in the quagmire of her own.

The amen-hallelujah exchange rolled smoothly throughout the sermon, until the Gathered quelled for the conclusion.

"Doesn't matter where you're born." Philip lowered his voice. "Doesn't matter who you know or who your kinfolk are. Doesn't matter where you've been or what you've done—good or bad. It doesn't even matter your opinion of your own self—high or low. Without God, you're hopelessly lost and stuck in the mire of sin. You're in need of a rescue. Won't you accept Jesus Christ as your Savior? He will make everything new and right.

"Sister Tucker, would you come to the piano? Saints, please pray. I'm wondering if there is anyone here tonight who is ready to be rescued. Are you ready to accept the Lord's mercy and goodness for yourself? Would you come forward tonight?"

Beulah May's eyes were closed. Her lips began to move. Henri was bogged down in his chair, aimlessly shifting his weight.

Betty Jo stood up and brushed past her aunt and grandfather. Her legs could not move quickly enough. She fell to her knees in front of the pulpit, sobs gurgling and sputtering out. She lost awareness of everything else, including the hand laid on her shoulder.

"Oh, God, save me!" she cried.

While Heaven came down and filled Betty Jo's soul; while Henri hung his head in indecision; while Beulah May prayed in the Spirit; and while Sister Tucker played a slow *Love Lifted Me*; the Reverend Philip Harris studied the stranger sitting in the back row. He had slipped into the Grange Hall during the sermon, his eyes darting around the room.

He was skinny with gently balding dark hair. His nose was long and his eyes close-set. His lips pursed together. Now his attention was focused on the commotion at the altar and his gaze was fixed on Betty Jo.

Henri thought he was dreaming. Time seemed to stand still as he watched his granddaughter kneeling at the front. She cried and carried on while Beulah May stood like an old oak tree nearby.

The Baptist preacher sat down in the chair next to him. The simple action convinced Henri that he was, in fact, awake.

"What a glorious time," he said, "when a sinner comes home!"

"Betty Jo ain't no sinner," Henri retorted. "She never done a bad thang in her life."

"We're all sinners." Brother Tucker paused. He opened his mouth, then closed it again.

Henri looked around the hall. Only a handful of folks remained. Quiet settled in the room. When Betty Jo finally stood, she was embraced by Beulah. They turned to walk toward their row. Surpassing the stain of tears on Betty Jo's cheeks, was a face aglow.

"Thank y'all fer waitin'," Beulah May whispered to Henri. "We're ready now. Are y'all?" She questioned him with her look. He answered by walking to the door.

The drive to the farmhouse was peaceful.

"Papa, thank y'all fer carryin' us to meetin'," Betty Jo said.

"It's late, Henri. Y'all kin drive yerself home," Beulah offered.

"Nah. I'll walk."

Without a goodbye Henri headed down the gravel drive to meet the county road. The wind and rain of the morning left a drape of damp, cold air. He pulled his loose coat snug around and quickened his steps.

He chewed on the religion he'd been fed the past two days. Leona had tried to convince him of *you need Jesus 'cause you're a sinner,* but he figured that life was more like a balance scale. Do enough things right, and you'd be with the good folks on one side. Do bad, and you'd start moving the other way. Most folks seemed to spend their time in between, moving back and forth.

He'd started out mostly on the good side, but the odds were really stacked against him. He found himself on the outs of most every circle. His dad abandoned him, his father-in-law rejected him, and times with

Leet were tough. Bitterness pushed him to the bad side of the balance scale, and the spirits kept him pinned down there. He gave up on goodness because the last thing he'd ever want to be was a hypocrite. Since the accident, though, it seemed the scale might be tilting the other way.

He arrived at the plank house. He stoked the fire and went to the bedroom. Digging under clothing odds and ends in the top drawer, he found the two mementos.

He sat down at the table and studied the photograph. Leona was pretty, but Charlene was the real beauty. There he stood, a husband and father not so worn out. He had failed the women in his life. Two were gone, but amends could be made through his granddaughter.

Then he opened the jewelry box and pulled out the necklace. Neglect had tarnished the silver. With a little effort, it could be shiny once again.

Yes, he thought, *I will keep moving back to the good side.*

*****

Denny Ron arrived at the plank house Monday morning. Henri released the handle on the pump and looked up as the old mare approached.

"Mornin', Henri," Denny greeted, making a pretense of tipping his floppy hat.

"Mornin'," Henri returned.

Denny Ron leaned forward. "Come to learn yer answer to the bus'ness proposition. What'd y'all say? Ready to git to work?"

"I'll not be workin' fer y'all." Henri focused on the overalled-man's face.

Denny Ron leaned back in the weathered saddle.

"But I'll tell y'all what I will do," Henri said. "I'll sell y'all the recipes and the still. I'll teach y'all the finer points and supervise yer first three batches to be sure they be quality. I'll do it all fer $500. Y'all pay me half up front and the other 'pon completion."

"Ridiculous!" exhaled Denny Ron. "That's 'most a year good wages!"

"Shorely yer connections will have funds." Henri shifted his weight. "Y'all will have a skill that'll last and a product that folks clamor fer. And I'll be outta yer way. Take it or leave it—makes me no nevermind."

Henri picked up the bucket and walked into the house. He poured a glass of water and took a deep breath as he raised it to his lips. The initial sip morphed into a gulp.

The mare neighed as it clomped close to the porch. "All right Henri," Denny yelled. "I'll agree to yer terms."

Henri set the glass down and stepped out onto the porch. "Five hundred dollars firm?"

"Highway robbery, ya ol' bootlegger—but yes. It'll take a few days to git the money." Denny Ron drew the reins up. "Meet me behind the mill Thursday 'fore first shift."

Henri nodded his understanding and watched as Denny and the mare blended into the Pineys. He returned to the warmer air inside the house, satisfied that he'd found a resolution to his quandary. He poured another glass of water and drank heartily.

*****

Betty Jo descended the stairs and glanced at the grandfather clock.

"Good mornin', Sugar! Much longer and I'd be greetin' with a good afternoon." Beulah giggled.

"Mornin', Aunt Beu. I cain't believe I slept so long!" Betty Jo added her own giggle. She walked over and kissed Beulah on the cheek.

"Well, after puttin' yer soul at rest last night, I 'spect yer body needed to catch up." Beulah May added, "No need to worry over the chickens and chores. Eddie will see to it through the holidays so's we kin concentrate on the book learnin'.'"

Betty Jo flopped onto the sofa. "Oh, Aunt Beu, when I first woke, I wondered if'n I had dreamed what happened last night. But my insides feel lighter than a feather!"

Beulah smiled. "It shorely was real, Sugar. You gave yer life to Jesus, and He made y'all new. Yer joy is from the inside out." Beulah pushed herself out of the chair. "Let's git us a bite to eat and then git to yer studies."

Papa came on Wednesday afternoon. Betty Jo was abuzz with all manner of conversation, but Henri was pure business.

With coaching from her grandfather, she drove the car to Joaquin. She brought it to a jolty stop in front of the mercantile. Red colored her face when she saw Mrs. Westly staring through the front window of the store.

"Wait here," Henri instructed. "'T'won't take long."

Betty Jo sat behind the steering wheel of the idling car. She occupied the time with thoughts of what it might be like to attend high school.

Papa stepped out of the mercantile clutching a small paper sack. "I think y'all're ready to go it alone. Why don't y'all drive me home? I'll be as quiet as a mouse and see how y'all git along."

Betty Jo used all her shoulder strength to turn the car to face the other direction. She cringed knowing an audience watched. Smooth starts and stops were going to take a lot more practice.

She sputtered through the gears as she drove the highway. Slowing to a crawl, she turned onto the county road, glancing at the Thorpe place on the right as she headed the vehicle toward the home of her childhood. She drove the road that many times she'd walked secretly to escape an angry Papa. Arriving, she pulled over to the muddy surface in front of the plank house.

"Good," Henri muttered.

Betty Jo turned and smiled at her grandfather. "Papa, thank y'all fer teachin' me. I shorely am grateful."

Henri nodded. "Take care now." He exited the car.

Betty Jo waited as he walked up to the porch. In spite of his limp and cockeyed posture, she thought this version of her grandfather quite good.

When Henri turned her direction, she waved. He nodded.

With cranks of the wheel, a series of lurches and mud splatters, she negotiated a three-point turn and headed back to the home of her womanhood. It occurred to her that she was living a blessed life. She had a personal faith, enough food to eat, was learning to read, and she understood for sure that she had kinfolk to whom she belonged.

When she parked the car at the yellow farmhouse, she stopped to give thanks. Then she wondered. *Why hadn't she thought to put Philip Harris on that list?*

Wednesday night Bible Study at the Baptist Church had more attendees than usual. To Beulah May's surprise, the young preacher was one of them. He sat near the front under the teaching of Brother Tucker. Also to her surprise was the aloofness in her great niece's face upon seeing him.

At the conclusion of prayer time, the conversational milling about commenced. Sister Tucker drew Betty Jo over to the piano.

Philip Harris approached Beulah May. "Mrs. Thorpe, may I speak with you?" he asked.

"Shorely, Reverend Harris," she replied.

"In confidence?" he asked, gesturing to a Sunday School classroom.

The pair moved into a smaller room, leaving the door open to the sanctuary.

"Beulah May, I want to thank you for the many kindnesses you have shown me since last summer," Philip began. "You have been supportive of my ministry, where other folks have shown, well, reservation."

"God is at work through y'all, Philip. It's clear to see. I'm pleased He brought y'all our way. You've bin a real blessin'," Beulah sighed, "through our difficult days."

"I have great affection for you all, especially for your sweet niece." Philip shifted his weight. "I plan to travel home soon and be with my family. My father has taken ill."

Beulah May interjected, "So sorry to hear."

"I'm not willing to leave Betty Jo." Philip's deep blue eyes met Beulah's raised eye brow. "Ma'am, may I have permission to ask her hand in marriage?"

Beulah was slow to respond. "It isn't my place to grant that permission. Y'all need to ask her Papa."

"I see," Philip said softly.

"I won't stand in yer way, but I would encourage y'all to pray more 'bout this. Betty Jo's not ready to be a preacher man's wife. She's a baby Christian and needs to grow in her faith. She's workin' hard on her book learnin', but she's not a good match fer y'all in that way." Beulah hesitated before adding, "And I don't think she's ready to unite with a man from such different kind."

Beulah placed her hand on the preacher's shoulder. "Forgive me if I've said too much, but give it more time, Philip. If'n yer love is meant to be, it'll wait." Beulah patted Philip's shoulder. "However y'all proceed, know that y'all have fellowship with us."

Philip stepped toward the open door. "Thank you, Mrs. Thorpe. May I still come visiting tomorrow evening?"

"Certainly, Reverend," Beulah replied. "We'd be pleased."

*****

Henri rose early. Not taking time to stoke the fire, he lit the lantern and dressed in his woolens. He pulled on his boots and coat and placed the satchel he'd packed the night before over his shoulder. It would be a long walk. Even though the thought of it tied his stomach in knots, he would take the river trail. It was shorter. He hadn't asked to borrow a horse or truck. That act, besides humiliating, would necessitate lying. Walking the river trail would also keep him out of eyeshot of the sheriff.

Won't be long 'til I'll have a truck again, he thought.

The trail was rougher than he remembered, and his eyes were hazy in the dark. In spite of the candle-lantern he carried, he stumbled frequently. Jolts of panic surged through him each time his feet faltered. The slightest incline gave cause to catch his breath.

Morning light filtered through the cloud-laden sky as the bridge came into view. The main path ascended to the highway, but Henri stayed low on the brushy foot trail that went under the bridge. As he neared the first stanchion, his feet halted. He looked up the steep embankment. The wreckage of the Model T was positioned impossibly between tree and brush, a carcass left exposed to the elements.

Henri lowered his head and moved his feet apart. The surge of dizziness began to subside. He'd been so sure of his plan. Bootlegging was what he knew well, and his reputation would bring him gain. Surely his memory would return in full once he saw the tools of his trade. He rubbed his temples. Just a few days, then he could buy himself some freedom.

Henri moved cautiously as he made his way under the bridge and to the sawmill. He found the wagon team behind a stack of logs on the edge of the woods.

Denny Ron sat on the buckboard, arms crossed as Henri approached. "Yer late," he said.

Henri nodded.

"This here's Charles," Denny Ron said. Without pausing, he pulled out a sealed manila envelope from inside his jacket and handed it to Henri. "Let's git on with it."

CHAPTER TEN

Betty Jo read the paragraph for the third time and shook her head. It made no sense, the numbers and letters mixed up and all. Beulah May had given her Jack Lee's old algebra book and told her she'd be on her own. Her aunt had taken her as far as she could go in the mathematics.

She stood up and stretched. "Aunt Beu," she called toward the back bedroom, "I think I'll go fer a walk. Won't be gone long."

Beulah emerged from the hallway shadow. "There's a package of cold cuts and cheese fer yer papa. Kin y'all walk that way?"

"Shorely," Betty Jo replied. It was a bit further than she'd planned, but she would hurry. The outing would be good for her brain.

She grabbed her coat, went to the kitchen to retrieve the butcher-wrapped package, and exited out the back door. The driveway and the county road were spongy underfoot. Both needed more road mix.

Philip Harris was coming to visit this evening. After a time of prayer last night, she knew what to do. Her walk to the plank house was sped by thoughts of how she should go about it.

Betty Jo stopped at the pump for a drink of water. The squeak did not bring Papa out of the house. She stepped up onto the porch and knocked on the frame of the screen door.

"Papa, y'all here?" she called out. "Papa?"

Betty Jo knocked on the door. Then she opened it and peered inside.

"Papa?" She stepped through the threshold.

The peg near the door was vacant and the cool of the house was the same as outside. She set the cold cuts on the table. Just to be sure, she walked to the back room. The quilt was tidily spread over the bed.

Then her eyes were drawn to the rough-hewn chest of drawers. There on top was the old photograph. How many times had she stolen peeks at it? Now it was in plain view. She walked over for a closer look. Her mother was beautiful and Papa seemed tall and strong, but it was Granma's image that brought a wave of longing.

Betty Jo was surprised at the shine of the silver frame but understood the source of the miracle. Next to the picture was a jar of silver cleaner and a rag. The paper sack from the mercantile was folded neatly. Her eye turned toward an old jewelry box. It was not something she recognized. Betty Jo reached out and picked it up, cradling it in both hands.

She shook her head and returned it where she'd found it. She walked quickly out of the bedroom.

She searched for a pencil with no success and concluded that her papa would understand. It was cool in the room. She'd leave the butcher's package on the table. He wouldn't be away for long, and she needed to hurry back home and finish preparations.

Beulah May ushered Philip Harris into the house.

"Might I take yer coat, Reverend?" she said, her hospitality set in motion.

"Thank you, Mrs. Thorpe," Philip said with a nod. "All right now, let's dispense with the formalities, shall we, Beulah May?"

Beulah smiled. "Betty Jo's been workin' on a fine dinner tonight."

"I truly am looking forward to it," Philip returned.

Beulah led the way to the dining nook and gestured to the master chair before moving to the opposite side of the table. Philip hurried to help with the chair. Light from a single candle danced on the walls with the movement.

"Thank y'all kindly," Beulah said.

The everyday dishes and utensils were set perfectly and water glasses were filled.

Betty Jo arrived with a serving bowl of mashed sweet potatoes. "Evenin'," she greeted.

"Good evening, Betty Jo." Philip returned. "It looks great! May I lend a hand?"

"Why don't y'all take a chair? I'll be back in a bit." Betty Jo exited the dining nook as Philip settled into the one chair made with arms. She returned with the chicken pot pie. Setting it down, she moved to the remaining place setting. Philip stood and assisted her with the chair.

"Thank y'all kindly," Betty Jo said with eyes focused forward.

"Philip, would y'all ask the blessin' ?" Beulah requested.

Philip bowed his head. Betty Jo stole a glance at the handsome Yankee. Puzzled, she noted the white strip of skin on the third finger of his right hand.

"Lord, thank You for this food and for this fellowship. Guide our steps as we seek to glorify You. Amen."

"Amen," the two women responded.

With Betty Jo in the role as hostess, the three coalesced into conversational pleasantries. Upon completion of the meal, Beulah May set the cloth napkin down and pushed back in her chair. "Why don't y'all retire to the sittin' room? We'll let our food settle 'fore dessert."

Betty Jo searched her great aunt's face. She stood, and to the clatter of dishes being gathered, led the guest to the comfort of the sofa.

"Delicious dinner, Betty Jo. Thank you." Philip said, his blue eyes smiling.

"My pleasure. Aunt Beu is a real good teacher of most ev'rythang—'cept algebra." Betty Jo giggled.

"Philip," she continued, "I'm so grateful for the Word y'all brought durin' the meetin's. I never understood my personal need for Jesus until y'all spoke so clearly."

"The Lord is always at His good work." Philip readjusted his posture, turning sideways to face Betty Jo. "It amazes me to see all of the changes in your life these past five months. I am thankful that God brought us together."

Philip reached out for her hand. "I will be heading back to Rhode Island—leaving Saturday. My father has taken ill, and I need to go home."

"Oh, Philip, I'm sorry." Betty Jo empathized.

"I don't know how long I'll be gone. I do know I want to continue to court you." Philip let go of her hand and reached into his pocket, pulling out a small handmade paper box.

Betty Jo caught her breath and held it.

"Betty Jo, would you be mine?" he opened the box to reveal his gold-plated ring. The initials NP were on the face with a 19 on one side and a 31 on the other. "Would you accept this as my promise to you?"

"Oh, Philip." Betty Jo released her breath. "Yer class ring belongs on yer finger."

Philip Harris leaned back.

"I, I cain't make any promises now. The future's just so unknown. My attention's on gittin' into high school and helpin' my kin. I'm, I'm not ready fer promises."

In her short life, Betty Jo had many times witnessed pain. It wrinkled the brow and hollowed the eyes. In her lowest points of abuse and neglect, she knew pain had stamped its shadows on her face as well.

What she saw as she looked at Philip was undeniable. Her words had written pain upon his countenance.

She rested her hand on his knee. "Oh, Philip . . . Y'all're a wonderful man, and I do care fer y'all. I just cain't accept the ring now."

"Now? Do you think someday you might?" he asked.

"I dunno." Betty Jo shook her head.

"I see," he said. "May I write?"

"Of course, Philip. It'll be good to know how thangs go with y'all." Betty Jo stood up, leaving her perplexed suitor alone on the small couch. She walked to the piano and picked up the autoharp case that was next to it. She returned to an unarmed chair.

Carefully she unlatched the case and pulled out her mama's harp. Picking up the tuning tool, she made a few adjustments. Then she began, singing a solo to the good man she'd come to know.

> *Down in the valley, valley so low*
> *Hang your head over, hear the wind blow*
> *Hear the wind blow, dear, hear the wind blow*
> *Hang your head over, hear the wind blow.*

Betty Jo paused her voice while continuing to strum. Then with conviction she sang.

> *Roses love sunshine, violets love dew*
> *Angels in heaven know I love you*
> *Know I love you, dear, know I love you*
> *Angels in heaven know I love you.*

Philip closed his eyes. Instead of merely overhearing the song like last summer, it was being sung for him. His heart began to calm and his lips formed a smile of resignation.

"My, goodness gracious!" declared Beulah May as she entered the room. "We all need some happy music."

Then the sounds of hand-clapping praise wafted from the sitting room of the Thorpe's farmhouse. It rose up like the mists after a storm and put to rest the souls of those who sang.

*****

Betty Jo was determined to park smoothly. She geared down and positioned the car next to the gas pump in front of the mercantile. The giant star on the sign above welcomed her. Bringing it to a complete stop, she waited, sitting at the wheel. It appeared the sign would be her only welcome as the help did not come.

She emerged from the vehicle and walked toward the store's entrance. As she reached the boardwalk, her route was blocked by a manfolk moving her direction. Being cautious to keep her eyes lowered, she attempted to sidestep the form.

"Afternoon, Miz Landry."

Betty Jo froze at the tone.

"Don't y'all look real perty today?"

Betty Jo brazened her eyes to meet the face of the Sheriff of Shelby County.

"Guess the help never showed to work. Lemme git it fer y'all." Sheriff Davis walked to Beulah May's car and began the task.

Betty Jo stood, watching, with muscles taut in indecision. Then she hurried into the shelter of the mercantile.

"Afternoon, Betty Jo. What kin I do fer y'all today?" the proprietor asked.

"Afternoon, Mr. Sam," Betty Jo returned, glad for the warmth of his voice and the woodstove. "Aunt Beulah sent me with a list to fill." Betty Jo handed the paper to him. Looking toward the storefront window she added, "And the gasoline."

"We'll do." The proprietor set a box on the counter and began filling it with the requested items.

Sheriff Davis came into the store surrounded by a fume of gasoline mixed with a burst of cold air. Looking at the box of goods, he told the owner how much fuel had gone into the tank. He stood leaning against the counter.

"Alrighty. I think that's ev'rythang. I'll put it on yer Aunt's account." The owner smiled.

"Thank-y'all kindly," Betty Jo said. She reached out to pick up the box.

"Allow me," the Sheriff said, not waiting for a response.

Trapped in the rules of decorum, Betty Jo backed away from the box. She walked to the automobile, with the Sheriff following. She opened the passenger door and stepped aside.

"Thank-y'all kindly," she quickly said.

"Miz Maisie was wonderin' if y'all might join us fer Sunday dinner, two o'clock." Davis gave a smile that did not reach his eyes. "Would y'all kindly extend the invitation to yer aunt?"

"Yessir." Betty Jo sped her walk to the driver's side. All she wanted to do was get home and nurse her unsettled insides.

*****

"Stop the wagon, Charles," bossed Denny Ron. "Git yerself down," he called over his shoulder.

Henri slipped off the tailboard, wincing with the jar. He was met by stony glares when the other two men reached him.

"Ya ol' fool!" Denny Ron exclaimed. "Y'all know better'n to cheat me!"

"It ain't that way," Henri pled. "I cain't 'member 'xactly how it all goes. The accident messed my mind, but it's comin' back. Give me a bit longer—another day or so," he urged. "Please."

Henri turned slightly and began to back away. Denny and Charles pressed him toward the edge of the embankment. "Y'all've wasted two days already!" Denny snarled.

Henri reached inside his jacket and pulled out the envelope. "Here—I got no intent for ill-gotten gain."

Denny Ron snatched the envelope out of Henri's grasp.

Charles swooped forward and shoved the old man.

Henri fell backward and tumbled toward the water's edge. His body flopped to a stop against the trunk of a tree.

Denny Ron glared at Charles. "What're ya'll doin'? We was just gonna put the scare in 'im."

"The fool ain't deliverin' and he knows too much." Charles grabbed a hammer from the wagon. "I'll finish it."

"Leave 'im to rot," Denny Ron said.

"Cain't be soft in this bus'ness," Charles said, brushing past Denny Ron.

"No, I said! Let 'im be!" Denny Ron grabbed his new business partner by the arm.

Charles threw off Denny's grip. Hesitantly, he retreated to the wagon and returned the hammer.

Denny Ron looked down at his long-time bootleg partner. They'd surely been through much together over the years. He never intended to let the old codger keep the money. He sure never intended to hurt him. Henri Landry really messed things up this time. Denny shook his head, then made his way onto the wagon, calculating what in the world he could do now to get business going.

*****

"Well, if'n that don't beat all," Beulah May sighed. "Y'all heard 'im right?"

"Yes, ma'am," Betty Jo answered.

Beulah sat down at the kitchen table. Betty Jo joined her.

"Bin years since we've fellowshipped." Beulah shook her head. "Somethin's up. Must be so," she mumbled.

"Y'all were friends?" Betty Jo asked.

"In school, we all palled around. But since then, we made diff'rent choices." Beulah added, "Time marches on. We lead separate lives now."

"I don't feel right 'round the sheriff," Betty Jo admitted.

"Oh, Sugar, neither do I," Beulah chimed. "But I think we oughter accept."

Betty Jo slumped into the chair; her insides churned with contention.

"Fer one, it's rude not to. Fer the other, God kin change hearts. He kin do amazingly more'n what we kin ask or think." Then Beulah grinned. "My real reason is I'm just plumb curious as to what that ol' big head is up to now."

Betty Jo stood abruptly. She ran up the stairs to her bedroom and retrieved the drawing she kept hidden in the dresser. She returned to the kitchen table.

"Y'all told me once to be careful who I ask questions of. I figured it was time to ask y'all." Betty Jo unfolded the paper and set it on the table in front of her great aunt. "The man in this picture resembles the sheriff an awful lot. Who is he?"

"Oh, Sugar," Beulah groaned. "Where y'all get this?"

"It was Mama's. Who is this, Aunt Beu?"

Beulah looked Betty Jo in the eyes. "This here is the sheriff's son, Jimmy."

Betty Jo emphatically articulated, "And who is he to *me*?"

Beulah's eyes closed, and she lowered her head. Silence boiled the emotions long suppressed.

"Perty shore he's yer daddy," Beulah whispered.

"Why y'all hide it? Why y'all never tell me 'fore this?" Betty Jo began to cry.

"Sugar, I . . . " Beulah had no more words.

"Y'all're the one who says it's never good to ignore truth." Betty Jo shook her head with the accusation, then softly added, "Y'all're a hypocrite."

"Oh, Sugar, I . . . " Beulah May lowered her head as tears slid down her face.

Betty Jo left the picture on the table and left the kitchen. She headed to the front door, took her coat off the hook, and left the yellow farmhouse at the junction of the state highway and the county road.

Beulah May Thorpe grieved. She knew she'd done right by her sister, Leona, honoring her wishes to shelter Betty Jo. It was the best way to keep peace. At the same time, Betty Jo was right. She had withheld the truth into her niece's womanhood, and that was akin to propagating a lie. She was a hypocrite.

Oh, when will this turbulence ever end?

Beulah turned the kitchen table into an altar. Confessing her pride and weakness, she pled for wisdom. Then she came boldly before the Throne to seek God's mercy and protection on Betty Jo's behalf.

After time suspended, Beulah stood to her feet. Her eyes fell upon the drawing of Jimmy Davis. Though it made her uncomfortable, she would leave it be for now. She put the items from the mercantile into the pantry. She would light the sitting room and keep watch, holding vigil in Jack Lee's chair.

Halfway to the plank house, the rain began to fall, increasing its vigor with each step Betty Jo took. By the time she stood on the porch, she was soaked and chilled. For the second time in as many days, there was no reply to the calling and knocking.

Betty Jo opened the door and entered the dark room. Shivering, she fumbled around until light from the kerosene lamp filled the room. With the illumination, she noted that the butcher's package remained on the table, the string still tied. She set about to make a fire in the stove gone cold dead, her movement made clumsy by urgency. Finally, a flicker became a flame. She was truly grateful that her papa had taught her the skill of fire.

Betty Jo removed her soaked coat and draped it over the back of a chair, positioning it close to the stove. She removed her shoes and socks and placed them strategically on the hearth. She stood shivering, attempting to dry out and warm herself.

Her thoughts caught up to her actions, and guilt overtook anger. She had dished up disrespect and served it to one who had provided only the kindest regard. She'd caused a needless confrontation and spoken words that could never be taken back. And nothing she'd done this evening alleviated the turmoil brought on by the strange interaction with Sheriff Davis.

She pulled a second chair over to the wood stove and turned it to face her. Kneeling, she asked for forgiveness, and then began to pour out her concerns. Words soon turned to pleading.

Oh, Lord, where is Papa? Please, you know I couldn't stand it if . . . Conviction gripped her heart. She ought not be praying about her feelings, but her Papa's well-being. *Lord, keep him safe.* And this thought led her to what was most important. *Save my papa, Jesus.* Betty Jo prayed until there were no words left. Soft groans expressed what she could not to the God who knew all.

*****

Henri squinted his eyes against the sharp pelts of rain stabbing his face. He could not discern where he was. The darkness was oppressive, and he shivered convulsively. He turned his head to find that his torso was wedged against a tree. Moving his limbs slightly, he became aware of the mud penetrating through his clothing. With no light, he could not make out shapes, and the only sound he heard was the pounding rain. He knew he must get up on his feet, yet he had no energy within himself to use. Closing his eyes, he rolled onto his side and curled his body against the trunk. Just a little bit of rest and then he could be on his way.

*****

Betty Jo knew that Aunt Beu would be worried, and she was eager to make amends. She also knew that it would be wise to wait until the weather settled down. She would keep a good fire going and stay at the plank house through the night. Papa might return and perhaps would need her company. She would watch and pray.

*****

As clearly as if she were right in front of him, Henri could see his granddaughter kneeling on a plain wooden floor. Her long, dark hair hung in wet drapes on her shoulders. Winding around her was a river with clear water as he had never seen before. Oh, how he wanted a drink! Above her was a ceiling of translucent jasper, and its yellow glow served as a canopy.

He focused upon her form. She lifted her head and raised her hands and began to sing.

Love lifted me.

Then she stood to her bare feet and moved slowly toward him. "Papa, please accept God's love." Inexplicably her image disappeared.

Henri knew he did not have much longer.

Jack Lee appeared with a grin on his face. "Come on, ya'ol' rascal," he said. Then Leona came to him, reaching out her arms in invitation. Charlene sat on the three-legged stool and played her autoharp and sang.

When nothing else could help, love lifted me.

Henri began to sob. He'd known people who loved him, but he had never known love. He'd never done good.

He clawed at the earth he lay upon and filled his fists with mud. He was just a fallen ol' fool who'd lived life in the mire.

"Oh, God!" he cried. "I'm so sorry." He gasped for air. "Please save me!"

Henri Landry was raised above the muck of Earth. He opened his eyes to a world of pure light. The crystal-clear river stretched toward him, and enveloped him in its eternal life-giving flow. And in an instant, all things were made new.

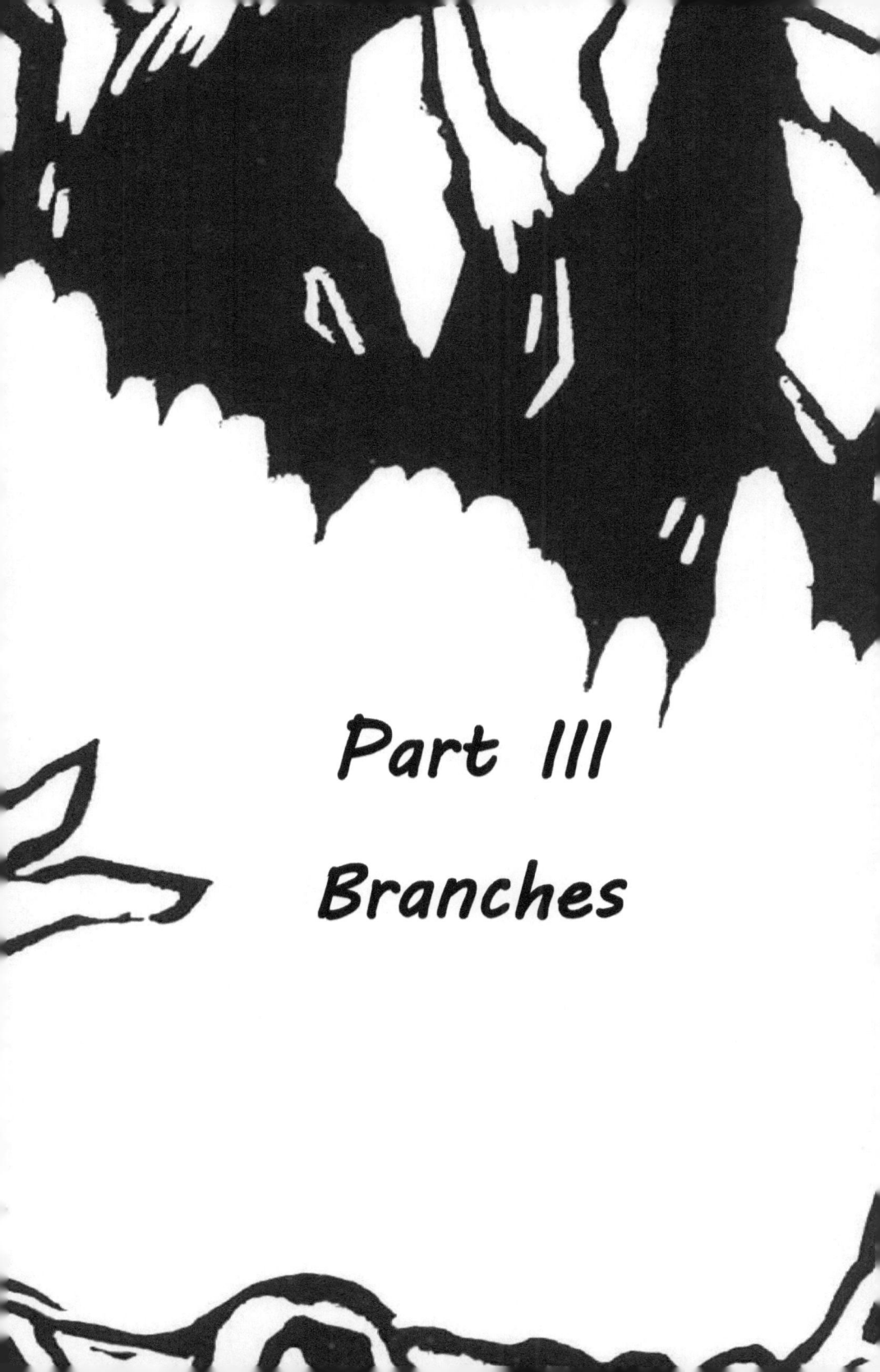

Part III

Branches

Debby L Wynkoop

CHAPTER ELEVEN

The weather settled. The mist dissipated as sunshine filled the sky. Betty Jo thought Papa might be found along the Sabine so she hiked the familiar trail downriver, searching—afraid of what she might find. The mud caused her steps to be erratic, impeding her progress. She turned around, aware of the need to get to the farmhouse and calm the anxiety caused by her abrupt and prolonged absence.

She approached the place where Big Tree once stood. She surveyed the gravesite of the fallen cypress. Brush and saplings grew out of its moss and mushroom covered carcass. Putrefaction is the way of the Pineys.

Betty Jo knew Papa was gone. She did not know how she knew. She just knew. Her mind wanted to linger—to hold memorial in the cathedral of the pines. Yet all things fall into a sequence of events, and to do so now would put the world out of order. Reluctantly, she moved again along the trail.

She had to get home to Aunt Beu.

Beulah May lifted the lid off the dutch oven and gave the stew a good stir. The carrots and potatoes were tender and the gravy had thickened nicely. She'd keep it and the cornbread on a hold temperature to wait. Surely Betty Jo would come home soon. Beulah stopped herself from sending Eddie out to fetch her niece. Involving Sheriff Davis would be a last resort. Betty Jo was grown now, and her God was great. *Casting all your care upon Him; for He careth for you,* Beulah recalled the scripture. She resolved to trust.

Betty Jo pushed aside her hungry and tired. She stepped onto the porch and cleaned her shoes on the mud scraper. It was proper to knock on the front door.

"Oh, Sugar," Beulah May sighed.

Betty Jo was reticent, her eyes cast low.

"Come on in." Beulah opened the door wide and stepped aside as Betty Jo crossed the threshold. "I 'spect we oughter talk."

Betty Jo removed the shoes that still held traces of her walk in the Pineys, hung her coat on a hook, and followed her great aunt to the sitting room. Beulah took position in Jack Lee's chair. Betty Jo sat on the sofa.

"I 'member the day ya'll were born," Beulah began. "Yer granma had a premonition that mornin'. Turns out her fears were realized. I promised her I'd guard my mouth concernin' yer daddy. Yer papa would have met any interference with fury, and the Davis clan would never admit paternity."

Beulah shifted her weight in the chair. "I honored yer granma's wishes. But I done a real disservice by keepin' to myself what y'all had a right to know, 'specially in yer womanhood. I regret the hurt and confusion it caused. I am truly sorry."

Betty Jo lifted her head and walked to her aunt's side. She knelt down. "Aunt Beulah, I'm ashamed fer my outburst. Y'all've only ever done me good. Disrespect shot out before I could even think. I guess it come from a real dark place. Please forgive me."

"Oh, Sugar, y'all're a true gift. Never ferget it." Beulah's arms reached out to her niece.

Crying, Betty Jo laid her head in her aunt's lap. Beulah stroked Betty Jo's tussled dark hair and hummed comfort.

"Y'all must be famished," Beulah said once peace settled. "Let's get a bite to eat."

Betty Jo stood to her feet. "Papa never came home," she stated, matter of fact. "No fire'd bin made fer some time, and the cold cuts were where I left 'em."

Beulah tilted her head.

"Aunt Beu, I prayed fer 'im most the night. At mornin' light, I searched along the Sabine. No hide nor hair."

"Oh, my goodness," Beulah whispered.

"He's gone," Betty Jo said. "I mean . . . in my spirit I believe he's .
. ."

"Dear Jesus," Beulah responded.

*****

The menfolk mingled outside the church in Joaquin, bedraggled from a chilled day of chores. Duty to Sister Beulah May compelled them to come. The sheriff moved about, hovering over the shoulders of the men as they conferred in urgent tones to divide the territory. There wasn't much daylight left.

Brother Tucker projected his voice. "Thank y'all fer comin'. Let's pray. Lord, we ask that the hidden thangs be revealed. Help us find Henri. Protect these faithful men as they search. Amen."

They went out two by two—on horseback, in old trucks, and on foot. They searched their place in East Texas, only to return to the House of the Lord after blackness fell with nothing to show for their efforts.

*****

Jimmy Davis leaned back in the wooden chair, crossed his arms, and stretched out his legs. "Y'all want me to do what?" Incredulity dripped from each word.

"Y'all heard me. Yer the one who needs to find Henri Landry." James Roy Davis stared his son down. "Time fer y'all to be the hero fer a change."

Jimmy winced and shook his head slowly.

"Church folk are fools," James Roy smirked. "They be searchin' the Texas side where we already run 'im out. I 'spect he took up with them bootleggers in Lou'siana—outside my jurisdiction."

Jimmy pulled his legs in and leaned forward. "Do tell."

"Boys workin' out of Shreveport bin takin' over territory. It's a big operation. Hurtin' our business. My guess is Denny and Henri got tangled up with 'em."

"How am I supposed to find 'im?" Jimmy asked.

"Are y'all dense, Boy? Start with the old wagon road out of Logansport—but just find the ol' bastard. If he's lost or hurt, drag 'im back. Y'all will earn favor with Betty Jo. But if he's workin', do 'im in, and drag his sorry corpse home. Y'all will still earn favor. No one need ever know a thang 'bout who done it. They know the kind of life he's lived."

"I dunno." Jimmy Davis wiped his forehead as if he'd been sweating.

"Don't fergit, Son, y'all're here to serve the family!" James Roy abruptly stood to his feet and handed Jimmy the Smith and Wesson Special. "Git goin' first thang in the mornin' while the folks are occupied with church."

Jimmy caressed the gun with his fingertips. "Yessir," he sighed.

*****

Betty Jo sat tall in the wooden pew, pulling her mother's sweater tightly around her. The dress Aunt Beulah had made for her return to school was crisp and stylish—a mismatch for the dated sweater that obscured it.

There were vacancies in the pews creating spaces for a cold draft to move about the parishioners. Heads huddled together and then turned her way. She received the looks with stoic nods. She was Henri's granddaughter, and she would deal with the aftermath of his disappearance. Aunt Beu had said once that these were her people. Of this, she was skeptical. What she knew was that Beulah May Thorpe was her nearest kin, and she belonged by her side, sitting in Joaquin Baptist Church on this Sunday in December.

The ritual of church attendance was now part of Betty Jo's life. Once she discovered the pattern, she had learned the how-to-greet and the when-to-stand and the what-to-respond. She set aside the conduct of the congregants and her own suppositions as to what they were thinking and took shelter in her Lord. She resolved to fellowship with Him.

When the singing and the speaking concluded, Brother Tucker gave the final prayer. "Dear Jesus, we thank Ya'll fer comin' to this ol' world, being born to be our Savior. Oh, Light of the World, shine in the darkness. We pray today for guidance and help in findin' Henri Landry. In Your precious name, amen." Congregants murmured their agreement.

Betty Jo echoed the amen and opened her eyes. Sister Tucker played a grandiose *Joy to the World* as the church goers slowly made their way toward the large doors.

Mrs. Westly positioned herself in the middle of the aisle. "Oh, Beulah May, we are so sorry to hear about Henri!"

Beulah received the hug, then turned and placed her arm around Betty Jo's waist.

"The not knowin' must be so difficult. Whenever did he go missin'?" Mrs. Westly asked, looking Beulah directly in the eyes.

"Thank y'all kindly fer the condolence," Betty Jo said. "Miz Westly, we do so appreciate yer prayers." She nudged her aunt. "We best be gittin' along."

Mrs. Westly hesitantly stepped to the side between rows of pews. "Why, certainly," she said. "Bless y'all," she added.

Betty Jo escorted her great aunt down the aisle. Maisie Davis, with coat buttoned, was waiting for them at the back.

"Beulah May," she whispered, reaching for Beulah's hand. "We certainly understand if'n y'all need to cancel dinner plans."

Beulah looked at Betty Jo before replying. "There be nothin' left fer us womenfolk to do but wait. Breakin' bread with y'all will help pass the time."

"Very good, Dear." Maisie offered a feeble smile. "Two o'clock then?"

Beulah nodded agreement, before she and Betty Jo walked to the door. They stopped to shake hands with Brother Tucker.

"The men will go out this afternoon," he assured them. "The Lord will answer our prayers. Have faith, yer papa will be found."

"Amen." Beulah May turned the statement into a prayer.

"Thank y'all, Reverend," Betty Jo returned.

*****

The Davis home sat on an acreage east of the county seat. The front of the large craftsman house was ornamented with bric-a-brac molding to welcome visitors who seldom came.

Betty Jo parked the car in front of the picket fence. She looked at her aunt. "Y'all shore 'bout this? I could offer apologies."

"Sugar," Beulah said, "We're here now—might as well go through with it. I cain't be sure what waits us inside, but I think we may be here fer reasons beyond our own selves."

Betty Jo took a deep breath and got out of the driver's side. She went around to open the door of the car for her aunt and stood guard until Beulah landed firmly on her feet. Together they passed through the fence gate and walked the path to the porch.

Betty Jo struggled to breathe.

Since she first understood that children have daddies, all Betty Jo wanted to do was meet hers. She was about to have dinner with her daddy's daddy. The realization swelled to the point of suffocation. *Sheriff Davis was her grandfather!*

In short order, the knock at the door was answered. Betty Jo had no time to lasso the wild thoughts in her head.

"Please come in," Maisie said, opening the door wide.

Betty Jo followed her aunt into the Davis house.

"Yer home is just beautiful," Aunt Beu said to the hostess.

"May I take yer coats?" Maisie offered. She gestured to the sitting room. "We'll hold dinner for James Roy. He's out organizin' the search, but should be back shortly."

"We are thankful fer his efforts," Beulah said.

Betty Jo and Beulah shared the settee, and Maisie sat down in a floral-upholstered arm chair. Her knees were tight together with her right foot tucked behind the left.

Betty Jo found respite in the quiet moment. She studied her surroundings. It was a tidy room. The woman opposite the area rug from her was a meek soul. Both observations stood in opposition to the sheriff's blustering persona. As she glanced back and forth between Aunt Beulah and Maisie Davis, her dread gave way to intrigue. An unspoken conversation was occurring.

Maisie's hand tremored in her lap. At last, a melancholic smile crossed her face. "Hard to believe how time has passed."

"And how much has transpired in its quick passage," Beulah added.

"How're y'all doin'?" Maisie asked.

"I miss 'im sorely," Beulah replied.

Maisie nodded sympathetically. "Yers was a precious love story."

Love story? Betty Jo never considered that Aunt Beulah and Uncle Jack were characters in a love story.

"It was good to see y'all in church this mornin'." Beulah lowered her voice. "How are y'all doin', Maisie?"

"Jimmy's returned home," Maisie said.

Anxiety flooded Betty Jo's thoughts.

Beulah looked at her hostess sincerely. "How are y'all doin'?" she repeated.

"Gittin' along." Maisie looked down at her hands. "Seems there is always . . . disruption."

"I trust the disruption is not harmin' y'all?" Beulah pried to the boundary of propriety.

Maisie raised her eyes to Beulah's face.

"Y'all're not without helpful friends," Beulah assured.

Recognition pushed anxiety away. Betty Jo was suddenly overwhelmed with a desire to hug this woman—to encircle her in womenfolk kindness.

"Sugar," Beulah said, "Miz Davis, yer granma, and I were girlhood friends."

"Truly so," Maisie said, her hand tremor accelerating. "I shorely am sorry fer the troubles that have come yer way. I pray yer grandfather will be found soon."

"Thank y'all, Miz Davis." Betty Jo's voice quivered.

"Please, call me . . . call me Maisie."

A door slammed. Heavy footfall sounded on the wood floor. Sheriff Davis, with hat fixed squarely on his head, stepped into the sitting room. "Afternoon," he said. "I'll join y'all at the table in a bit."

Maisie stood quickly.

"Miz Maisie, I kin help y'all get the food on," Betty Jo said.

"Thank y'all," Maisie said as she led the guests out of the sitting room.

Before all of the food had been brought in from the kitchen, James Roy joined Beulah at the dining table—his hat removed and his remaining hair slicked back.

"When was the last time y'all seen Henri?" he questioned.

"Wednesday mornin'," Beulah answered.

"Wednesday past?" James Roy scoffed. "Why in the world y'all soundin' the alarm—gettin' folks riled up?"

"Because somethin' is terrible wrong," Beulah answered.

"How do y'all know that? God tell y'all?" scoffed Davis.

Beulah met the sheriff's eyes. "We know," she said firmly.

"Lands alive, Beulah May. We cain't carry on so over a hunch." Sighing, Sheriff Davis crossed his arms. "Henri back in the business?"

"Now, James Roy, y'all know I do not oversee Henri's affairs."

"He had no horse. Y'all loan 'im Jack Lee's truck?

"No, sir."

"Well, the searchers are out agin, lookin' 'round the east woods. I be thinkin' he left the area with someone." James Roy paused before adding in a soft voice, "If'n that's the case, could be nigh impossible to find 'im."

Beulah turned from the conversation as Maisie and Betty Jo completed the final trip from the kitchen and sat down. James Roy asked Beulah to say the blessing. Betty Jo took security in her eyes being closed. She was not sure she would be able to look at the man sitting across the table from her aunt. As Beulah prayed, Betty Jo felt the warmth of her aunt's hand patting her knee under the table.

Beulah concluded, "Bless this food and the hands that prepared it. In Jesus' name, amen.

"Thank y'all fer the invitation." Beulah smiled as Maisie Davis began to pass the food around the table. "The ham smells delicious—just like Christmas dinner."

Betty Jo was not sure she could keep any food down, yet she understood her obligation. She served herself small portions, but not too small as to be noticed.

With the business of the food served, table sounds—scrapes and clinks and proper affirmations of deliciousness—filled the space where conversation was absent.

After chasing a butter bean about her plate, Betty Jo succeeded in getting it into her mouth. She chewed slowly and thoroughly, finally managing to swallow.

James Roy broke the silence. "How're y'all plannin' to manage the property now that Jack Lee's passed?"

Maisie's fork, bearing a piece of ham, suspended midway to its destination. It quivered in her hand.

Beulah looked James Roy square in the eyes. "Jack Lee and I were blessed with two wonderful children and our lovely niece." She turned her head sideways and smiled at Betty Jo. "Maisie tells us that Jimmy's come back home."

James Roy pursed his lips.

"Do y'all think he'll be 'round a while?" Beulah pressed.

The table sounds came to a stop.

"I do 'spect 'im to make a life here in Shelby County. Don't know if'n it'll be Center or Joaquin where he was born and raised," James Roy answered.

"I see," said Beulah.

"What about y'all, young lady?" The Sheriff made a pretense of looking at Betty Jo. "What does yer future hold?"

Betty Jo's shoulders stiffened. She focused on the wall just behind the shoulder of James Roy. With a courage not of herself, she answered. "We cain't say about the future, sir. Ours is to live today. And today, I am concerned that Papa be found."

"Of course, dear," Maisie Davis assured, attempting to smooth the bristle emanating from her husband.

"*Sufficient unto the day is the trouble thereof,*" Beulah recited.

Table sounds resumed.

With a bite of sweet potato, Betty Jo commandeered her emotions. It was strange to sit at a table with grandparents she'd never known. Stranger still was that no one spoke of this relationship. But by far, the strangest thing was that her papa was gone forever.

"If he's in Shelby County, we'll find 'im fer shore," Sheriff Davis tersely added as a benediction to the meal.

*****

Betty Jo stretched out on the bed and bundled in the patchwork quilt. Alone in the room where she was born, she prayed for understanding. No revelation or confession had come from the strained Sunday dinner. The dramatic juncture she expected did not occur.

Papa being gone was nothing new. Papa never coming home would change her world. The thin string that physically connected her to the man she had both hated and loved was severed. The emotional cords, however, tightened with each passing hour.

A light rap sounded. "Sugar?" The door slowly pushed open. Beulah's frame filled the space. "Come to check on y'all."

Betty Jo pushed herself up and leaned against the headboard as Beulah walked in the room and sat on the edge of the bed. Betty Jo could sense the rapid expansion and compression of her aunt's chest.

"Strange," Betty Jo said. "Ev'rythang's so strange."

Beulah nodded understanding. "Clarity will come. In due time."

In the quiet, the women sat in kinship.

Beulah reached out and patted her niece's hand. "As y'all wait, put yer hope in the Lord. Isaiah 40:31 is fer y'all, Sugar." Arduously, Beulah stood and left the bedroom.

Everybody leaves, Betty Jo mused. *Mama, Granma, Jack Lee, Dottie, Philip . . . Papa. How can anyone bear to love?*

*****

Betty Jo lowered the history book in her hands. It was difficult to concentrate. While she could sound out most of the words, many she did not recognize. Every time there was a lapse in progress, her thoughts turned to Papa. He had yet to be found.

In spite of the challenges, she enjoyed reading stories of the nation's founding. The more she read, however, the more questions she had. Where were her papa's people when all of this was taking place? They were never mentioned. And if all men were created equal, why didn't folks act like it? The Colored, the Cajun, the poor—they surely weren't treated the same as the townsfolk or land owners. Being in the mercantile taught her that.

Engine sounds and the crunch of gravel captured Betty Jo's attention. She marked her spot and placed the book on the end table. She moved to the window as the sheriff's black patrol car approached.

"Aunt Beu!" she called. "Sheriff's coming!"

Beulah May emerged from the kitchen, towel still in hand. "Shorely?" she questioned, joining Betty Jo at the window.

The women turned, donned their coats at the entrance and made their way to stand side by side on the porch. Betty Jo linked her hand through the crook of her aunt's arm.

Sheriff Davis pulled the car to a stop and got out. A younger Davis exited the passenger side. Car doors slammed shut in sync, and together they approached the porch. The sheriff touched the brim of his hat. Jimmy Davis stood quietly next to his father. Betty Jo tightened her hold on Beulah's arm.

"Y'all 'member my boy, Jimmy?" the Sheriff asked.

"Afternoon, ma'am," Jimmy said to Beulah in monotone.

"This here's Betty Jo," Sheriff Davis continued. "Henri's granddaughter."

Jimmy briefly looked Betty Jo's way before lowering his head.

"Jimmy's bin out lookin' fer Henri. Found 'im this mornin' in the Pines on the Lou'siana side."

Betty Jo nudged even closer to her aunt.

"Sorry to tell y'all that he's gone. Bin gone quite a while."

"Seems he'd fallen down the river bank," Jimmy said. "Likely hit his head. 'Spect the cold did the rest." Jimmy lifted his eyes. "Truly sorry, ma'am . . . Betty Jo."

"Took the liberty to carry 'im to the undertaker," Sheriff Davis said. "The body's wrecked bad."

Silent tears began to roll down Betty Jo's cheeks.

Beulah sighed. "Thank y'all."

For the first time, Betty Jo looked at Jimmy Davis. "Thank y'all fer findin' my papa."

Jimmy nodded acceptance but offered no more words.

"Our sincere condolence," James Roy perfunctorily said as the two men turned to go.

Beulah and Betty Jo watched the sheriff turn the car around and drive away. When the silhouettes of the Davis men disappeared from view, the women turned to each other in somber embrace.

The sky was threatening. Eddie stood with a group of men in the periphery—shovel still in hand. Beulah had arranged for a simple pine box and an immediate burial. The location of Henri's internment had been a matter of discussion. Papa would have resented being in the Morris family cemetery, yet it was proper for him to be laid to rest near Mama and Granma. Beulah, ever the pragmatist, extolled the advantage to Betty Jo of having all of her dear ones in the same location. Where one is laid to rest should be to the benefit of those left, she had said. Of course, the decision was confirmed to Betty Jo when she learned of the *No Colored, No Cajun* policy of the nearest cemetery.

Betty Jo declined to view Papa's body. She chose to keep him pictured as she saw him last—standing on the porch of the plank house, nodding goodbye. She would trust the undertaker and the death certificate.

Word had spread that Henri Landry had been found. While he had no folks or friends, a few gathered at the graveside in support. Sister Tucker escorted Aunt Beulah over the bumpy ground and stood on her other side. Brother Tucker was positioned to offer a few words. Betty Jo hugged her mama's autoharp to her chest. The cold would affect the pitch of the strings, but she was undeterred.

The preacher prayed and read scriptures of comfort. The handful of folks sang songs Papa would not have known. The uncertainty of Papa's spiritual condition hovered over the proceedings. Words were carefully chosen. No one mentioned Heaven.

With a nod from the reverend, the work crew advanced.

Her papa, the man who raised her, was lowered into the ground. What she had hoped for six months ago, was now reality; yet she stood sorrowful.

"Ashes to ashes . . . dust to dust," Brother Tucker began the recitation of the final words.

Betty Jo gave the autoharp to her aunt to hold. She bent down and scooped a fistful of damp soil. Her hands were ice cold, as if the life blood had ceased. The clod landed on the pine box with a gentle thud of finality. One by one, others followed in the ritual. She wiped her hand on her coat, oblivious to the stain it left.

Taking the autoharp from her aunt, she balanced it carefully in her arms and began to strum.

> *Dors, dors, Mon père*
> *'coutes la rivière, 'coutes la rivière*

Finishing, the tears began to flow.
"Goodbye, Papa," she whispered.

CHAPTER TWELVE

Betty Jo wedged the wooden crate against her hip and surveyed the place where she was raised. The hand-hewn planks and hardwood posts stood as memorial to Papa's hard work and ingenuity. Now the little house he made and its contents were handed down to her. She stepped onto the porch, not really sure where to begin the task.

Aunt Beulah and some of her church ladies had offered to help with the clean-out, but Betty Jo knew it was her responsibility alone. Exams were next week, and she needed to be free of this burden. She would be unable to concentrate on book learning until this chapter of her life was closed.

She entered the house. The butcher-wrapped package of cold cuts remained on the table, and the chair that was her altar last Friday night remained next to the stove. Time was suspended in the empty stillness.

Betty Jo lit the lantern. Despite the chill, she chose to not make a fire. She went to the bigger of the two back rooms, treading on soles of guilt. She had been forbidden from this room, though after Granma passed, she would sneak in and snoop around on occasion. Even then, the little box on top of the chest of drawers was something she had not seen until last week.

She picked up the photograph. Glancing in the yellowed mirror hanging on the wall, she looked back again at Papa, Granma, and Mama. She clearly saw the resemblance—the shape of her face, her wavy hair, and body posture. Then she imagined a photograph of the Davis family. She looked in the mirror again. She might have a similar nose shape and eyes more close-set eyes like the Sheriff and Jimmy. It occurred to Betty Jo briefly that she in no way resembled Maisie Davis. Oh, well, sometimes it worked that way in families.

Betty Jo placed the framed photograph in the wooden crate. Then she reached for the old jewelry box. Still conflicted about the right to do so, she lifted the lid to find a silver necklace. The tear-drop shaped pendant was as shiny as the photograph frame. Papa had also tended to it recently. She lifted the necklace out of the box and turned the pendant around. Words were engraved: *Love always.*

Betty Jo knew she'd found treasure and wondered about Papa's intent. She returned the necklace to the box. She set it on top of the photograph. She also planned to keep the cypress chest, Granma's Bible, and her quilt. She would sort through and organize the household goods. They would be of use to whoever might reside here next.

She began the process of separating the clothes into piles. Wearable clothes would be given to Eddie to distribute to needy pickers. Usable fabrics would go to the Baptist Women's Missionary Alliance for quilting and patching. She would place the oil-stained-beyond-hope clothes into a burn pile.

Betty Jo examined her Papa's flannel shirt. She hesitated before putting it into the crate. Finally, she came to Papa's suit—the very one he wore in the old photograph. A tinge of guilt crept into her mind. It would have been proper to have Papa buried in it, but circumstance did not permit. There were several egregious holes made by hearty moths. Still, she put it in the usable fabrics pile.

The silver comb was one of only a few of her granma's personal items remaining. Strangely, there was nothing in the plank house that would have belonged to her Mama, but Betty Jo was content. The autoharp was more than enough.

What Betty Jo most hoped to find, she did not. Perhaps it was time to take a trip to Center.

"Yes, it was yer granma's," Beulah May simply said, turning to tend the pot of beans.

Betty Jo walked to the kitchen table and sat down, staring at the necklace in her hand.

"I never seen it . . . I have never seen it before," Betty Jo corrected herself.

"I 'spect that be true." Beulah tapped the wooden spoon twice on the lip of the dutch oven. She formed a patty with the corn meal mixture and slid it into the melted lard in the cast iron skillet. "My daddy—yer great grandpa—gave it to her years ago."

"Shorely . . . Surely so?" Betty Jo replied.

Beulah laughed and placed three more patties into the skillet. "Now, Sugar, no need puttin' on airs. School'll accept y'all on yer exam scores, not if'n y'all sound like a Yankee."

Betty Jo smiled. "Just practicing my grammar, Aunt Beu."

Beulah turned to face her niece. "Just don't y'all go gettin' the big head now," she said with mock sternness.

Betty Jo calculated each word. "Why do you expect it is true that I have never seen it?"

"Well, honestly, Sugar!" Beulah exclaimed. "I'll tell y'all the story over supper if'n y'all promise to talk regular agin."

"Yes, ma'am," Betty Jo returned. "Shorely."

With corn cakes and beans on the table and the blessing said, Beulah began the story.

"I told y'all how yer granma and papa took up with each other without my daddy's blessin'?"

"Yes, ma'am," Betty Jo affirmed.

"Daddy was a wise man, but he was stubborn. Disownin' yer granma was a terrible burden on the family. Mother grieved over it fer the rest of her days. No one would admit mistakes, so bitterness was mixed into the pot and it stewed into a strange love-hate brew."

While Beulah ate part of her corn cake, Betty Jo chewed on the words.

Beulah swallowed and continued. "Yer poor mama . . . she really didn't know what it was to have grandparents. One year fer Christmas, Daddy bought the autoharp. He'd bin on business in Dallas. The folks gave it to yer granma to give yer mama."

"I never knew it came from Great-Granddaddy," Betty Jo interjected.

"Yer papa was none too pleased 'bout it, but yer granma persuaded 'im. I'm so thankful! It has brought such good over the years.

"It hurt Daddy to see his daughter and granddaughter livin' so poor when he owned so much. He had influence on ev'rythang and everyone 'cept his own family."

Beulah May pushed back from the table. "Be back in a bit," she said as she slowly stood.

Betty Jo began the supper clean-up. When Beulah returned, she held a jewelry box. It drew Betty Jo back to the table.

"Several years after the autoharp, Daddy and Mother gave Leona and me these." Beulah opened her box to reveal an identical necklace, with the exception that hers bore the darkened tarnish of time. She pulled it out and turned it over. Betty Jo bent over to read the inscription.

Love always.

"It fell to me to give Leet hers. At the time, yer papa wouldn't allow let her to come to family gatherin's. She tried to hide it from him. Sorry to say he found it when he was drunk, and it sent him in a rage. I put mine away after that—never knew what happened to Leet's . . . 'til tonight.

"I suppose the gift was Daddy's way of makin' amends. Sadly, it just brought grief. Guess Daddy finally understood the truth. When yer family, yer forever connected. There's no disownin' yer own.

"Seems yer Papa was gettin' ready to give y'all yer Grandma's necklace. Mebbe he came to understand it, too."

*****

The brisk wind helped push the car door shut. Cold rain would begin soon on this Monday morning. Betty Jo looked up at the courthouse—standing tall in the mist, guarded by turret-topped columns. She could not have imagined a more intriguing castle.

This was her third trip to Center. The first time was to visit Granma in the hospital. She'd only glimpsed at the courthouse as they drove by, but it could not be missed. It was positioned prominently in the middle of the town square. After Granma passed, Betty Jo descended into a world of make-believe. She was sure that having seen this structure was the catalyst for the stories of princes and castles she had created.

Her second time to come to Center was also a trip to the hospital. Last summer, she sat in the back seat of this very car. The angst of the moment transcended the passage of time. She always thought the town was far away, but it didn't take that long to get here today.

Betty Jo shook off her musings and hurried to the passenger side to assist her great aunt. With one hand securing her hat and clutching a purse with the other, Beulah May looked up at the edifice.

"Shorely is glorious. Like an Irish castle in the middle of Shelby County," she said.

The pair walked inside and found the records office. An amiable clerk, dripping with sweetness, filled their request. "Here y'all're," she said. "Ask y'all just to look and not touch."

Betty Jo studied the details of each certificate.

> *Certificate of Live Birth*
> *Betty Jo Landry*
> *Female*
> *Born: October 28, 1915*
> *Birthplace: Joaquin, Texas*
> *Father: unknown*
> *Mother: Charlene May Landry*
>
> *Death Certificate*
> *Charlene May Landry*
> *Age: 17*
> *Passed October 28, 1915*
> *Joaquin, Texas*
> *Cause of Death: Childbirth*

The only surprise on the certificates was her mother's middle name. Everything else she knew well; yet to stand witness to the legal documents—to see for herself the truth in writing—filled Betty Jo with sadness. No one had claimed to be her father, and she was the cause of her mother's death. These two facts were irrefutable.

Betty Jo opened the door for Beulah to leave the building. A bluster of sideways rain awaited them. She took care to steady her great aunt as they proceeded down the walk.

"Sugar, we all have one more stop 'fore leavin' Center." Beulah pointed across the street and the two made their way to the business side of the block. *T. L. Murphy, Attorney at Law* was in gold letters across the plate glass window of the building they entered.

"Good mornin', Beulah May. Blustery day," the receptionist greeted them. "Make yerself comfortable. Mr. Murphy will be right with y'all."

"Thank y'all," Beulah replied, removing her coat to hang on the coat tree, before sitting down in an unarmed chair.

Betty Jo followed her great aunt's lead, and sat in the chair next to her. "Never knew Mama was named after y'all," Betty Jo whispered.

"Well, fer me, I suppose, but mostly fer yer great grandma. *May* was her maiden name," Beulah explained.

Betty Jo was confused. Mama gave her a name unrelated to any kin. Betty Jo thought it was to keep Papa appeased, yet her mama had a family name.

"Won't take long," Beulah said to her niece when T. L. Murphy emerged from his office. "Just a few papers to sign."

The drive back to Joaquin took longer. The fiercely falling rain made it difficult to see the road. By the time they pulled up to the school, the squall had abated.

They entered the office of the small-town school. The secretary looked over her glasses at Beulah May. "Y'all the guardian?" she asked skeptically.

"Not official, Mabel Dee," Beulah said.

"Y'all have a birth certificate?"

"No ma'am, but it's on file at the Courthouse," Betty Jo answered. "I come . . . I came to primary school here. My teacher was Miz McDonald."

"Remind me yer last name?" the secretary asked as her shoes clicked across the hardwood floor.

"Landry. Betty Jo Landry," Betty Jo responded.

The secretary's feet stopped for a moment before continuing to the file cabinet. Betty Jo wondered why this Baptist church lady seemed so different here in the school office.

Mabel Dee bent down, pulled out the lowest metal drawer, and began riffling through the files. Finally, she pulled one out and stood up.

"Here we are," she said to herself. "Looks like y'all completed through second grade." The secretary turned to face Betty Jo. "Y'all never returned?"

"No, ma'am," Betty Jo replied, fairly certain the secretary knew the answer to her own questions.

"It'd be quite unseemly to have, well, a young woman in the third-grade class." The secretary walked back to her desk.

"Mabel Dee, we shorely agree," Beulah said. "Betty Jo would like to enroll in high school."

The secretary placed the file on her desk, sat down, and scrutinized the one born illegitimate. "Plenty is learned between second grade and high school."

"Betty Jo has been schoolin' at home," Beulah responded. "I talked with Mr. Filmore few weeks back. He said if'n Betty Jo could pass the exams at semester fer junior year she could enroll second semester."

The secretary sighed. "Why, she'd be missin' two and a half years of credits!"

"Mr. Filmore said he'd figure a way fer Betty Jo to catch up to her peers," Beulah pressed. "I take 'im at his word."

The secretary frowned. "Lemme me check with 'im."

"Of course," Beulah May said diplomatically. "All we need today is the testing schedule fer each of the junior courses. As fer enrollment, Betty Jo kin enroll her own self. She turned 16 autumn past."

The secretary acquiesced. She pulled out the necessary papers, and in perfect cursive wrote the schedule for the seven tests. Betty Jo shifted her weight from foot to foot as she waited.

Thank y'all," Betty Jo said when the secretary handed her the paper.

"Have a lovely day, Mabel Dee," Beulah said.

Beulah May and Betty Jo left the school office. The secretary, with pursed lips, slowly shook her head from side to side.

The women walked into the hallway and out the front door. Betty Jo placed her hand in the crook of her aunt's arm as they descended the steps, wet with rainfall.

She looked at the schedule once they were inside the car.

"I dunno if'n I kin pass all these tests."

"Fer shore will be hard. But our God is a mighty Help," Beulah assured. "One more errand and y'all kin spend the rest the day studyin'."

"Mornin'," the proprietor of the mercantile greeted as Betty Jo closed the door. "Guess it's still mornin'."

Betty Jo smiled as she walked to the aisle with the crochet needles and thread.

"Mornin', Sam. Not too many thangs today," Beulah said as she approached the counter, handing him the list. Mostly need to pick up the post."

"Shore thang." The proprietor set to work filling the list.

Sheriff Davis emerged from the back room and slipped around the counter. He nodded at Beulah. His greeting was met with scrutiny.

Mrs. Westly was drawn to Beulah. "Oh, Beulah May, how are y'all? So sorry to hear of the loss of Henri, but must be a relief to know fer shore." She turned to look at the sheriff. "Heard tell yer boy, Jimmy, was the one who found 'im."

"Yes, ma'am," Davis acknowledged. "Proud to say so."

Betty Jo was content to stay away from the conversation. She studied the thread. She knew she could borrow Aunt Beu's crochet needles and use some of the starch, but where could she get the money to purchase the colored threads?

"We're so thankful fer Jimmy's effort. Laying Henri to rest properly was a blessin'," Beulah said to Mrs. Westly and Sheriff Davis.

Betty Jo moved back to Beulah's side, marveling again at her great aunt. She always seemed to say just what was needed without saying too much.

The proprietor returned from the back room with two letters in his hand. He added them to the little box of groceries. "Anythang else?" he asked.

"Add the tab, please," Beulah answered.

The click and ching of the register sounded. Beulah counted out exact cash and coin, laying it on the counter.

"Thank y'all, Sam," Beulah said.

Betty Jo reached for the box, but was intercepted by the sheriff.

"Allow me," he said.

The proprietor looked at Betty Jo. "My sympathies on the loss of yer papa."

Betty Jo braved a look into his eyes. They were misty gray. The kindness she saw there eased her tension momentarily. "Thank y'all," she said sincerely, before assuming her place at Aunt Beulah's side.

"Goodbye now," Beulah said to Mrs. Westly.

The three exited the store and walked the obstacle course of mud puddles to the car, pausing for a brief conversation when they arrived.

Mrs. Westly watched from the store's front window. "Well, I'll be . . . " she said to no one in particular.

"Mrs. Westly," called the proprietor, "will there be anythang else today?"

The sedan turned onto the highway. Betty Jo waited until the steering wheel released itself. "Why y'all suppose the sheriff's makin' nice?"

"Dunno, but 'spect it'll be clear after he comes to call," Beulah replied. " 'Til then, let's not get carried away supposin'."

When they arrived at the Thorpe house, the two set about the task of putting items in the pantry. Beulah sat at the kitchen table with the letter addressed to Mrs. Jack Lee Thorpe in her hand. Betty Jo followed her with the letter addressed to Miss Betty Jo Landry.

Beulah May opened the envelope with the return address marked Houston, Texas. She pulled out the letter and read aloud:

December 13, 1931

Dear Cousin,

I trust my reply finds you in good health. We share in your sorrowful loss of Jack Lee, and send our deepest sympathies. We take comfort that he is with the Lord.

I would be pleased to accept your offer. It is an answer to prayer as to what I ought to do next. While it has been good to be with my sister, I do not relish the city life. I sense the Lord drawing me home.

I will return by February. That should give us enough time in advance of planting to get organized.

Suzanne and I send our best wishes to you and all the kinfolk for a Merry Christmas. Give Betty Jo an extra hug for me.

Love,
Dot

"Thank Y'all, Jesus!" Beulah exclaimed, throwing her free hand up in the air.

Betty Jo grinned at her aunt's enthusiasm.

"A burden's bin lifted!" Beulah returned the letter to its envelope and set it in the middle of the table. She added, "With Dottie Sue managin' the bus'ness and Eddie operatin' the farm, the kids and I kin go 'bout our own affairs. Y'all will be able to concentrate on yer schoolin'."

"Makes me glad," Betty Jo said.

"Go on, now . . . read yer letter," Beulah urged.

Betty Jo opened the envelope, uncertainly. Was she expected to read aloud?

Beulah May lifted herself from the chair and walked to the stove to begin warming leftovers for lunch. Her actions answered Betty Jo's query. Betty Jo unfolded the three hand-written sheets. Relieved, she saw that Philip printed rather than used cursive.

December 15, 1931

Dear Betty Jo,

I wanted to write to you the very first day I arrived back in Providence, but I entered a hectic situation. The Sovereignty of God has directed my steps. I came home at just the right time to be of help to my family.

My father is gaining strength and appears to be recovering from the stroke. We praise the Lord it was not an illness unto death. As he is convalescing, I feel the Lord's presence near. It is a blessing to serve my father and offer encouragement to my mother. Since I arrived home, I have been able to see all of my brothers and sisters.

My father has decided to put his affairs in order. Many times, one stroke is followed by another. While no one knows their appointed time to die, it is good to be prepared spiritually and practically.

God, in His great grace, has been teaching me many valuable lessons. I pray that the fruit of the Spirit will continue to grow in me.

Betty Jo lowered the pages. *So many big words!* She understood the gist of the letter, but reading it was slow-going. Why did Philip use big words when he knew that she was just learning? Doubt filled her mind—her reading skills were not sufficient for high school.

Oh, how I've missed being near you, Sweet Betty Jo!

My thoughts are divided between Rhode Island and beautiful East Texas. I wonder how you are doing. Are you remaining with Sister Beulah, or have you returned to live with your grandfather? How are your studies going? Most importantly, are you growing in your new faith?

While we have no promise between us, I have told my family about you. It's only fair since your family knows about me.

My family? Betty Jo pondered. She was an orphan.

They all send their best regards. And I send my love.
                                        Sincerely,
                                        Philip

Love. What kind of love did he mean? Could there be love without promise?

Betty Jo read the letter three more times. Each time, the big words became easier. She had learned to read around words she didn't know to figure them out, and hoped doing so would help her pass the exams.

Conviction pressed on her thoughts. Here she was thinking about herself when the Harris family was going through a difficult time. She folded the letter and returned it to the envelope. Closing her eyes, she began to pray for the family miles away from her, and for the handsome Yankee preacher.

Debby L Wynkoop

CHAPTER THIRTEEN

One week after Papa's burial, the Davis men came to visit. While the arrangements had been made two days prior, it was still a dreaded surprise to Betty Jo.

Beulah May gestured to Jack Lee's chair and the sheriff sat down, hat in hand. Jimmy Davis moved to the wood chair. After tending to the coats and hat, Betty Jo sat on the edge of the sofa—right foot tucked behind the left, hands folded in her lap.

"Maisie won't be joinin' us?" Beulah inquired.

"She sends her regards," James Roy Davis replied.

"May I offer y'all coffee?"

James Roy answered, his raised hand in a *stop* posture. "No, thank y'all."

Jimmy fidgeted with his hands before resting them on his knees. Betty Jo watched his knuckles slowly whiten. Without moving her head, she looked down at her own. Were the fingers similar?

James Roy drew a deep breath. "As y'all know, Jimmy here's come home—makin' a fresh start."

Jimmy Davis lifted his head. Betty Jo was swarmed by jabbing pins and needles on her insides.

"Ma'am, Betty Jo," Jimmy began. "Years ago, Charlene and I snuck around in the Pineys, behind Henri's back. And, well, liberties were taken that ought not have bin."

Silence swept the air out of the room.

"Are y'all my daddy?" Betty Jo asked bluntly.

The sheriff leaned back in the big chair. Beulah's eyebrow raised. Jimmy Davis lowered his head once again. "I'm sorry," he whispered.

"If'n y'all're my daddy, why y'all leave me an orphan?" Betty Jo blurted. "Seen my birth certificate: *Father unknown*. Seen a death certificate: *Charlene May Landry*. Got nothin' that says Davis!" Betty Jo sensed the flushness of her face.

Beulah looked back and forth between the sheriff and Jimmy. "Good heavens, James Roy, why y'all comin' out with this now?"

"Time to repair the damage. Jimmy wants to make thangs right," he answered.

"Damage?" Beulah May expelled the word from her mouth. "Betty Jo's not like a fight in one of yer Blind Pigs, when y'all come to clean up afterward! She's not goods y'all need to fix somehow!"

"Ma'am, I truly am sorry fer my mistakes." Jimmy said. "I'd like to . . . "

"Y'all made mistakes, no doubt," Beulah interrupted. "There's shore a lot of *I* in what yer sayin', but be assured—Betty Jo's no mistake!"

Jimmy turned his attention toward Betty Jo. "I'd like fer us to get to know each other. Would that be all right with y'all?"

Betty Jo squeezed one hand, then the other. She was definitely awake. She'd imagined this moment for years—picturing herself overjoyed and running into her daddy's arms. She'd thought up hundreds of explanations as to why he'd left her. Now it was happening, and it was nothing like her dreams.

"Jimmy," Beulah said. "Where y'all bin these past years? Might be of help fer Betty Jo to understand."

With a slight clearing of the throat, Sheriff Davis leaned forward in the chair and looked at his son.

Jimmy looked back at Betty Jo. "Yer papa kept me away from y'all. I finished school, and then the army found me. When I got out, I took a job in the oil fields." He looked around the room before continuing. "I'll be honest—got myself in trouble. Served time in the state prison."

James Roy leaned back.

"Bound and determined to make a new start, and I understand I have responsibilities," Jimmy concluded.

"The Good Lord is forgivin' and merciful, fer shore." Beulah couldn't keep herself from testifying.

"Yes, ma'am," Jimmy Davis said appreciatively. He turned to face Betty Jo. "We'll leave y'all to yer thoughts. But if you'd consider havin' a talk, Mother'd love to have y'all to the house, anytime yer inclined. It'd be our pleasure."

Jimmy Davis stood to his feet, followed by the Sheriff. Betty Jo met her obligation to retrieve the coats and hat and see them out the door.

"Goodbye fer now." Then as an afterthought Jimmy said, "Betty Jo . . . what a good name yer mama chose."

Betty Jo shut the door behind the Davis men, walked back to the sofa and collapsed into it.

Beulah sat at the secretary in her bedroom—elbows down, hands folded, head bowed and eyes closed. Her prayer posture had changed in recent years. She missed the humbled state of mind brought on by the simple act of kneeling, yet she understood that the Lord looked on the heart.

O, taste and see that the LORD is good.

She meditated on the scripture before making her petition known.

Lord, I cain't understand what's goin' on here. I bin tryin' to keep my mind on what I know is true and not be supposin', but it is difficult. I'm greatly burdened.

Beulah leaned back and lifted her head and raised her hands.

Jesus, help us! Protect us from evil. Direct our steps. Give me wisdom fer right counsel and wisdom when to keep my ol' mouth shut.

Beulah's prayer quelled. Her head and hands lowered and a sustained silence followed. Then she prayed again.

Y'all promise that all thangs work together fer good to those who love God and are called accordin' to His purpose. And we do. And we are. Amen.

*****

Mr. Filmore ushered Betty Jo into the English classroom. The students who were already seated stared as she made her way to an empty desk at the back where the teacher indicated. She concentrated on taking deep breaths, but they were jolted out of rhythm each time a student entered the room and looked at her with a puzzled face.

She knew that Aunt Beulah had used her considerable influence and persuasiveness to get this opportunity. It was Aunt Beu who spoke with the teachers. It was Aunt Beu who developed a study plan and taught her and quizzed her. It was Aunt Beu who won the principal as an ally. With everything that had happened lately, Betty Jo wanted to back out. She wasn't ready. But for all her aunt's efforts, and more importantly, reputation, she simply could not.

Betty Jo was grateful that the grammar test was first. She thought it might be the best of the day's three tests.

During the lunch period, Betty Jo walked to the mercantile, relieved to find it wasn't too busy for a Friday. The proprietor looked up when she entered the store. "Afternoon, Betty Jo," he greeted. "Be right with y'all."

"Afternoon," she replied in return. She walked down the aisle to study the thread until the chings and clangs of the register subsided and the footsteps faded away.

"What kin I do fer y'all?" the proprietor inquired.

"Mr. Sam, I was wonderin' if . . . " Betty Jo's voice tapered off.

"Go, on . . . " he encouraged.

"Well, I was lookin' to buy crochet thread." Betty Jo leaned in a bit and whispered, "But I don't have any money. I was wonderin' . . . well, might there be chores I could do?"

The proprietor crossed his arms and sighed. "Yer aunt has money. Y'all not ask her?"

"Well, sir, it's so's I kin make her a present."

"I see." He stepped out from behind the counter. "Why don't y'all show me which thread and how much—and mebbe we'll figure a fair exchange."

Betty Jo led Mr. Sam to the thread and pointed out the three colors and how much she thought she'd need.

"Alrighty, then. Come this afternoon and ya'll kin get started," he said.

"Thank y'all," Betty Jo said. "Be back right after class."

The bell on the door alerted the entry of a customer. Betty Jo approached a puzzled Mrs. Westly.

"Betty Jo—"

"Lovely day, isn't it?" Betty Jo greeted as she scurried out the door.

"Y'all're back late," Beulah asked more than said.

"Yes, ma'am," Betty Jo muttered.

Beulah reminded herself that her niece was grown now. "How'd y'all do?"

"They were hard. I finished them, but I was the last one each time. Don't think the teacher was all that pleased to be waitin' on me." Betty Jo frowned.

"Don't be discouraged, Sugar," Beulah said. "Y'all have the weekend to study fer the next ones. I'll let y'all know when supper's on."

"Yes, ma'am."

*****

Sister Tucker continued to play the piano as congregants mingled among the pews. Betty Jo's head was so full of facts and ideas that she struggled to concentrate on the sermon delivered by Brother Tucker. It was something about the long-awaited Jesus. Laughter lifted from parishioners as they chatted in the aisles afterward. Aunt Beulah was particularly lively this morning. Betty Jo guessed it was because she learned yesterday that her children and grandchildren were all coming to celebrate Christmas with her this year. Considering the troubles of the past weeks, it was good to see Aunt Beu smiling.

A young lady approached. Betty Jo recognized her from the revival meetings and previous times she had attended church. "Weren't y'all at the school, Friday?"

"I was," Betty Jo answered.

"Yer Miz Thorpe's niece?" she asked.

"I am. Name's Betty Jo."

"I'm Mary Ann," she said. "Y'all be comin' to our school now?"

"Not fer shore." Betty Jo hesitated. "Y'all a junior?"

Mary Ann nodded. "I am. I kin tell y'all fer shore I'm ready fer a break."

Betty Jo smiled, relieved that the young lady her age did not seek to entangle by asking more questions.

"Hope to see y'all agin." Mary Ann's friendliness soothed Betty Jo's busy mind.

Once home, Beulah May excused Betty Jo to her book work. After all, Jesus was the Lord of the Sabbath and He understood the need to prepare for the rest of the exams. Betty Jo resolved to tend keenly to study. There were two more days of tests and two more afternoons doing chores at the Mercantile. She didn't want to wish her life away, but she would be truly glad for Wednesday to come.

*****

Like a fairy dancing, the broom moved about the floor of the store. The testing was over. Betty Jo had done her best and completed them all. While she was pretty sure her efforts weren't enough, her heart was light. She had thrown off the burden of doing a difficult thing. Tomorrow they would know the official results.

"After y'all finish the sweepin', we'll reconcile," the proprietor called.

"Yessir." Betty Jo danced the broom down the final aisle. She heard the door open and shut followed by a strong footfall that came to a stop at the end of the aisle.

"Afternoon, Betty Jo," the man's voice sounded. "Didn't know y'all worked here." He moved closer to her.

Betty Jo looked up, wondering why Jimmy was so skinny and the sheriff had a pot belly. "Just doing a few chores fer Mr. Sam."

"Glad I caught up with y'all," Jimmy started.

Caught up. Betty Jo wondered at the word choice.

"Mother would like y'all to join us fer Christmas dinner." Jimmy's eyes implored. "I'd be pleased to carry y'all there. What d'y'all say?"

A vine was trying to wrap itself around her. "Please send my regrets to Miz Maisie," she said hesitantly. "The kinfolk are comin' in, and I promised Aunt Beu to be of help." Betty Jo knew immediately that she'd allowed too many words out her mouth.

"Y'all have kinfolk—closer kin I'd dare say—not so far away," Jimmy pressed.

The vine tightened.

"Perhaps another time." She began to move the broom aimlessly over where she'd already swept.

"New Year's Day then?" Jimmy persisted.

Betty Jo was trapped by her own words. "Yes, that would be lovely."

"I'll come to pick y'all up at noon. New Year's then." Jimmy Davis added, "Merry Christmas, Betty Jo."

"Merry Christmas." Betty Jo finished the chore—the broom now marching to a dirge.

When the front door opened and closed again, Betty Jo put the broom and cleaning supplies away and met the proprietor at the counter. He carefully cut the lengths of crochet threads, bundled them, and placed them in a sack.

"Here y'all are," he said, handing the sack to Betty Jo. "I'm perty shore Beulah May will love yer gift."

Betty Jo was glad she had two days to immerse herself in making the ornaments.

"Thank y'all, Mr. Sam," she said with a smile. "Merry Christmas."

Every square inch of the Thorpe house was filled with kinfolk. Young cousins squirmed and wiggled throughout all the crevices. Betty Jo took refuge in the attic nook of the solo dormer. She would have preferred spending time in the woods, but the weather was unpleasant. So, she bundled up her thoughts and snuggled into Granma's quilt.

Most of her life, she occupied places alone. When she spent time with Dottie Sue last summer and later moved in with Aunt Beu, she had found companionable routines that were comfortable with silence. The noise of all the kinfolk in the house was truly joyous, but tiring. Aunt Beulah was in seventh heaven to be surrounded by all her people. She suspected more kin came this year to be near her great aunt in the aftermath of Uncle Jack's passing.

Betty Jo, however, needed respite before returning to the festivities. No one would notice her absence. After all, she had never been part of the Thorpe traditions before. She was beginning to wonder if she would feel the same about returning to school. Would it be too many people for too long, and would she be able to manage it for three and a half years?

She pushed thoughts of school to the side and set about to write a letter to Philip. So much had happened in such a short time! Where should she begin?

December 24, 1931

Dear Philip,

Merry Christmas! Thank you for the letter. I am glad that you are with your family. I am living with Aunt Beu. All the kin are here. There is a big party tonight. I took seven tests. I only passed two. I can still go to school. I will be a freshman. Papa died. It was an accident. Jimmy Davis is my daddy. He wants us to get to know each other.

Thank you for praying for me.

Sincerely,
Betty Jo

Betty Jo would ask Beulah to check the letter to make sure there were no mistakes once everyone left. Maybe she could send it Monday.

She could hear banging on the piano. She had hidden out long enough. Gathering the three packages wrapped in newsprint and twine, she made her way downstairs.

Two older cousins were warming up on their instruments as children banged keys on the piano. Betty Jo peeked into the kitchen where taffy was being pulled. A host of kin were decorating between rounds of molasses cookies. She found Aunt Beu sitting in her chair, taking a break from activity. Betty Jo knelt on the floor next to her.

"Aunt Beu, Merry Christmas," she said, holding out the packages.

"Well, Sugar, what have we here?" Beulah exclaimed.

Betty Jo smiled. "Go ahead. Open them."

Beulah fingered the twine on the package on top. "Now?" she asked.

Betty Jo nodded.

Beulah May unwrapped the first gift. "Oh, goodness," she whispered as she caressed the blue crocheted stars, each with a loop for hanging. "They're lovely!"

A crowd of cousins began to gather.

She opened the next package to find a solitary golden angel whose cone-shaped attire was suitable for the top of a tree. "How clever!" Beulah gasped with delight. The third package contained three crocheted red bells, complete with dangling clappers. "Y'all make all of these?"

Betty Jo nodded. "Granma taught me. Aunt Beu, I want to thank y'all . . . fer ev'rythang."

Beulah reached for Betty Jo's hand. "Oh, Sugar, I will cherish them."

With the new ornaments hung on the tree, the party moved to the piano. Ruth Ann shooed the young ones away from the bench. "Let's sing!" she said as she gave an introduction. Betty Jo retrieved the autoharp from its case and joined the violin and guitar.

Joy to the World, the Lord is come!

Betty Jo rose early. It was cold in the attic and the cot was uncomfortable. Though it was still dark, she imagined seeing the green of the pines through the dormer window.

Using the wash basin she prepared the night before, she cleaned herself, put on one of the new dresses, and adorned her neck with the silver pendant. It would be challenging to descend from the very top of the house without disturbing anyone, but years of sneaking around an angry papa had taught her a few tricks.

When she arrived in the kitchen, she wrapped an apron around her, tying it securely behind her back. She lit the stove and set about making the first brew of coffee. Pecan pancakes and scrambled eggs were on the menu for breakfast, and the preparations for the ham dinner needed to be made.

Before too long, Aunt Beulah entered the kitchen. "Isn't the house nice and quiet?" she said, smiling.

Betty Jo turned to greet her great aunt. Around Beulah's neck was the matching silver pendant, polished and shiny.

"Oh, it's beautiful, Aunt Beu!" Betty Jo exclaimed.

Her aunt beamed with pleasure. "'Bout time I wear it—glad y'all have yers on. My daddy would be so thrilled! Merry Christmas, Sugar," Beulah said as she wrapped Betty Jo in a hug.

Beulah May cleared the kitchen of everyone except her children, their spouses, and Betty Jo. There was business to attend to before they left for their own homes. They gathered at the table. Beulah gestured for Betty Jo to sit at her right hand.

"Thank-y'all fer hostin' such a fine celebration," Bernie's wife, Kathleen, said.

"It has been delightful." Ruth Ann sat next to her husband, Walter.

"Mother, how're y'all doin'?" Bernie asked. "Is there anythang y'all need?"

"I miss yer daddy very much," Beulah replied. She reached out to pat her great niece's hand. "Betty Jo here is a real blessin'. Cousin Dottie has accepted our offer. She'll be home 'fore plantin'. The way I see it now is she'll manage the properties and investments. Eddie will take a bigger role overseein' the farmin' and all. I'll be needin' to compensate 'im more."

"Eddie's a good man," Bernie said. "And Dottie's a quick one, fer shore, but is she trustworthy?"

Of course Dottie was trustworthy! Betty Jo struggled to hold her tongue. It seemed this was a not a conversation she should be a part of, and she wondered why Aunt Beulah insisted on her presence.

"I think so, Brother," Ruth Ann answered. "She wants a new beginnin', and she's certainly proven she kin be loyal."

Beulah continued. "I'm afraid there's vultures hoverin' over us—folks hopin' we'll sell fer cheap. Some who'd like to take advantage—swoop in to snatch our inheritance. I think it best to keep all our holdin's, and wait out this depression best we can.

"There's somethin' else y'all should know. Daddy Morris planned to have two heirs—me and Leona. He disowned Leet after she married Henri—cut her off completely. It was terrible. Daddy came to regret his choice. Fact is, the necklaces Betty Jo and I are wearin' were a Christmas present he gave Leet and me years ago."

Beulah turned the pendant over. "*Love Always* he had engraved on them. He so wanted to make amends and set thangs right, but sadly, he passed away 'fore restoration could happen.

"Bin prayin' long and hard 'bout this. While God is our Balm of Gilead, He has shown me what I kin do to brang healin' and return thangs to how they oughter to be."

Beulah took a deep breath that rose above those who sat frozen around the table.

"Betty Jo is the sole heir of Leona. Y'all're are my heirs." Beulah looked at Bernie and Ruth Ann. "I had the will redone. It's on file in Center at T.L Murphy, Attorney at Law. Daddy's property will be divided three ways upon my death: Bernie, Ruth Ann, and Betty Jo—y'all each have a third share."

Bernie opened his mouth to speak, but was stopped by his mother's stern look.

"Betty Jo, yer inheritance will be held in trust 'til y'all turn 25 years or graduate from college—whichever comes first. Whatever life choices y'all make 'fore then will be of no consequence regardin' the will."

"Mother, I don't think— " Bernie's words were cut off.

"This matter is settled," Beulah said forcefully. "And it is right." Softly, she added, "Many families never have the chance to repair mistakes of the past. We do, and we are blessed."

Betty Jo was not certain what all had taken place or what it meant. She could only think about her aunt saying the word, *college*, and kept wondering why.

"We should be gettin' on," Kathleen said.

The meeting adjourned, and the Bernie Thorpe family said their thank y'all kindlies. Bernie kissed his mother on the cheek formally.

Ruth Ann and Walter and their offspring were the last to leave. Betty Jo walked out to the porch with Aunt Beau to say goodbye to them.

"Betty Jo, I wanna thank y'all fer takin' good care of my mama," Ruth Ann began. "It's a comfort to know y'all're here."

"Yer mama is the one takin' good care of me." Betty Jo smiled. "I think y'all're much like her. Y'all would've raised me well, if given the chance."

Beulah reached an arm around Ruth Ann and one around Betty Jo, encircling them in embrace.

The tight-knit circle had grown bigger.

*****

Resettled in the guest room, Betty Jo curled up and began reading *Heidi*, the book Aunt Beu gave her as a gift. It was the first book, besides Granma's Bible, that she owned. Thinking about a story someone else had created was a new experience. She had always made up her own. Now as she read, she was discovering a world very different from the Pineys—a place of mountains and snow and goats. Yet the more she read, the more she saw her own story—an orphan girl with a mean grandpa.

Aunt Beulah was resting. She had very little time to recover from Christmas company before regular Sunday service, but she insisted on attending church anyway. Now they were snacking on leftovers and nestled inside the house for the rest of the day.

In the evening, Beulah proofread Betty Jo's letter. "Y'all done real good. Proud of y'all, Sugar," Beulah said, handing the letter back to Betty Jo. "I think y'all kin get it in the post tomorrow as is."

Betty Jo smiled her thanks. "Aunt Beu, y'all said an inheritance would be mine when I turned 25 or graduated from college. I was wonderin' . . . how d'y'all 'spect I could go to college? I couldn't even pass the junior tests."

"Yet. Y'all haven't passed them yet." Beulah patted Betty Jo's hand, rose from the table, and left the kitchen.

Betty Jo sighed. Philip was a college man, educated in the Bible and other subjects. He needed to find himself a nice Yankee college girl. As for her, she couldn't imagine what the future held, but it would be a miracle if a girl like her could finish high school.

Debby L Wynkoop

CHAPTER FOURTEEN

Beulah brushed the curtain to the side and peered out the front window. Jimmy had come to carry Betty Jo to a Davis family gathering. What unsettled her the most was that her niece made the plans and didn't tell her until last evening. *Why the need to keep it quiet until the last minute?*

Beulah thought back on the conversation with the Davis men. Something was askew, but she couldn't pinpoint it. If only she could visit privately with Maisie. She might get understanding.

What am I thinking? Understanding came from God alone. She was being a busy body. Best to occupy herself serving the Lord.

Beulah retreated to the kitchen to check on the black-eyed peas in the 16-inch dutch oven. Bits of ham floated in and around the legumes. She'd mixed up the corn bread batter and pulled the canned collard greens, saved for this very day, out of the pantry.

Eddie was out fetching the faithful pickers and their families in the work truck. Serving the traditional meal to the workers was a New Year's tradition started by her mother and daddy many years ago. Today it fell to her alone to carry it on.

The sun came out and joy began to rise up from her insides. Giving was a blessing.

Lord, cause yer people to prosper this year.

Beulah sat in her chair as the sun began to disappear. Her old bones were just plain tired, but her heart was lively as it moved toward a new idea. While she wasn't sure there were enough resources to implement it, she was certain that God would supply and that Dottie Sue was part of His provision. Beulah reached for her Bible. She would wait upon the Lord and renew her strength.

Headlamps cast uniquely shaped shadows in the sitting room. An open door waved a draft into the house.

Betty Jo hung up her coat and joined her aunt. "How was yer day?" she asked.

Beulah looked up from her Bible. "Good. Real good. Eddie brought over a couple dozen folks. We dished up some real good food." Beulah smiled. "How 'bout y'all?"

"Not shore," came Betty Jo's taut reply.

Beulah gave her a quizzical look. "Oh?"

"I cain't decide if it was good or bad."

Beulah leaned a bit forward in her chair.

Betty Jo searched for words. "Sheriff Davis is . . . well, he bothers me. I like Miz Maisie. And Jimmy—should I be calling 'im Daddy?—just don't have anythang much to say to me. I cain't think of a word fer it all."

"Awkward?" Beulah suggested, leaving be her niece's question.

Betty Jo nodded. "Awkward. Sounds 'bout right."

The pair sat in amiable quiet. Betty Jo pondered if she should elaborate on one of the conversations with the sheriff, but then thought better of it. Mixing things together wouldn't be good. She best build a wall between the two families.

Betty Jo stood, leaned over, and kissed Beulah on the cheek. "Think I'll finish the book." She smiled. "See y'all in the mornin'."

"Good night, Sugar."

Betty Jo settled into her bedroom and tried to concentrate on the make-believe story that seemed so real. Her mind kept traveling to this new and crazy chapter in her own life. It seemed to be a story someone else was trying to write.

She didn't know anything about her inheritance or what it even meant, but spending the afternoon around Sheriff Davis told her that he wanted it.

*****

Mary Ann caught up to Betty Jo on the steps of the high school. "Good mornin'—glad to see y'all," she said.

"Mornin', Mary Ann," Betty Jo returned. "How're y'all?"

"Guess I'm ready to git back to it," she said, shrugging her shoulders.

They entered the building. Betty Jo stopped in front of the first of the four classrooms across from the office.

"Aren't y'all in my English class?" Mary Ann asked.

"I'm . . . well . . . this is my classroom," Betty Jo said softly.

"Y'all shore 'bout that?" Comprehension crept onto Mary Ann's face before she could stop her words. "Mebbe see y'all at lunch?"

Betty Jo managed a weak smile and turned to enter the freshman math class. She chose to sit in the back, thinking she would be more inconspicuous among the other students. When roll was taken, she averted her eyes to the stares. During the algebra lesson, she tried to place her full attention on the teacher at the chalkboard, but whenever he turned his back to write, antics from three boys would erupt.

After class was dismissed and the teacher exited, the main distractor turned on her. "Landry? Y'all're Cajun. What're y'all doin' here?"

Betty Jo stood up and pushed past the ruffian and made her way between the desks. Quickly, she walked to the science classroom where she chose a seat in front nearest the door. She returned each stare that came her way. As the teacher began the biology lesson, she listened with great interest, connecting the things he talked about to the plants and animals of the woods she knew so well.

During lunch period, Betty Jo sat down to eat leftover cornbread and the hard-boiled eggs from the box lunch Aunt Beu packed. She imagined her mama, Dottie Sue, Jimmy, and their pals sitting together at lunchtime in this very building.

A cluster of young ladies entered the room and sat down. Mary Ann introduced Betty Jo to the girls in the junior class, but interactions did not continue beyond the pleased-to-meet-y'alls. Betty Jo was pretty sure she would not be palling around with any of them. She wouldn't concern herself with friendship. She was here to learn.

*****

January days passed in the fog of routine. Betty Jo loved learning and was relieved that the embarrassment of illiteracy was being washed away. Yet, she came to despise going to school. She knew how to stand up to bullies, but their jibes were tiring. What she didn't know how to manage was the dismissiveness of some of the faculty.

Philip's letter arrived in the post on one of Betty Jo's more discouraging days.

January 10, 1932

Dear Betty Jo,

Happy New Year!

I am trusting God for His very best for you in this year ahead. May you sense the Gentle Shepherd guiding you each step along your way.

It was a shock to learn of Henri's passing. He seemed to be doing so well at the time of my departure. I'm truly sorry for your loss.

I am curious how it was confirmed that Jimmy Davis is your daddy. I wonder why that knowledge was presented to you at this particular time.

The church here had a Watchnight Service on New Year's Eve. My brother came to stay with our parents so I was freed to attend. It was refreshing to wait on the Lord in prayer. As the old year ended and the new one began, I was reassured that our God is in control of all the circumstances of our lives.

I am confident that He has a special plan for your life. I am hopeful that His plan for you will include me.

Love,
Philip

Betty Jo set the letter in her lap. *Special plan*? She was struggling through her days just trying to do something normal.

*****

The waters of the Sabine kept flowing. Rigs kept pumping oil. Sawmills kept producing lumber. Yet there still were not enough jobs and income to fill the needs. In cupboards throughout the region, supplies of canned vegetables waned, and hunger tip-toed its way inside.

Trains kept passing through. Single men, and even families, rode the rails searching for hope. Early in February one of those trains brought Dottie Sue Dawson home. She stepped off into Logansport with her hair tucked under a hat and red lipstick freshly applied. In one hand she held her purse and in the other, a suitcase. Her eyes were locked in steely determination. She was prepared to meet the demons of the past.

Betty Jo had experienced a variety of embraces in her young life. In the hospital, she had laid her head on her grandmother's wilting body and felt a weak response. She knew her loved one would not be much longer on the earthly side of Jordan. Granma was leaving. Lost in sorrow, Betty Jo never uttered goodbye.

In bursts of irreconcilable frustration, Betty Jo would flee to the yellow farmhouse. There she'd be swooped into folds of comfort—hidden in the safety of her great aunt's bosom.

She'd offered a quick hug to Philip Harris the last time she'd seen him. Then she stood on the porch, chilled with regret, and watched him disappear into the night.

But her most memorable embrace was the one wrapped in hope upon her reunion with Dottie Sue.

"Oh me, oh my, Girl" Dot took a step back to examine her young friend. "Y'all're shorely a sight fer sore eyes!"

Dot's words slowed as she added, "Beulah May told me 'bout Henri. I am grievously sorry."

Betty Jo received the sympathy with a slight nod. "How've y'all bin, Dottie Sue? How was yer time in Houston?"

"Well, let's sit a spell and I'll do tell," Dot said, laughing.

Conversation was not exhausted before the battle to suppress yawns was lost. Heavy eyed, the women said good night. Betty Jo laid on the old cot, happy she would spend the next day in Logansport.

There was something else she wanted to talk about—something she couldn't tell Aunt Beulah.

Betty Jo studied the banner on the wall behind the simple pulpit. *Jesus Saves.* Her heart rejoiced that she now understood its truth. She hadn't been to the little store-front church since summer. The benches and lack of décor were in contrast to Aunt Beu's well-established church. The music was lively, with a guitar playing the lead role. It still shocked her that Coloreds were a part of the gathering.

Betty Jo glanced sideways at Dottie when Deacon Delbert stood behind the pulpit to preach. The look on Dot's face caused her to smile.

After the closing prayer, the deacon preceded the folks to the door, greeting each one as they exited. Delbert reached for Dottie's hand as if to shake it, but then held it still.

"Sister, so glad to see y'all!" he exclaimed.

"Good to be home," Dottie replied with a smile before withdrawing her hand.

Then the lay preacher turned to shake Betty Jo's hand. "My sympathies in the loss of yer grandpa. How y'all gettin' along?"

"The Lord's my comfort," Betty Jo replied.

The two women stepped outside and walked to Dot's lumbered house to share Sunday dinner for two.

"Dottie Sue, kin I tell y'all somethin'?" Betty Jo asked as she finished washing the first plate.

"All we bin doin' is talkin'," Dot giggled. "Of course, y'all kin tell me somethin'."

"I don't like school." Betty Jo washed the second dinner plate.

Dottie turned to look at Betty Jo. "Not ev'rybody does."

"I like the book learnin' and all," Betty Jo said.

"Then what don't y'all like?" Dot asked.

"The goin' part . . . goin' to class." Betty Jo answered. "I shore don't see doin' it fer three more years."

The pair finished in the kitchen and sat on the furniture that only a few days prior was dressed in dust-covers.

Dottie resumed the conversation. "Y'all made friends?"

"Mebbe one, but I . . . " Betty Jo searched for the right words.

"Don't have much in common?" Dottie provided.

Betty Jo nodded.

"Listen, Girl, school's a good way to git educated, but there's other ways, too. Most folks I know teach themselves. They learn by doin'. Like how y'all taught yerself the autoharp. Books kin teach, and now y'all kin read. Y'all kin learn from other folks in yer life. Biggest thang to gittin' educated is bein' curious and persistent."

Dottie's words confirmed what Betty Jo had been thinking. "But Aunt Beulah shorely wants me to go to school—get a diploma and all. Why, she even thinks I oughter go to college. Can y'all imagine that?"

Dottie lowered her voice. "Seems Beulah May is livin' in the past. I 'spect she wants y'all to accomplish what yer granma never attempted." Dottie looked Betty Jo in the eyes. "We all have diff'rent paths to take. Y'all just need to figure which one the Lord's callin' ya'll to."

When their reunion and sharing time was over, Betty Jo readied herself to return to the Thorpe house. As the friends reached out for a goodbye-for-now hug, they each brushed aside guilt for what they had withheld.

*****

The secretary entered freshman homeroom and placed a note on Betty Jo's desk. Its delivery gained her unwanted attention and brought anxiety. *Come to the office after class,* it read.

Upon dismissal, Betty Jo walked across the hallway and opened the door to the office. The secretary looked up, left her desk, and stepped to the counter.

"This was dropped off fer y'all," Mabel Dee said, pushing a large envelope toward Betty Jo. "Not sure why the post weren't used," she muttered.

"Thank y'all," Betty Jo picked it up, surprised at its bulkiness.

Mabel Dee returned to her desk. "Next time y'all need to use the post."

"Yes, ma'am." Betty Jo said mannerly before leaving the office.

Curiosity pressed in on Betty Jo, but she would wait until she was alone to open the envelope. Once outside, she headed straight for the sedan.

A voice called to her. "Hi, y'all!"

Betty Jo stopped. "Afternoon. How're y'all?"

"Shore glad it's Friday," Mary Ann answered. "Say, I know y'all don't come to Sunday School, but our class is havin' a little social Sunday afternoon. Y'all should come. It'd be fun."

"Thank y'all kindly," Betty Jo said. "I'll think on it."

Mary Ann's shoulders sagged.

"Fer shore I'll come to service. See y'all Sunday," Betty Jo confirmed with a smile before quickening her steps to the car.

She drove to the plank house and opened the envelop. Grabbing the three-legged stool and a butter knife, she sat on the porch. She slit the top of the envelope and pulled out two items. The first was letter-writing paper.

> *Betty Jo,*
> *Let's go fishing!*
> *Meet me where Big Tree once stood,*
> *tomorrow morning.*
> *I'll explain the picture then.*
> *Jimmy Davis*

The second was a picture on thick art paper. It mesmerized her.

Black ink, heavy as sin, portrayed Big Tree prone on the floor of the woods. Fat and sturdy, with a vine wrapped around, it obstructed the path. Its absence from the canopy allowed sunlight to stream down.

Same style of art. Different position of the subject. Sometimes things just were. Sometimes they meant something. Betty Jo determined to figure out which was true in this case.

She tucked the letter and ink picture back in the envelope. She would do some cleaning, and make sure everything was in order. The house with its household goods would be Eddie's new home. It was a way to improve his compensation and more convenient for him to be closer to the barn and boss.

The decision came with mixed feelings. It would be hard to let go of her childhood home, but the more she got used to the idea, the better it seemed. The old shack could quickly become a burden. This way it would be a blessing.

"Mornin', Aunt Beu," Betty Jo said as she entered the kitchen, dressed in bib overalls.

"Mornin', Sugar." Beulah May looked up from the newspaper. "What're y'all's plans fer the day? Nice and calm outside."

"I need a bit more time at the house to git it ready fer Eddie. Then I think I'll go fishin'." Betty Jo went to the stove and served herself grits from the pot.

"A fry would be real good," Beulah said.

" 'Xactly what I was thinkin'," Betty Jo smiled.

She ate the grits quickly, downed a glass of milk, and headed to the barn to get the fishing pole, basket, and tackle.

As Betty Jo walked to the plank house, it occurred to her how easy it was to slip back into sneakiness. It seemed to be a nature she had inherited.

She walked the county road to the open field just beyond the house. She cut across it and found the connecting path to the river trail. Swallowed by the deep woods, she hiked until arriving at the big bend. She slowed her gait.

Jimmy Davis leaned against the giant remains of Big Tree, nestled between sprouting shrubs and decaying limbs. "Glad y'all come," he greeted.

"Mornin'. What should I call y'all? Betty Jo asked.

"Jimmy be just fine," he answered. "Shall we?"

The pair descended the slope to the river, fighting back new-growth bramble until they landed at the well-known fishing spot.

"Y'all go fishin' with my mama?" Betty Jo asked as they prepared their poles and lines.

"Fer shore. We all went fishin' and swimmin' and all. This was one of the favorite spots. Changed since then." Jimmy looked over at the upper reaches of Big Tree that lay at the water's edge.

"Ev'rythang changes," Betty Jo acknowledged. "Was Mama good at fishin'?"

"Naw. She'd usually stay up above to do her sketchin'," he answered.

"The picture in the envelope—she make it?" Betty Jo asked.

"Shorely did. Gave it to me. Kept it all this time." Jimmy secured the bait on his hook. "Thought y'all should have it."

"But in the picture, Big Tree's on the ground. It didn't fall 'til last summer."

Jimmy Davis sent his line into the water. "I think she made a picture of what she was hopin' fer."

Betty Jo stood still. When no more words were added, she began to fish and figure. She considered the other ink drawings her mama had made and the poem she had written. Why was it that Mama never gave the poem to Jimmy?

When the fishing slowed, Betty Jo had a basket half full. Jimmy seemed ready to pack it up.

"Why y'all keep the picture all this time?" she asked.

"To remember," Jimmy said, starting his way up the river bank.

Betty Jo followed closely.

Once at the top, he continued. "Yer papa and my daddy—they might have bin diff'rent kind, but they were woven from the same cloth. Growin' up in their shadows weren't easy. No matter what we did, seemed we couldn't please our own daddies. Yer mama wanted out of Henri's house perty bad. She talked 'bout plans and dreams and thangs. Guess she figured if it weren't fer her daddy, she could see the light of day."

They hiked out of the woods together.

"Thank y'all fer goin' fishin' with me." Jimmy added, "Mebbe we kin do it agin sometime soon."

Betty Jo nodded. "Thank y'all fer the picture and fer tellin' me 'bout it."

Jimmy disappeared, heading south. Betty Jo walked the road to the north, contemplating. Her mama never got a chance to live her plans and dreams. She never got outta Papa's shadow until circumstances pushed her out. By then it was too late.

Didn't seem Jimmy Davis got too far away from his daddy's shadow either.

*****

Beulah set down her copy of the *Plainsdealer*. Reading the business page and futures was always Jack Lee's job. He had the business head and the farming skill. She was glad Dottie Sue would start managing soon. Dot had good sense—as attested by the money she helped Henri make. Ill-gotten gain, Beulah supposed. It could have been a blessing had her brother-in-law not squandered it all on spirits and gambling.

Dottie arrived promptly, delivered by the piston-thumping Chevrolet. Beulah was curious about Dot's friendship with the lay minister, but did not broach the subject. Once the simple chit chat subsided, the conversation turned to business matters. Beulah opened the books and explained the holdings of the Morris Estate. Dot asked questions and clarified the role she would assume. Adding Eddie to the meeting, a plan was formulated—when to plant, what, and how much.

After Eddie left the conversation, Beulah asked Dottie Sue about her experiences working the soup kitchen in Houston. Then she ventured her one-more-thing.

"Folks are hungry 'round here. Folks passin' through on the rails are hungry, too." Beulah paused.

"Poverty shorely is a curse," Dot nodded in agreement.

"The Lord has blessed us." Beulah May knew it was time to get to the point. "We oughter obey Him and feed the hungry. I'd like to start a soup kitchen, of sorts. What d'y'all think it'd require?"

With a passion Dottie Sue had never known before, she discussed with the matriarch ideas on the topic—ideas she realized she had already formulated. *The Lord returned her home for such a time as this.*

*****

Betty Jo looked forward to weekend visits with Dottie. She loved the freedom of driving to Logansport in Beulah May's sedan, but it was more than the outing. Betty Jo felt a bond beyond friendship with Dottie. Seemed Dot didn't expect anything out of her.

The door opened on her knock. "Afternoon, Betty Jo," Dot greeted. "Come on in. Did y'all have a good week?"

"It was mostly good," Betty Jo replied. "I kin use some help with the numbers and all—if'n y'all don't mind."

"I 'spect we kin find the time." Dot smiled. "What was the 'good part' of mostly?"

Betty Jo set her bag down. "Teacher put together a women's ensemble. She chose me and Mary Ann to be in it. Meets a bit at lunch period each day. Gonna do some songs fer graduation."

"How delightful!" Dot exclaimed. "Y'all decided to keep in school then?"

"Just a couple months left. A person kin do most anythang fer a couple months," Betty Jo said wryly.

Dottie nodded.

"Doubt I'll return," Betty Jo added. "A diploma's just too far off."

"Y'all tell yer Aunt Beu?" Dottie asked.

"No, ma'am. Keep waitin' fer the right time."

"Might be better sooner," Dot said. "One thang's fer shore, now's the right time to help me in the kitchen. We have company fer supper."

Betty Jo set the table properly for three, using china from the hutch. She would have preferred it to be just two places. She noted with amusement the extra effort Dottie took to gussy up. She also noted a change in her friend's countenance. The closer to suppertime, the less the girlish chatter. Quiet settled solemnly.

Before the clock chimed 7:00, the deacon stood at the door with hat in hand. Under his Sunday suit was a white shirt with a starched collar.

"Evenin', Sister Dottie," Delbert greeted.

"Evenin', Brother Delbert," Dot replied. "Please come in. Let me take yer hat."

Delbert looked across the room. "Hello, Betty Jo. How're y'all?"

"Fine, thank y'all," Betty Jo returned.

The three took seats in the small sitting room. Betty Jo played the part of the third wheel quite well as Dottie and Delbert discussed the completion of the planting campaign.

"That Miz Thorpe, ain't she just a blessin' to all around!" Delbert exclaimed when he learned of the start of the feeding program. "Reminds me of the Shunamite Woman."

"The Shunamite Woman?" Betty Jo asked, interested at last in the conversation.

"Why shorely," Delbert said. "*Second Kings* tells the story of the woman of Shunem. She had means and was well respected in her town. When she saw a need, she took care of it, and God blessed her fer it."

"That does sound like Aunt Beu," Betty Jo smiled.

"Well, our main course is compliments of Beulah May." Dottie stood up. "Think it might be time to enjoy it."

Supper conversation was propelled by Delbert's stories. Betty Jo laughed out loud a time or two, but was puzzled at Dottie's reserve.

After dessert, Brother Delbert pushed back from the table. "Delicious!" he said. "The chicken fried steak—so good. Topped off with chocolate cake? Well, I've my fill of goodness!"

"Glad y'all enjoyed the meal," Dottie replied. "Why don't y'all relax while we git the table cleared?"

Betty Jo was confused. Dot loved to clown around, and she surely did like the deacon. *What's gotten into her?*

After the food was put away and dirty dishes stacked for washing later, the two women sat on the settee. Delbert's head tilted slightly as he studied Dot's face.

Dottie looked first at Betty Jo and then Delbert. "I wanna tell both y'all somethin'. Somethin' important. Somethin' no one 'round here knows."

Betty Jo's eyes widened in alarm at the timbre of Dottie Sue's voice. Delbert sat frozen by the words of magnitude.

Tears welled up in Dottie's eyes. She took a deep breath.

"I palled around with Betty Jo's mama in high school." She looked at Delbert. "Charlene was my very best friend.

"There were others in our group. Jimmy Davis bein' one of 'em. Jimmy, the son of Sheriff Davis. We all went to school together—that's before the Davis family built their home nearer to Center.

"Both Charlene and I fell in love with Jimmy. He was pushy, like his daddy, and a whole lot spoiled; but there was a kindness in him, and he was very handsome.

"I think Charlene saw him as a ticket out of Henri's house. I saw him . . . Well, I was tired of bein' the good girl, the Sunday School teacher, the obedient daughter. Jimmy was my ticket to rebellion."

Delbert interrupted. "Why y'all tellin' this? The past is just that—past. Y'all're a new creation in Christ."

"That's true," Dottie Sue replied. "But the consequences of my sin has bearin' on both y'all." Dottie Sue hesitated before adding, "I prayed long 'bout tellin' y'all."

Betty Jo shifted in the chair.

"Jimmy Davis played the field." Dot looked at Betty Jo. "Told y'all yer mama was a real beauty. She attracted menfolk like crazy. Yer papa was very protective. He had his eye on Jimmy 'specially. We all shot the breeze by Big Tree, but Jimmy never let hisself get caught alone with Charlene.

"My parents weren't aware of what was goin' on. I found myself gittin' looser and looser with Jimmy, until we were . . . well, perty soon I was with child."

Betty Jo's eyebrows furrowed.

Delbert lowered his head.

Dot continued. "Jimmy left me high 'n' dry, of course. He weren't 'bout to claim paternity. I took responsibility—told my folks. Shorely did disappoint 'em. They set 'bout to make arrangements to send me away.

"One mornin', the baby I didn't want miscarried. My sorrow found no comfort, fer after the miscarriage, all I wanted was my baby."

Dottie looked at Betty Jo. "Yer mama got pregnant 'bout the time I was grievin'. I stuck with her 'til y'all were born—'til she passed.

"I know, Girl, this is all so complicated. Y'all're Charlene's daughter, and even though Henri kept me clear, y'all've always felt like my own. Yer the daughter I never had.

"Delbert, I told y'all I was a tainted woman. Sadly, the ugly doesn't end there. I took up with one manfolk after another. Denny was my most steady, and he has hisself a wife.

219

"I may be a new creation, but I was a mistress." Dottie Sue Dawson sighed heavily. "Sometimes more in life is needed than forgiveness. I'm so sorry."

The deacon lifted his eyes. "Folks know who y'all were, Dottie Sue. God, alone, knows who y'all will be. But I know who y'all are, and that's what matters to me."

Delbert stood and retrieved his hat. Dottie hurried to followed him. "See y'all at church." Turning the knob, he let himself out.

Dottie returned and sat again on the settee next to Betty Jo.

"Dot, y'all're sayin' Jimmy Davis is my daddy and yer baby's?"

Dottie Sue exhaled the toxic breath of a secret rotten with time. "No, Girl. Jimmy Davis is my baby's daddy, but he's not yers."

Betty Jo had never driven at night. Her clammy hands gripped the steering wheel as she crossed the bridge. Trying to shake the image of the skeletal remains of the Model T, she blinked rapidly. She had to get across the bridge and to the other side.

She had nowhere to run, she had no plan, and she didn't even know what it was she wanted.

Dottie Sue knew who her daddy was but refused to say. She would not even tell her why she wouldn't say. Folks were lying, and Betty Jo did not know who to believe.

Never good to ignore truth. Well, truth was like water slipping through her hands—there for a while, but then dribbling away.

She drove past the yellow foursquare farmhouse. She had to get her head on right. Running into her great aunt's embrace would not solve this problem. Beulah May was pretty sure Jimmy Davis was her daddy. The Davis clan were acting as if he were. But Dottie Sue said he wasn't.

She wanted to shake the whole thing off, but just couldn't. *Oh, why does matter so much?*

Before she realized it, the sedan was parked in front of Joaquin Baptist Church. No lights were on inside, but the parsonage was lit. Betty Jo exited the car and walked up the front steps. The door was unlocked. She pushed it open.

Once her eyes adjusted, she walked down the aisle. The wooden cross behind the pulpit drew her like a magnet. She knelt down at the altar bench and poured out her heart.

Her prayer had no beginning. It found no amen.

A halo of lantern light entered the sanctuary from the side door.

"Might I help y'all?" a man's voice asked.

Betty Jo, startled, stood up to face the intrusion.

"Ah, Betty Jo . . . " his voice drifted off. "Be back in a bit."

She did not know if she should leave or sit on a pew or fall back on her knees. She stood, helpless.

Soon the lantern light returned. The reverend and his wife stood side by side.

"May we be of help, Betty Jo?" Sister Tucker asked.

Betty Jo was pretty sure the preacher and his wife could not be of help. No one could help this mess of her life.

Brother Tucker turned to his wife. "I'll be next door." He made his way out of the church.

Sister Tucker walked to Betty Jo's side and put an arm around her. "Come, dear, let's sit." Then she coaxed Betty Jo to the first pew.

Betty Jo stared through the shadows at the cross. "All I ever wanted was a daddy and mama." She closed her eyes.

When she opened them again, Sister Tucker was still by her side. "It's the middle of the night, Betty Jo. Come on over to the parsonage and git some rest.

Like a sheep being led by a shepherd, Betty Jo followed the pastor's wife. Sleep came quickly.

*****

Beulah May sat in Jack Lee's chair with her Bible in her lap. The sound of the back door interrupted the morning quiet.

Betty Jo walked in the room slowly.

"Thought y'all were stayin' over fer Dot's church," Beulah said.

"Decided to come home early," Betty Jo answered. "Need some alone time, if'n y'all don't mind. I'll be up in my room."

Beulah's eyes followed her great niece as she ascended the stairs. Her heart flooded with compassion for her charge. Betty Jo wasn't telling everything, but she had eyes to see. The unknowns of her niece's past were relentless in their quest to disrupt the present.

Lord, help her press on.

Betty Jo settled onto the bed. She was tired of trying to figure things out on her own. Her thoughts turned to the man from Rhode Island.

April 2, 1932

Dear Philip,

How are you?

I am sorry it's been so long since I've written. I don't know what I should write. The little things aren't important and the big thing is a burden.

I wish you were here so we could sit on the porch and talk.

Sincerely,
Betty Jo

CHAPTER FIFTEEN

Aunt Beu and Dottie Sue sat at the kitchen table examining business figures over cups of coffee. Eddie was in the barn repairing equipment. Betty Jo sheepishly went about serving herself breakfast. Going fishing when everyone else was working didn't seem right.

"All yer studies complete?" Aunt Beulah looked up from the ledger.

"Just one assignment. I'll write it this afternoon," Betty Jo replied.

"Mind if I tag along?" Dot asked. "We're almost finished here."

Betty Jo poured a cup of coffee. She hadn't thought Dot would be working on a Saturday, and she surely hadn't considered the possibility of someone else going with her. She sensed her great aunt assessing each detail of the moment.

It was confession time.

Betty Jo sat down at the table. "I'm meetin' Jimmy Davis at Big Tree—sort of been a standin' date. He asked if we could git to know one another, and well, it's been pleasant."

Betty Jo took a sip of coffee. Dottie and Beulah looked at each other.

"If'n it's all the same to y'all, I'd still like to go," Dot said resolutely.

"Y'all're welcome—just wanted y'all to know who I was meetin'."

Jimmy Davis leaned his hip against Big Tree and looked at the sky overhead. Light filled the space. It was the way things should be.

Betty Jo appeared around the bend with a shadow following behind.

He stood tall and squared his feet. He recognized the woman.

"Don't 'spect I need to make introductions," Betty Jo said when they arrived. She hurried to descend the slope to the river, disturbed by the steeliness in Jimmy's face.

Dottie Sue and Jimmy followed Betty Jo's movement with their eyes, then turned to stare at one another.

"What're y'all doin', Jimmy?" Dot crossed her arms. "Betty Jo is none of yer concern."

"I'm lookin' after Charlene's girl, Dot," he answered. "Could ask the same of y'all. As much my concern as yers."

"No," Dottie said emphatically. "Not the same. I'm kin."

Before Jimmy could stop them, words catapulted from his mouth. "I am, too!"

"Please, y'all oughter leave her be," Dottie Sue implored. "I dunno what Sheriff is up to, but don't be part of it."

"Aren't y'all high 'n' mighty?" Jimmy's retort dripped sarcasm. "Y'all bin hangin' pretty tight to Miz Thorpe these days. After the Morris money are y'all?"

Money? Dottie was filled with understanding. "Jimmy, listen now. The hidden thang will be revealed, and when it is, it'll brang terrible pain on Charlene's girl. Don't let yer daddy cause more ruin."

Jimmy Davis clenched his teeth together. He bent down, picked up his pole and tackle, and walked away. Dottie Sue glanced down and saw that Betty Jo was occupied with fishing. She knelt on a carpet of ferns and prayed. Wiping her tears, she joined Betty Jo at Sabine's side.

Though Betty Jo wondered what had transpired between Dot and Jimmy, she did not ask. Privacy was to be respected.

"Here ya'll're," the proprietor said as he handed Betty Jo the mail.

"Thank ya'll," Betty Jo said, rifling through the stack. Her smile broadened when she recognized the handwriting on the letter from Providence.

"I 'spect ya'll're the only one 'round to git a letter from Rhode Island," Mr. Sam said, grinning.

Betty Jo's eyes sparkled with delight. "Have a real good day, Mr. Sam." She waved as she stepped outside. Noting that the bench in front of the store was unoccupied, and the coast was clear, she sat down to read the letter.

April 15, 1932

Dear Betty Jo,
We are in a time of grieving. My father had a second stroke which he did not survive. While we do sorrow, we do not grieve as the world grieves. Our hope is fast and sure.

We are moving Mother into my sister's home in Providence. My oldest brother will settle affairs. While it is difficult, we see the wisdom in selling the family home.

Life changes. Someday there will be a final, great change. Until then we occupy and strive to do the Father's will.

Lord willing, I will return to Logansport soon. I look forward to sitting on the porch and talking with you; and I am eager to share your burden.

Love,
Philip

*****

Dottie Sue and Betty Jo packed up the camp kitchen. The sparse shade at the little town's center was proving inadequate for feeding the folks. The days were getting warmer. This Saturday had seen the most served, and for the first time, people were turned away. They would need to make adjustments.

Betty Jo hummed *He's Got the Whole World in His Hands* as she took a box to the sedan. Learning songs and singing in the women's ensemble was her favorite part of school. They would perform the songs at graduation in two weeks. This would be one part of school she would truly miss.

Sheriff Davis pulled his patrol car up to where Dot was working. Hanging his head out of the window, he slapped the side of the car. "Hey, y'all're encouragin' vagrants in town! Don't do it agin!"

Dottie gaped at the lawman.

Betty Jo closed the trunk of the car and walked briskly to her friend's side.

The sheriff got out of the car and walked to the women. "Afternoon, Betty Jo." The greeting he offered Betty Jo was incongruous with his aggression toward Dottie Sue. He attempted to soften his voice. "Y'all cain't use public property."

Dot's disgust showed on her face as if she were in an outhouse on a hot day. She continued with her task.

The Sheriff turned to Betty Jo. "Why don't y'all come up to the house tonight? Miz Maisie would love a visit. Yer daddy could come 'n' carry y'all."

"No, thank y'all—but please let Miz Maisie know I'll be sure to visit with her at church tomorrow."

James Roy shifted his weight. Hesitating, he tipped his hat and returned to the car.

The women watched as he walked away.

"Well, aren't y'all a sly one," Dottie whispered.

"I'm tryin' real hard to keep myself from gettin' tangled," Betty Jo replied.

With the last of the supplies in the car, the weary pair headed back to the Thorpe place. Beulah May greeted them with sweet tea, a smile, and a load of questions.

"Why, that stinker!" she exclaimed upon hearing the sheriff's directive. She went inside to make the cobbler for Sunday's dessert.

Betty Jo was glad Dot invited her to help with the feeding program. It was a good use of her Saturday, more so than fishing. It also helped soothe her thoughts regarding her friend. Dot was a kind woman. Betty Jo was sure she must have a real good reason for not telling who her daddy was. She wondered, though, *Is part of a truth still truth?*

"Dottie Sue, if'n Jimmy's not my daddy like y'all say, then why the sheriff keepin' up the charade?"

Dottie Sue stopped the porch swing. The evening song of birds replaced its squeaks and creaks.

"Y'all have to ask yerself—if Jimmy *were* yer daddy, what would the sheriff stand to gain?" Dottie hesitated before adding, "Davis is a taker. That's just what he does—take."

*****

Jimmy Davis stood on the sidewalk in front of the school. He was eager to hear the dismissal bell. The heat was moving in on him.

At last, a stream of youth flowed out the front doors and down the steps. He received a few speculative glances, but his mission was too important to get sidetracked. Betty Jo finally exited the building—chatting with a young lady her age. In her arms she held a bundle of books.

Jimmy stepped forward. His movement caught her eye.

"See y'all tomorrow, Mary Ann," she said.

A curious look crossed her friend's face. "See y'all," she said slowly before continuing down the walk.

"Afternoon, Betty Jo." Jimmy stepped closer.

"What brangs y'all in front of the school buildin', Jimmy?" Betty Jo asked forthrightly.

"Hopin' we might have a talk—somewhere private."

"Perty busy today. Next week is finals, and I be needin' to study." She shifted the books in her arms.

"Won't take terrible long," Jimmy implored. "Kin I buy y'all a sodie? Then mebbe we kin sit at the church grounds?"

"All right. Grape's my flavor." Betty Jo smiled. "I'll walk on over."

"Be right there," Jimmy said as he hurried off to the mercantile. He was glad Betty Jo agreed to talk with him. Today was a good day. His daddy was busy investigating a theft in Center.

Jimmy found Betty Jo sitting on the grass under an oak tree in the church yard. He took a deep breath and approached her with the two bottles of soda. He handed Betty Jo the grape and sat down, taking a swig of his Pepsi Cola.

He would assume a matter-of-fact tone, even though his insides were torn. "I'm 'fraid I misled y'all." He raised the bottle to his lips and sipped. "I'm not yer daddy."

"I know," she said.

Jimmy squirmed. *What all had Dot told her?*

Betty Jo looked at him. "Y'all never actually said ya were."

They sipped on the sodas, contemplating the situation.

"If'n y'all knew, why go fishin' with me and all?" Jimmy asked.

"Y'all were Mama's friend. Plus, yer the right age and I wanted to know what it'd be like to be 'round someone who could be my daddy."

Her answer stirred tenderness into his mind.

Betty Jo lowered the soda bottle and looked Jimmy in the eye. "Why, Jimmy? Why y'all actin' like yer my daddy?"

Jimmy Davis understood the need to build walls and protect family matters, but what defined family had become blurred. He had rehearsed the beginning of this conversation, but hadn't prepared anything after it. Words came slow.

"Fer the sheriff. Daddy got me outta prison—course I s'pose doin' his biddin' got me in prison in the first place—but he got me out, and I owed 'im. It become more'n that, though. Gettin' to know y'all was like bein' with yer mama agin. Guess I was relivin' the good ol' days."

Jimmy cleared his throat. "Betty Jo, I won't say any more, but take care. Put as much distance as y'all kin between yerself and the sheriff."

He stood up. "I'm gonna miss our fishin' outin's." Before Betty Jo could speak, Jimmy Davis walked away.

*****

The three women relaxed under the big oak. With improvements to the outside kitchen, the Thorpe property became the home of the feeding program. For Beulah May, it required a change of heart. She always kept her distance from the vagrants and low-lifes, but now everyone was thrown into the same batch of dough in Great Depression's mixing bowl.

Dot was glad for the permanent location. It saved packing and preparation time and allowed her to focus on procuring and managing supplies. She had insisted on a strict serving schedule. The policy was simple—serve until either the food ran out or the line was vacated.

The cornbread was the hearty part of today's meal. The Red Bean soup had a thinner broth than normal, but even so they ran out. While Betty Jo enjoyed the serving part, she dreaded the turning away part.

The piston-thumping Chevrolet rolled down the drive. Brother Delbert, wearing denims and an unbuttoned shirt that revealed his white tee, got out of the car. He walked across the grounds.

"Mind if I join y'all?"

The smile of the women served as affirmation. He sat down, cross-legged, on the grass next to Betty Jo.

"How'd it go today?" he asked.

"Real good," Beulah answered.

"Gettin' more efficient," Dot said. "Folks know where and when to come."

"God is blessin'," Delbert responded.

"Dottie and Betty Jo are such good workers!" Beulah added, "We be needin' to figure more help when school starts agin."

Dottie Sue threw a glance at the young woman. Betty Jo's face washed in helplessness. Beulah caught the look and paused.

"Aunt Beu," Betty Jo began. "I won't be returnin' to school."

Beulah leaned forward in her chair, eyebrow raised.

"I think there's another path I'm to follow," Betty Jo offered.

"But, Sugar, y'all done real good—got good grades, enjoyed yer sangin' and all, made a new friend. Why the sudden change?"

Betty Jo looked at Dottie and then back to her aunt. "Not so sudden, fer actual. Bin thinkin' it most semester."

"I had no idee." Beulah sighed as under a heavy weight.

"Sorry I didn't tell y'all," Betty Jo said. "I didn't want to disappoint. But in hidin' it I handed y'all a bigger dose."

"Might help yer aunt if she knew the reasons," Delbert prodded.

Betty Jo fought off the offense of his intrusion, recognizing the wisdom of his words.

She spoke slowly. "Don't have much in common with the other students. I'd be nigh 20 years 'fore graduatin'. "

"Y'all have a big future ahead—don't give up on the diploma we all workin' so hard fer."

Betty Jo pushed the retort that flew through her brain to the side.

"Yer shorely right. Betty Jo does have a wonderful future," Dottie affirmed. "Y'all know the proverb well—'Trust in the LORD with all thine heart and lean not unto thine own understanding. In all thy ways acknowledge him, and he shall direct thy paths.'

"It says *paths*. Once we choose the narrow road that leads to life, there's more'n one path we kin take. We don't all walk the same way."

Beulah May leaned back into the wood chair—her head now lowered.

Delbert closed his eyes, silently moving his lips.

"Aunt Beulah, thank y'all fer teachin' me to read and helpin' me with the subjects and all. Thank y'all mostly fer teachin' me 'bout Jesus and how to walk with Him. Yer effort won't be in vain. I'm not stoppin' learnin'. I'm just not returnin' to school."

Beulah lifted her head. Great aunt and niece locked eyes in a truce of acknowledgement.

As the fireflies began their show, a hush slipped into the circle of the four souls. Rest was found.

"I have some good news fer y'all," Delbert said. "Reverend Harris is returnin'. Should be in Logansport in a week or so."

A breeze rippled through the leaves. Delbert smiled. Dottie contemplated. Betty Jo joyed. And Beulah May Thorpe praised, "Glory be!"

Beulah May and Betty Jo moved out to the porch on the Lord's Day late in June. Betty Jo worked on the strings of the autoharp, turning the tuning wrench until one by one the strings were pitched correctly.

She had hoped for a visitor all day long. Even in the morning she found it difficult to think about the sermon. Music would pass the time and ease disappointment's sting.

Philip Harris had arrived on the Louisiana side, but she hadn't heard from nor seen him. Tempted as she was to spend the weekend over at Dot's, it didn't seem the thing to do. She needed to carry Aunt Beu to her church and steady her in the coming and going. There needed to be a smoothing of the wrinkles in their relationship.

Finished with the tuning, Betty Jo strummed a simple chord progression. Beulah caught the pitch and began belting out a tune in her resonate, alto voice.

> *By and by, when the morning comes,*
> *when the saints of God are gathered home,*
> *we'll tell the story,*
> *how we've overcome;*
> *for we'll understand it better by and by*

Betty Jo took the high harmony, third above. One song flowed into another as the night sky settled upon them.

"That sure is pretty," a voice called from the gravel driveway, rising above the women's joyful noise. "I know it's late, but I was wondering if you all could spare some food."

The familiar voice and manner of speaking brought light to the shadows. The man-shape moved to the porch.

"I came from Logansport, and the day got away from me." He smiled broadly.

"Philip!" Tears slid down Betty Jo's cheeks.

Beulah rose to hug his neck. "Praise God from whom all blessin's flow!"

Betty Jo carefully set the autoharp down. This time, the hug would not be quick or regretful.

Beulah May excused herself, leaving the preacher from Rhode Island and the girl from the plank house to their reunion.

Releasing from their embrace, the pair moved to the porch swing. They rocked back and forth, joying in each other's presence.

"Sorry I did not come to see you sooner," Philip apologized, breaking the silence. "I wanted to be sure there would be plenty of time for a proper visit. With preaching at the Gospel Tabernacle this morning and talks concerning camp meeting, I knew this evening would be the best opportunity."

Philip reached for Betty Jo's hand. "I want to hear all about the little things, and I want to share the burden of the big thing."

Betty Jo caught her breath. "I'm so sorry fer the loss of yer daddy," she whispered. Philip received the comfort, pressing more tightly as they held hands.

"What was it like, havin' a father and all?" Betty Jo asked.

The young preacher tilted his head. "Well, my father was my teacher. From the time I was little, he showed me what it meant to love God and care for others."

"If yer daddy taught y'all, then why'd y'all go to college?" Betty Jo asked.

Philip laughed. "Good question. Well, he gave me the foundation of faith, but I needed to learn all the particulars if I was going to teach others. *James* says not too many should presume to be teachers. It's a big responsibility not to be taken lightly.

"My father was a very kind and gentle man. He was steady. It's still hard to think of this world without him."

Philip turned his head to look at Betty Jo. "Until I met you, I never thought what it would be like to not have a father. I also never considered what it might be like to have a bad one."

Betty Jo nodded. "That's Jimmy Davis. His daddy's bad."

Philip considered the notion before speaking. "Some men crave power. You said in a letter that Jimmy Davis was your daddy?"

"He come . . . he came over with the sheriff. Sheriff claimed it to be true. Beulah thought it was. Dot told me later that he wasn't, and when I thought 'bout our talks and times together it occurred to me he never actually said he was.

"I enjoyed fishin' with 'im and all. Bein' 'round 'im made me picture what havin' a daddy would be like. But I never liked it when we were 'round his daddy. Before school let out, Jimmy visited with me.

Said he wasn't my daddy and that I oughter keep away from the Sheriff."

"So, you still don't know who your father is?" Philip asked.

"No, but the sheriff still acts like his son is. Seems Dottie's the one who knows, and she won't say. It's all very strange. The not knowing is the burden, but now I've started wonderin' if it even matters."

Philip responded, "We first learn about love from our parents. Whoever fathered you, for whatever reason, left you. He forfeited paternal rights and the privilege of knowing you. But you have a Heavenly Father who loves you and longs to be with you. It's from Him you can learn."

Betty Jo pondered Philip's words. Maybe not knowing was a good thing.

*****

"Won't y'all change yer mind and come along?" Dottie asked.

Beulah waved her off. "Y'all go on and have a good time now. I'll see y'all back here fer the fish fry."

Dottie returned to the passenger seat. The blue ribbon in her swooped-up red hair bobbed around with the movement. Philip hurried out of the car to open the door for Betty Jo. The four settled in for the drive to the county seat.

"I never bin to a parade before," Betty Jo said enthusiastically.

"Glad we kin carry y'all there," Delbert said.

The carefree miles passed quickly. The town square and surrounding blocks were bustling with activity. People, wagons, and automobiles filled the streets and walkways. Delbert found a place to park a few blocks from Nacogdoches Street. They got out of the car and walked to the parade route, searching for an opening in the line of people.

"So many folks!" Betty Jo whispered to Philip as they squeezed into a space. She took in the sights and sounds—flags displayed from the courthouse and lampposts, parents herding their children about, and happy voices that rose above the hard economic times.

In a short while, an honor guard marched the U.S. and Texas flags before them. In a solemn act of allegiance, hats were removed and hands were placed on hearts. Rangers on horseback immediately followed. Then entries of frivolity mixed with those of civic purpose passed by: kids pulling decorated carts holding a dog or younger sibling, the mayor on horseback waving, and a ragtag marching band played *Dixie*.

The Christian Temperance women were greeted with subdued applause as they marched by with their banner, *Abstinence from all Things Harmful*. Most secretly wished prohibition itself would pass on by. The Democrats of Shelby County were met by cheers. The KKK did not have an entry in the parade, but their presence was felt among the public. Near the end, Sheriff James Roy Davis with Miss Maisie sitting prim in the passenger seat, drove his patrol car down the route. The onlookers quieted until he passed. The final entry was the Veterans of Foreign Wars. Sitting on benches in a long-bed wagon were those who served in the Spanish-American War. Walking behind them were veterans of World War I. The crowd applauded their respect to the men and their service.

The four friends milled about the courthouse lawn and watched the various activities—three-legged races, egg toss, and pie eating contest. Needing a public privy, Philip excused himself. Then with his mind on the future, he walked quickly to rejoin Betty Jo. He did not notice the pot-bellied man with arms crossed blocking the walkway in front of him until the last moment.

"Excuse me," Philip said, attempting to sidestep the man.

"There be no excuse fer the likes of y'all," the scowling voice said.

Philip looked the Sheriff square in the face. Narrow-set eyes sparked with hostility.

"Y'all don't belong here. Take yer Yankee self and git back north. Folks 'round here don't need what yer preachin'. We all doin' just fine without y'all."

Philip squared his feet. "Are you finished?"

"No. One more thang. Back away from Betty Jo. Y'all will never be a part of her life."

Philip held his tongue, and stepped briskly around the sheriff, befuddled at the brash aggression.

"Boy, I'm warnin' y'all!" the voice called. Philip's feet stopped, but his body did not turn. "Y'all best be on yer way."

Philip walked on to join Betty Jo at the watermelon bust. On the outside he acted relaxed and playful. In his spirit he knew battle lines were being drawn.

*****

The small group of saints assembled on benches in the stuffy store-front. To conserve church resources, Brother Delbert brought his lantern. The shadows it cast danced on the walls and ceiling as if to celebrate the time of jubilee. Betty Jo noted that her aunt and the pastor were the only ones there from Joaquin. She smiled at Dot who sat quietly on the periphery.

"Brother Tucker, would y'all open in prayer?" Delbert asked.

The pastor of the Baptist church stood and raised his voice. "Lord, we ask fer guidance and direction in our plans—that souls may be brought into yer kingdom," he concluded.

In Delbert's hand was a written list that Betty Jo suspected was composed by someone other than himself. One by one, he brought up points of logistics and they were discussed. It had already been decided to hold the meetings the week before cotton harvest. The church men prayed for the Spirit to have His way, but they were practical in their planning.

Delbert began to address the challenges. "Where should the camp meetin' be located?" he asked.

Beulah was ready with an answer. "There's a piece of land along the highway in the north woods that'd be perfect."

"Think the lumber company would loan us use?" asked Delbert.

"They don't own the land, they lease it," Beulah replied with a smile. "Be glad to have the camp meetin' there."

"Well, glory!" a church man exclaimed.

Delbert continued to the next point on the list. "The men bin busy stitchin' canvas, but we still don't have enough."

"We could do like ol' times," a wrinkle-crested fellow suggested. "Use brush fer what we lack."

After arrangements were made for constructing the tabernacle in the woods, Brother Delbert turned the floor over to Philip Harris.

"Let's go to prayer. Pray that people will be drawn to God. Pray for me as I bring the Word. Pray for yourself and what the Lord would have you do. And pray that no weapon being formed against this work would prosper."

Betty Jo turned and knelt at the bench where she had been sitting.

While others prayed aloud at the same time, she preferred to pray in her thoughts. *Lord, show me what my part is. Please use me somehow for Your glory.*

Sheriff Davis got out of the patrol car and approached the volunteers as they put the crossbeam into place.

"Y'all need to stop what yer doin' right now!" he blustered.

Delbert stepped away from the task.

"Y'all in charge here?" The sheriff's eyes narrowed.

Delbert thought better of answering the question. "Is there a problem, Sir?"

"This here's private land," Davis asserted.

"Truly so. We've got permission from the landowner," Delbert replied.

"Y'all got proof?"

"Not directly, no." Delbert admitted.

"Then stop what yer doin' and git off this property." Davis ran his hand across his belt buckle.

"Yessir," Delbert sighed. He turned around and walked to the men. Shaking his head, he answered their questions.

James Roy Davis returned to his car, leaned against the door panel with his arms crossed until each volunteer left.

"Oh, that man!" Beulah exclaimed. "He cain't stand it if'n he doesn't have complete control in this county. I 'spect he thinks folks gettin' saved and gettin' close to Jesus will put a dent in his bus'ness. Well, so be it!"

"We cannot suppose what his motives are," stated Philip.

"Mebbe not, but I'd shorely love to give 'im a piece of my mind!" Beulah's exasperation ascended above the evening sounds.

Delbert spoke calmly. "Now Sister Thorpe, let's 'member that we wrestle not 'gainst flesh and blood—"

Beulah bellowed, "Right now I wouldn't mind if someone wrestled that ol' man to the ground and pinned 'im fer good!"

Before Betty Jo could stop it, a giggle bubbled out of her. She covered her mouth for a moment, but the laugh insisted on having its way. Soon, the other three joined her.

"All right," Beulah said, regaining her composure. "I'll write a paper with permission and send Eddie out in the mornin' with it. He kin help finish the tent. Hopefully the rain will hold."

On the porch of the yellow foursquare farmhouse in the summer air, a prayer meeting was held well into the night.

*****

Debby L Wynkoop

Philip Harris knelt in the sawdust at the makeshift altar. He had
arrived early for the first night of camp meeting, assured of the scripture
text and message the Lord put on his heart. Yet he was troubled.
Deacon Delbert encouraged him to let loose and give himself to the
unction of the Holy Spirit. Brother Tucker admonished him to preach
the Word without getting sidetracked by emotion. He respected the men
of God, but he was pretty sure he wouldn't be able to please them both.
Sometimes it wearied him being the outsider. He wanted to be
accepted—even admired. Lately, he found feelings of wishing to
impress a certain young lady creeping into his thoughts. He cared too
much about what people thought of him. Pride was like pesky unwanted
plants choking out the crops. It was time to humble himself and let the
Lord do some weeding.

He rose from the altar and looked back. The benches were filling
rather quickly. Dottie Sue had made the rounds, inviting everyone she
knew, with the exception of Denny Ron. The Lord would have to send
someone else in that case. Former customers, hobos from shantytown,
pickers and sharecroppers had come. She moved the feeding program to
the tabernacle site for the week to encourage attendance.

The guitarist from Logansport began to skillfully play and sing,
cueing the folks to gather under the covering of quilted canvas and
brush. The coal-oil lanterns were being lit.
Everybody ought to know he sang three times with the Gathered
echoing. *Who Jesus is* they sang together. Then, verse by verse, the
leader musically described the character of the Son of God.

Enthusiasm swelled into sweet worship as one song flowed into
another. Philip raised his hands, overwhelmed with expectancy.

Beulah stood at the back, swaying side to side. Betty Jo joined her
after the meal was served and the clean-up completed. She brought one
of the few wooden folding chairs with her. The benches would certainly
bring discomfort to her aunt.

Betty Jo surveyed the Gathering. She had never seen so many
Coloreds in one place and at one time. She still felt discomfort with
their presence and knew it risked ire. She began to sing, and her
concerns washed away. Closing her eyes, she was swept into deep
fellowship. She knew that her only response could be complete
surrender to Almighty God.

When she became aware of her surroundings once again, Philip was standing at the front, asking the people to be seated. She prayed with her eyes open as he preached repentance and love.

Then he made the appeal. "God is calling you to turn from your sins, accept His salvation, and follow Him. Come, don't wait any longer."

Sinners hurried to the altar. Some fled the tabernacle. Reverend Harris paced back and forth as church men and godly women moved forward to pray with individuals. Saints worshipped where they were seated.

A girl, barefoot and wearing a flour-sack dress, timidly walked down the sawdust aisle. She knelt on the far side of the altar. Betty Jo recognized herself in the young girl—in every way except . . .

Pray with her. Betty Jo bowed her head in her hands.

Not for her. With her.

Beulah leaned over. "There's a girl needin' prayer."

Betty Jo looked up. Philip caught her eye from across the tabernacle.

This is impossible, she thought.

With Me all things are possible.

Standing to her feet, Betty Jo began the journey of obedience—traversing the landscape of humanity until she arrived at the altar on the far side. She remembered the night of her angst and how Sister Tucker sat with her. Betty Jo knelt next to the girl. She remembered how Aunt Beulah had kept a hand on her shoulder the night she accepted Christ. She put her arm around the child.

The girl opened her eyes.

"My name's Betty Jo. Kin I pray with y'all?

The girl kept her eyes forward. "Is it true? God loves me?"

Betty Jo smiled. "Of the thangs I know, it's the most true. He loves y'all so much. When y'all ask Jesus to come into yer heart, He washes away the bad and gives y'all His good."

The girl braved a look at Betty Jo.

"Doesn't change the circumstance or the folks in yer life, but He gives y'all true life. I know. Six months ago, I invited Him in and I'm so glad I did.

"Would y'all like to ask Jesus into yer heart?" Betty Jo asked.

While Beulah May Thorpe rejoiced to see God's hand moving, while Dottie Sue Dawson observed the good God was working out of her tainted past, while Philip Harris sensed a new call on his life, and while Betty Jo Landry led a colored girl in the sinner's prayer; the men in white hoods and robes came, torches in hand.

Brother Tucker ran to the flames. "Please . . . don't do this, Men. This is a holy place."

"Fer shame, Tucker. Y'all know better'n this," a muffled voice spoke.

Brother Delbert ran to Philip's side. "Gotta git the folks out! Coloreds first!"

Awareness flooded the Gathered. "Oh, God," was the mournful prayer of many as they scrambled to get away.

"Run to the woods 'n' hide!" Betty Jo urgently whispered to the girl whose name she did not know.

Dottie Sue hurried to Beulah May to escort her to safety. To her surprise, the matriarch headed straight for the cluster of hooded darkness and stood by her pastor's side.

"What's the meaning of this?" Beulah barked. "This is my property, dedicated to God. Y'all git along!" She waved her hand as if shooing away flies.

"There'll be no mixin' the races!" yelled the leader whose robe did not fully conceal his belly bulge.

"James Roy, don't y'all be doin' this evil thang!" Beulah May confronted.

"Step aside ol' woman," a young, gruff voice commanded.

Dottie and Brother Tucker sheltered Beulah as the klansmen surged forward. They spread out, igniting the brush and the canvas, smashing coal-oil lanterns, and chasing the Coloreds into the woods.

The remaining saints huddled together, helpless to stop the blaze. While families and friends were relieved in reuniting, fear gripped them for those who had to flee.

"My guitar," the song leader moaned, shaking his head in disbelief.

Philip's face was ashen white. Brother Tucker put his arm around him. "Son, y'all best git on the other side—stay outta Shelby County fer a while."

CHAPTER SIXTEEN

The intense work of harvest could not erase the image of the torched tabernacle. It was engraved in the minds of everyone who bore witness, and it unsettled all who heard about it. Still, work needed doing and that's what the folks of the Pineys did.

After a long, humid Saturday laboring at the machine shop, Delbert returned home to an invitation.

"Dottie took the afternoon off and asked if we could break bread together this evening." Philip smiled. "I took the liberty to accept. Her cooking is much better than mine."

Delbert smiled. "Lemme clean up a bit and we'll head over."

When the two men arrived, Dot arranged the picnic pork, beans, and fried okra on a small table placed in the yard. A pitcher of sweet tea and mason jars stood nearby at the ready.

"Smells good," Delbert declared.

They consumed the meal heartily. Dot waited until the men started their second round before broaching the subject that would not leave her thoughts.

"We cain't give up," she began.

Delbert and Philip simultaneously ceased chewing.

Delbert swallowed. "Give up?"

"We've a responsibility to the folks who came to camp meetin'. We've been fearful or busy or I don't know—but aren't we to go and make disciples?"

"It took a while to account fer all the Coloreds, Dot," Delbert responded. "We're blessed that none were, well, lost."

"What do you propose, Dottie Sue?" Philip asked.

"Light drives out darkness. What about a baptismal service tomorrow afternoon? Right out in the open, at the Big Eddy on the Lou'siana side? Give a chance fer new believers to declare their faith."

"And put action to ours," Philip added.

"I kin git the word out. What'd y'all say?"

*****

243

It rained in the night, muddying the waters of the Sabine more than usual. Philip did not know exactly how the communication happened, but folks showed up on the bank of the river at the appointed time. *Jesus, keep us safe* he prayed.

Even though he knew he'd have more fences to mend afterwards, Brother Tucker came to lend a hand. After all, he was a preacher of the gospel and spiritual matters were his priority.

"In case we're bein' watched, it would help if 'n y'all baptized the Coloreds." As the pastor said it to the Yankee, he cringed, but reality called for prudence.

One by one, they waded in the water. One by one, they confessed faith. One by one, a prayer was offered. One by one, they went into the water to rise in abundant life.

Philip Harris looked back to the bank to see if anyone else was ready. Betty Jo, holding hands with the young colored girl, waded into the waters. The precious child came to him. The woman he loved went to the Baptist Preacher. Beulah May stood on the bank, guarded on either side by Sister Tucker and Dottie Sue. Nothing could keep her from witnessing the grandchild of her dear sister publicly declare her faith.

And at a distance, on the other side of the river, obscured by the woods, the Sheriff of Shelby County scowled. He was losing control, and it felt none too good.

*****

"Sugar, pick me up when y'all're finished in Center," Beulah directed.

Betty Jo looked at her aunt quizzically. She had not anticipated this stop at the Davis home. She glanced at Dottie in the back seat and found only concern in her eyes.

"It'll be fine," Beulah said as she opened the passenger door. "Miz Maisie 'n' I haven't visited in quite some time."

Dottie quickly got out and saw Beulah May up the porch steps and to the door. She backed away once she heard footsteps responding to the knock. Returning to the car, she assumed the passenger seat and looked at her young friend.

"Gonna have to trust yer aunt knows what she's doin'. Let's hurry our errands, though—just in case."

Beulah disappeared into the craftsman home. The sedan pulled away, headed for town.

"This is a surprise," Maisie Davis said softly as she smoothed the skirt of her house dress. She led her visitor into the house and gestured for Beulah to take a seat, answering the unspoken question that James Roy was not home.

"Bin a while since we talked." Beulah attempted a nonchalant tone. "How're y'all doin', Maisie?"

Maisie studied her shaking hand before placing the calm one on top. She lifted her gaze. "How y'all manage it?" she asked.

Beulah waited for more words to come.

"Y'all bin through hard times, but always so at peace."

"The joy of the Lord is my strength," Beulah responded, "and I never had to live in the same house with my troubles."

Maisie closed her eyes momentarily.

Beulah shifted her weight in the chair. She didn't know how much time she might have. "Betty Jo has herself a suitor. I 'spect a weddin' may be in the near future."

Maisie smiled weakly. "She's a lovely young lady—spittin' image of her mama. I kin see Leet in her."

"I kin see some Davis, too," Beulah added pointedly. "Pardon my bluntness, but we need to know. Is Betty Jo Jimmy's daughter?"

Maisie lowered her eyes again. "Jimmy moved out after a fight with his daddy. It was 'bout Betty Jo." Brush strokes of sadness darkened the eyes of Maisie Davis. She shook her head from side to side. "I once thought Jimmy was her daddy. I wanted to think it." She looked at Beulah, tears streaming down her face. "But now I know it's not so."

Pain swelled inside of Beulah May's chest as hues of realization surfaced. "Oh, Jesus," she sobbed.

The women fellowshipped in the sorrow of the unspeakable.

Betty Jo and Dottie knew Beulah was troubled, yet they chatted about the purchases made and the menu they were developing. They would not pry into their elder's concerns. To do so might betray a confidence. Like all matters, it would come to surface in due time; and like all folks, they would be supposing in the meantime.

*****

Standing on the porch, hat in hand, the young man rapped on the screen door. He had chosen an evening after the busyness of the cotton harvest subsided and when he knew Betty Jo was staying over at Dottie Sue's house.

He rapped on the door again.

Moving steadily across the sitting room and to the entry was the face of the woman of noble character.

"Good evening, Sister Beulah," he greeted.

"Evenin', Preacher Philip," she returned.

"I was hoping we might have a talk?"

"Why, shorely. Give me a bit and I'll be with y'all.

The visitor understood his place was to be seated and wait on the porch. In his mind he had already waited long enough, but he knew that God's timing wasn't the same as his.

After a while, Beulah May pushed the screen door open with her hip and stepped onto the porch carrying a tray with a pitcher and two glasses. She set it on the little table. Without asking if he wanted any, she poured the young man sweet tea and handed it to him.

"Thank you, kindly," he said.

Pouring a second glass, she sat in her porch chair. "What a pleasure to have yer company this evenin'," she said. "Sometimes this house is just too big fer one soul."

"Yet it has been used to bless so many," Philip noted.

Beulah sighed, and spoke aloud to remind herself. "The Lord is faithful, even when thangs git difficult."

The Shunamite woman and the preacher listened to the evening sounds, each in lost in their own thoughts.

"May I ask you a question?" Philip leaned forward.

"Course." Beulah May wrapped a second hand around her glass and braced herself, happy to have other thoughts to consider.

"How do you see that Betty Jo has changed since the last time we spoke in regard to her?"

Beulah took a sip of her tea and lowered the glass. "Well, she's grown fer shore. She kin read 'n' write and kin study and learn fer herself. She's more social. She's workin' real hard. I think she's at peace with matters of kin and family. Most important, she's grown in her faith."

"And have I changed since you first met me?" Philip asked.

Beulah raised her eyebrow and tilted her head. "I see the fruit of the Spirit growin' in y'all. Yer more patient. Seems y'all understand the ways 'round here better."

"Ma'am, do you think we're ready to marry?" Philip's expression belied a boyish charm.

Beulah took another sip of tea. "There be many challenges to marriage. No one's ever ready fer 'em all. From what I kin tell, y'all're ready to be united and face them together."

Philip exhaled. "Who do I ask for her hand?"

"No one. But if'n y'all ask fer a blessin' y'all shorely would have mine."

"Ma'am, might I have your blessing to marry Betty Jo?"

"Yes, Philip Harris." Beulah smiled. "May the Lord bless y'all together."

Philip beamed his joy and jumped up to give Beulah a big hug.

"One thang I'd ask," she said as Philip pulled away. "Have the weddin' after her birthday, once ev'rythang is settled down and the weather more pleasant."

Philip grinned. "Well, that would be just one more opportunity for patience to grow." He leaned over and kissed Beulah's cheek.

"Dottie Sue, we cain't be spendin' time fishin' at Big Tree. There's too much to do today."

"We bin workin' hard," Dottie countered. "Beulah says it's time fer a break."

"But it hasn't cooled any." Exasperation colored Betty Jo's tone.

Dot kept walking, pole in hand. "We kin cool off in the river."

"Fer heaven's sakes, Dot. Y'all're actin' odd." Betty Jo shrugged and followed her friend. They moved down the county road, beyond the plank house where Eddie now lived, and into the clearing.

"What's yer hurry?" Betty Jo asked even though she knew there'd be no answer. Dottie could be a stubborn one at times. Into the woods and on to the river they went.

They arrived at the bend in the trail. Dottie slowed to a stop when they came to the site of the fallen Big Tree. She stepped to Betty Jo's side and kissed her cheek.

Standing between Betty Jo and Big Tree's decaying trunk was a man in a white Yankee hat and summer suit. His soft, blue eyes drew her to him.

Her eyes held unspoken questions.

"In this place your mother loved to be, I would like to ask you a question." Philip removed his hat and smoothed back his sweaty blonde hair. Taking a knee, he pulled out a small jewelry box and opened the lid. Then he looked up into her face.

"You are so beautiful, inside and out. In you I've found a treasure to be cherished for a lifetime. Betty Jo Landry, will you marry me?"

Eyes wide open, she saw the expansive green backdrop of her life. This was the world she had known. Now it would be the place of her new beginning.

"Yes, Philip, I would love to be yer wife!"

As the couple embraced, Dottie and Delbert moved in from each side for hugging and laughing and the patting of backs.

"Oh me, oh my, Girl, let's see that ring," Dot dramatically whispered.

The blue jewel sparkled in the sunlight that came through the opening of where Big Tree once stood.

"It's beautiful, Philip. But...it's too much."

"This is Mother's ring. She wanted you to have it. She welcomes you to our family.

It occurred to Betty Jo that she would have kin of her own choosing. The circle was getting bigger.

*****

"Cain't believe Mother spent money fer this shin dig," Bernie mumbled.

"Brother, you bin sour long enough," Ruth Ann scolded.

Bernie stifled a guffaw.

Ruth Ann threw him a stern look. "Y'all need to shape up. Don't be stealin' Mama's joy." Softening, Ruth Ann patted his arm. "Enjoy yerself. Lord only knows how much time we have with her."

Ruth Ann walked to the table and poured herself a cup of punch. Surveying the room, she marveled at the variety of folks who'd come to the engagement party. A handful of attendees from the two churches intermixed, minus a few like Mrs. Westly who objected to the possibility there might be dancing. Mary Ann and a couple other high school friends showed up. Laborers from both sides of the river and the hired man, Eddie, enjoyed respite from their hard work. A seemingly endless supply of cousins, in varying degrees of removal, were guests of her mother. Community folks were interspersed throughout. Even Mr. Sam from the mercantile was in attendance, with his wife on his arm. They filled the Grange Hall at Haslam and spilled out onto the grounds.

The decorations were created from the flora of the woods, the hors d' oeuvres simple and tasty, and the entertainment was a tip of the hat to Betty Jo's Papa. The three-man band played accordion, fiddle, and a washboard zydeco—alternating between Cajun tunes and Southern folk songs. Cousin Dottie sure had a way of organizing and getting big jobs done well.

Ruth Ann was relieved, however, that no Coloreds were present. She had not pressed the issue, and trusted that her mama would not tempt a hateful response. Celebrating an illegitimate East Texas gal's upcoming marriage to a Yankee with Cajun music was enough of a social quandary for one event.

Philip Harris and Betty Jo moved around the hall and the grounds, greeting guests with small talk and receiving congratulations. Betty Jo wore the dress Aunt Beu and Uncle Jack had given her last year on her birthday. The bodice only needed to be let out a little. Philip wore trousers and a button shirt, skipping his Yankee suit for a more casual appearance. Betty Jo was content to leave the talking to Philip, only prompting on occasion to assist with the niceties.

At the turning point of the party—the point where some folks were fixing to leave while others were cranking up enthusiasm—Beulah May asked the musicians to take a break. Dottie signaled the guests to gather inside.

"Thank y'all, dear friends, fer comin' to celebrate the engagement of my niece, Miz Betty Jo Landry to the Reverend Philip Harris." Beulah smiled from ear to ear as she gestured to the young couple. "We're so thankful fer yer lives and we pray God's richest blessin' on y'all."

As the celebrants clapped and cheered, an unwanted presence entered the Grange Hall. His boots pounded the wood floor as he stepped toward Betty Jo. Folks backed up, making way as a sudden hush fell. He stopped a couple yards from her, took his index finger to lift his hat up enough for his narrow eyes to be seen.

"Y'all forgettin' somethin'?" Sheriff Davis challenged.

Betty Jo's brain could not process the turn of events. She felt constricted. A vine wrapped around her and was about to pull her under.

"Yer a Davis!"

Betty Jo winced as a gasp swept through the room.

Bernie stepped to his mother's side to restrain her from intervening, ready to protect her should harm erupt.

Davis locked eyes with Philip. "Y'all never asked permission, and her daddy shore wouldn't give it. No Yankee's marryin' in. Told y'all once before. Fer the last time, git out of my county!"

In the kerfuffle that ensued, Dottie Sue hurried from the back of the hall and positioned herself in front of Betty Jo.

"Woman, this has nothin' to do with y'all," Davis growled. "This here's a family matter."

Dot raised her voice for all to hear, eyes intensely focused. "Tired of yer lies, Sheriff. Jimmy's not her daddy!"

James Roy stood frozen—uncertain as how to respond.

"Y'all're the father! But yer shore no kind of daddy!" Velocity of emotion propelled Dottie Sue and words spewed out of her mouth. "Y'all raped Charlene. Y'all took what ya wanted. She ended up dead. Dead!"

The sheriff staggered backward, as if a dagger had been thrust into his chest.

"Y'all took Henri's bus'ness—tried runnin' 'im off the cliff. Y'all wanted 'im dead. Y'all tryin' to worm yer way to take land that's not yers. Now yer tryin' to take the future from Charlene's baby girl."

Sheriff Davis lunged toward Dottie, but the deacon from Logansport intercepted and bound him with muscular arms.

"No, Sir. No more takin'!" Dottie yelled, shaking uncontrollably.

Sheriff Davis knew he had calculated incorrectly. He should not have come alone. He should not have confronted in public. He'd gotten careless in his old age, but he truly did not think anyone would resist. He was the one in charge, after all.

Betty Jo's legs no longer held her. She melted to the floor. Her hands covered her face as she drowned in shame.

As silence was the true companion of Job, so silence fell around Betty Jo. One by one the guests left, knowing full well the news of the evening's event would carry throughout the region. Deeds done in darkness eventually come to light. Sheriff James Roy Davis had already lost favor among the common folks, but now he would lose credibility and allies, too. His only gain would be disdain.

Strewn about, as if branches after a storm, those in close fellowship sat throughout the hall. Compassion filled the space and left no room for words. Singing could not bring inspiration. There was no movement, nor action that could possibly make it better.

Love, Himself, was all that could help.

*****

With her humiliation complete, Maisie Davis had nothing more to lose. She took time to put on a dress and style her hair. While she wasn't invited to the wedding, she would provide a gift. She opened the front door of the craftsman house with her good hand. A letter, a paper with an address, and a crisp bill were tucked into the one that incessantly quivered. She would walk until she found a youth she could trust with the errand. If she had to, she would walk all the way herself to make the delivery. She would defy her husband. She no longer feared the consequences.

October 27, 1932

Dear Jimmy,

Saturday is Betty Jo's wedding. Your father has worked himself into a frenzy concerning it. I fear he will ruin the day and cause even more sorrow. Please intervene. Give my best regards should you have opportunity.

Love,
Mother

*****

As clearly as if he were standing before her, Betty Jo saw her papa leaning against his pristine Model T. The green of the Pineys surrounded him. His face was soft and unmarred. He stood aright and held out his hands, palms up—his fingers perfectly clean. She focused her mind upon his image. He was where he should be.

Compelled, Betty Jo walked, then ran, to join him. She could not get to him quickly enough. This was the grandfather she always wanted. This was the man she always needed.

She placed her hands in his. He squeezed them lightly and then let go. Putting an arm around her shoulder, he turned her to the side. Together they stood looking into the dense green.

Without explanation, a man-shape emerged. He wore a white summer suit. He approached with steady, resolute steps.

Henri reached out to shake his hand. He held onto it. Lowering his left arm, he took hold of Betty Jo's right hand and placed it into the young man's hand. For a precious moment, the hands of the trio merged. Then slowly, Henri withdrew.

Perfect peace settled upon the scene.

Betty Jo gazed into brilliant blue eyes. She did not see her papa back away and vanish into the light. When she turned her head, he was no longer there.

Betty Jo opened her eyes to the dark of the bedroom. She looked side to side. Today she would marry the one she loved. Somehow, in the depths of life's mystery, she had been gifted a blessing.

Betty Jo studied the silver-framed photograph once again. Her papa was dressed in the only suit he'd ever owned. The fabric was in excellent condition—no moth holes or fading. Her dear, stalwart grandma was by his side with an appearance untainted by the cancer that had begun to grow. The mama she never knew was positioned just in front of them, with eyes fixed in a can't-make-me look, and a crown of lush black hair. This was Betty Jo's family—imperfectly beautiful.

None of them could stand as witness today when she would become the wife of the Reverend Philip Harris. Yet, they were intrinsically with her. She was a product of who they were and what they did was the beginning of her story. Now she would take up the pen and write the rest.

Dottie Sue completed the final touches on Betty Jo's hair. Placing her hands on the shoulders of her best friend's daughter, she whispered. "Yer lovely, Betty Jo. Yer mama would've bin delighted to see this day."

Betty Jo smiled at Dot in the mirror, blinking back tears.

"Are y'all ready fer the somethin' old?" Cousin Ruth asked the young woman she would have raised as her own.

Betty Jo nodded.

Dottie stepped back as Ruth Ann approached, lifting the pendant out of the old jewelry box. The polished silver caught a glint of light and sparkled. Ruth Ann unclasped the chain, placed it around Betty Jo's neck, and refastened it. The three women looked in the mirror, satisfied.

Love always.

"Oh, Sugar!" Aunt Beulah exclaimed, out of breath, as she stepped into the upstairs bedroom. "Yer so beautiful! We all're just plumb proud!"

Betty Jo stood and turned to face her great aunt. The corsage of golden mums was a perfect match for her dress and countenance. Smiling, she said, "Aunt Beu, how kin I ever thank y'all? Ev'rythang's just perfect!"

"So pleased to be a part of yer special day." Beulah reached for Betty Jo's hands and held them firmly. Then with a quick kiss on the cheek, Beulah May moved to the door. Looking at the other two women, she said with a smile, "Let's leave Betty Jo to her thoughts."

"I'll knock when everyone's in place," Dottie Sue said as she left the room.

*****

Philip Harris paced back and forth on the porch of the two-story farmhouse. Even though the day was cool, sweat had soaked the dress shirt under his suit. Brother Delbert stood on the top step, keeping his eyes fixed on the county road beyond the parked cars and hitched horses. Both men prayed aloud.

Unrepentance brings grief, and foolishness wreaks havoc. While the Almighty forgives, and while forgiveness is commanded, there are fences that need to be guarded. Conflict was not their intention on this joyous day, but they were putting on the full armor of God should it come their way.

The arrival of the guests tapered off, and Sister Tucker began the prelude. Dottie Sue stepped out to the porch to retrieve the groom just as the black patrol car turned onto the gravel drive.

"Dot, head on inside." Delbert said. "We'll come in a bit."

Dottie Sue stepped back into the house, just on the other side of the screen door.

The car squeezed in to park. The lone figure of Sheriff James Roy Davis emerged—white hat squarely on his head. As he shook out the cuffs of his dark pants, his belly-bulge jiggled. The bolo tie swaggered as he walked to the porch.

A man-shape appeared from the edge of the woods.

"Sheriff, what is your intention?" Philip asked forthrightly, his pacing ceased as he moved to Deacon Delbert's side.

"Stand back, Yankee," he answered. "I'm gonna have an understandin' with Betty Jo."

The man from the edge of the woods came more clearly into focus with each foot pound and bob of the head.

"No, sir," Philip replied. "Turn around and leave."

"You know who yer talkin' to, Boy? I'm the sheriff of this county, and I come fer what's mine!" James Roy asserted. Separating his feet squarely, he leaned forward. "I kin make yer life miserable," he added with a growl.

The man reached the side of Sheriff Davis.

"No more, Daddy! No more!" he yelled.

Startled, James Roy Davis fell out of his stance.

Dottie Sue returned to stand behind Delbert.

"Charlene's girl is gonna to marry, and y'all have no place or say here."

James Roy turned with shock toward his son.

"Now leave these good folks be!" Jimmy Davis was emphatic.

"That's enough!" James Roy erupted with a backhand swat that Jimmy nimbly evaded.

The sheriff surged toward the porch steps. Jimmy grabbed him from behind, and stopped his momentum. The Davis men stumbled backward, but stayed on their feet.

Jimmy let go and stealthily positioned himself between the sheriff and the porch. "No, Daddy! Time to leave." He ducked the fist headed toward his face. Before James Roy recovered from the effort, Jimmy shoved him back—once, twice, a third time.

"Git in the car," he commanded his father.

James Roy stepped forward only to be met with another shove. Puzzled, he looked at his son as if seeing him for the first time. "Remember, Boy, y'all're here to serve the family!"

"And I am," Jimmy said slowly, meeting his father's eyes with fierceness.

Sheriff Davis tilted his head.

Jimmy held fast his position.

James Roy slowly turned around and shuffled to the car.

Jimmy Davis looked at Philip. "I'm sorry fer the trouble. Mother sends her best regards."

He stood in the drive, waiting until the black patrol car turned on the county road before following—walking away from the Thorpe home and his half-sister.

*****

Betty Jo looked at her reflection in the mirror. Growing up, she could have never imagined being special. The Good Lord revealed just how much He loved her and brought people into her life who helped her understand her value. Now she was uniting with Philip. Everything was good. Everything except. . .

As she thought about the circumstances of her existence and the close kin she had lost, a frown crept to her face. *No, don't be sad. No sense in dwelling on the if onlys or what ifs. Today is what is.*

She was marrying Philip, with dear ones here to witness, and the thought took her breath away. She relaxed.

She smoothed her dress and attached the embroidered veil Aunt Beulah had so carefully made. With her thumb, she adjusted the sapphire engagement ring Philip's mother had given them. Something new. Something blue. She fingered the silver treasure at her neck. Something old. It was all present.

Forgetting what was behind and pressing forward.

No more plank houses. She would live in a home built on Solid Rock.

She was ready. Now she would wait. This was something she knew how to do well.

The knock at the door came at last. Fluttering on the inside and glowing on the outside, Betty Jo reached for the knob and opened it.

Dottie Sue stood with a grin on her face. "Girl, it's time," she said. "Oh me, oh my, it's *really* about time!"

Betty Jo giggled. The laugh brought emotional balance.

Aunt Beulah stood at the bottom of the stairs and gave a nod. Sister Tucker played the slightly out of pitch chord seven times on the piano, and the guests scattered throughout the house rose and turned toward the stairs. The march began.

Betty Jo descended the steps alone, holding a bouquet of yellow roses. Philip stood next to Brother Tucker. He looked at his bride with a bright face, like the light that came down through the opening in the sky where once Big Tree stood. It was a glorious beam.

Of all the things in her young life that caused her to wonder—of the river's curves and the expansiveness of woods, of crawdad pinchers and catfish whiskers, and the pure white of a cotton ball—of all the things she knew, what stood before her was the greatest wonder of all creation. Philip, the man with just one name.

At the bottom of the stairs, she slipped her arm around her Great Aunt Beulah.

"Who gives this woman to be married to this man?" Brother Tucker began.

"Her kinfolk do," Beulah May answered.

The ceremony was short. Applause filled the house to the couple's sweet kiss. Then Sister Tucker played and voices sang convention-style, four-part:

> *Love lifted me, love lifted me*
> *When nothing else could help*
> *Love lifted me*

Out the front door, holding hands, the new pastor of the church in Logansport and his young wife entered the world. The guests were close behind. As backs were patted and necks were hugged, the tables were prepared for dinner on the grounds.

And on the banks of the Sabine—within view of Big Tree's great fall—a young cypress, ripe with growth, lifted its arms to the sky and gave praise.

Discussion Questions

Part I: ROOTS

Chapter 1

1. From this opening chapter, what do you discover about Betty Jo and Henri and their relationship?
2. *"Nothing about that scene seemed right"* hints at the main metaphor used throughout this story. Have you ever come across a situation that left you unsettled? Did it foreshadow anything or did the feeling dissipate?
3. Betty Jo came to understand that she both hated and loved her grandfather. Is it possible for hate and love to co-exist?
4. Every family group has its 'skeletons in the closet'—actions taken in the past that fortify tensions in the present. What can be done to ease those tensions?
5. ***Proverbs 15:1*** *A soft answer turneth away wrath: but grievous words stir up anger.* Words once heard or read never leave. How, as a practice, can we guard our words?

Chapter 2

6. Why did Jack Lee and Beulah May want Betty Jo to see the wreckage?
7. Henri never allowed Betty Jo to attend church with her great aunt. What was the reason he gave for this? Do you think there were other reasons?
8. *"It's never good to ignore truth,"* Beulah said. Is there ever a time to conceal the truth? Under what circumstances would you withhold truth from those nearest you?
9. What was Betty Jo's motivation in secretly leaving the Thorpes?
10. ***Hebrews 9:27*** *And as it is appointed unto men once to die, but after this the judgment.* Beulah prayed about the situation, not knowing how to pray. She recalled scripture that points to the sovereignty of God. Have you experienced a time you didn't know how to pray? What did you do?

Chapter 3

11. What social norms (manners) does Betty Jo appear to understand? Are there any social norms in this story that seem to be unique to the time and place?
12. ***Psalm 122:1*** *I was glad when they said unto me, Let us go into the house of the LORD.* Church attendance and Biblical references were entrenched in the society of the Bible Belt. Compare the two churches Betty Jo has attended. Which church would you choose to attend and why?
13. What was the root of Betty Jo's recurring feeling of shame and guilt?
14. *"Running all the time leads nowhere fast."* Why were Dottie Sue's days difficult?
15. *"We don't be needin' luck. We be needin' to pray fer God's answer."* Delbert, the lay minister, was reminding the group of the importance of prayer. How can a person develop the practice of prayer in daily matters? What role does prayer play in your everyday life?

Chapter 4

16. What were the surprises Betty Jo encountered after Papa's accident?
17. Had Betty Jo fallen from Aunt Beulah's favor?
18. If you were visiting Henri Landry during his recovery, instead of Brother Tucker, how would you have responded to him?
19. Why do you think Philip Harris is attracted to Betty Jo?
20. *Philippians 4:19* *But my God shall supply all your need according to his riches in glory by Christ Jesus.* Betty Jo was puzzled by this scripture. Were God's people really poor? Tell about a time that God supplied a need for you.

Chapter 5

21. What is the root of Henri Landry's bitterness?
22. What were the pressures Jack Lee faced? How do we *fulfill the law of Christ* by *carrying one another's burdens?* Can a person carry too many burdens?
23. *Matthew 5:45B* *for he maketh his sun to rise on the evil and on the good, and sendeth rain on the just and on the unjust.* Beulah was frustrated that something bad happened to Jack Lee. When something occurs that "is not fair" how do you respond?
24. Dot fumed when Philip confronted her, pointing out the truth. Why? Do you think it was Philip's place to do so?
25. Betty Jo *"focused on the silhouette of a single green leaf as it shimmered, surrounded by a chorus of leaves. It was so different from Big Tree."* What is the symbolism of this passage?

Chapter 6

26. Henri was more cooperative when Betty Jo came in the evening to tend to him. What brought on this change?
27. Why, do you think, had Betty Jo been kept from knowing the circumstances of her birth and her mother's death when Dottie seemed to know many of the details?
28. *"There's no end to these wounds,"* Beulah gently said. *"There kin only be healin.'"* This seems to be a contradiction. What do you think Beulah meant? Is there a situation in your life where wounds remain present? What can bring about healing?
29. *John 8:32* *And ye shall know the truth, and the truth shall make you free.* Dottie Sue used these words of Jesus as motivation to confront the Sheriff. What is the truth we should know? Is truth always freeing?
30. What do you think Sheriff James Roy Davis and Jimmy discussed?

Part II: TRUNK

Chapter 7

31. Why did Henri refuse to give Betty Jo the autoharp?
32. Beulah May mused that marriage is complicated when marrying an outsider. In this story, who are the outsiders and what makes them so?
33. What did Philip have that Betty Jo recognized she didn't have? What do you think Betty Jo has that Philip does not?
34. *Ecclesiastes 4:12* *and a threefold cord is not quickly broken.* What was the source of discontent for the scheduled meetings in Haslam? When, in terms of social groupings, have you seen a *threefold cord* be a bad thing? When is a *threefold cord* a positive thing?
35. Describe the relationship and history between Henri Landry and Jack Lee Thorpe.

Chapter 8

36. Different cultures have varying traditions concerning death. What similarities and differences do you see between your traditions and those described in this chapter?
37. *"Pretending was better than real life."* Why would Betty Jo feel this way?
38. Betty Jo observed the *circles of fellowship* at the wake and recognized that she was outside of those circles. In our lives, what can be done to make the circle bigger to include those who are socially left out?
39. What prompted Henri to visit his granddaughter and give her the autoharp?
40. *John 14:1* *Let not your heart be troubled: ye believe in God, believe also in me.* Beulah, in her grief, lost her song. Have you been through a similar time? What happened that led you to be able to sing once again?

Chapter 9

41. How has Henri changed since the accident? How do you think he will *redeem the time*?
42. Contrast Beulah May's view of goodness with Henri's view of goodness.
43. *2 Corinthians 5:7* *(For we walk by faith, not by sight:)* Beulah quoted this verse at the end of Sunday dinner. What does *walking by faith* mean? In this story, what are examples of characters *walking by faith*?
44. What will be Philip's response to Beulah's unsolicited advice?
45. What was Henri's motivation in getting into a business arrangement with Denny Ron?

Chapter 10

46. ***Philippians 1:6*** *Being confident of this very thing, that he which hath begun a good work in you will perform it until the day of Jesus Christ.* Philip tells Betty Jo that *the Lord is always at His good work.* In this story, how is Betty Jo changing?
47. Why was the encounter with the sheriff at the Mercantile unsettling to Betty Jo?
48. After Betty Jo confronted Aunt Beulah, why did she run to the plank house?
49. *"Her thoughts caught up to her actions."* Tell about a time you acted out of emotion, only to regret it later. If faced with a similar situation today, how would you respond?
50. Read ***Revelation 1:1-5***. What does it mean to be saved?

Part III: BRANCHES

Chapter 11

51. Beulah was worried about Betty Jo's safety and their relationship. *Casting all your care upon Him* came to her mind. Why was it that in times of gladness and times of concern, Beulah would recall scripture?
52. Betty Jo again finds herself in Joaquin Baptist Church after a tragic event. How is her attitude and behavior different from the first time?
53. What do you think is Maisie's story? What was it that Betty Jo recognized in her?
54. ***Isaiah 40:31*** *But they that wait upon the LORD shall renew their strength; they shall mount up with wings as eagles; they shall run, and not be weary; and they shall walk, and not faint.* Why did Beulah May tell Betty Jo that Isaiah 40:31 was for her?
55. *"The thin string that physically connected her to the man she had both hated and loved was severed. The emotional cords, however, tightened with each passing hour."* Can you identify with Betty Jo's feeling? Can there be a physical severing while emotional connection increases?

Chapter 12

56. Why did Betty Jo want to clean out the plank house by herself?
57. What good had the autoharp brought over the years?
58. Why did Betty Jo's mother give her a name unrelated to any relative?
59. Finding the silver necklace prompted Betty Jo to ask Beulah about its history. Beulah concluded by saying that *when yer family, yer forever connected. There's no disownin' yer own.* Do you agree with this statement? Why or why not?
60. ***I Corinthians 13:13*** *And now abideth faith, hope, charity, these three; but the greatest of these is charity.* Can there be love without promise?

Chapter 13

61. What was the reason the Davis men gave for claiming paternity at this time? Do you think there is another motivation?
62. ***Romans 8:28*** *And we know that all things work together for good to them that love God, to them who are the called according to his purpose.* In her prayer, Beulah claimed this promise. Have you ever been involved in a circumstance that was bad, but later you could see how it worked out for good?
63. Jimmy Davis *caught up* with Betty Jo at the mercantile. What made her think twice about that word usage? Why did she feel she had allowed *too many words out her mouth* during that conversation?
64. What did the silver necklaces represent to Beulah? How did she intend to set things right in her family? Is it possible to correct the mistakes of the past?
65. What are Betty Jo's doubts and concerns at this point in the story?

Chapter 14

66. What, do you think, are the *demons of the past* that Dottie Sue is prepared to meet? How does one maintain the balance between leaving the past behind and dealing with unresolved issues?
67. In what way does Betty Jo lack commonality with her peers? Do you think Dottie Sue empathizes with her?
68. What, do you think, is the significance of the picture Jimmy gave to Betty Jo? Why would he give it to her now? Did Betty Jo's secret meeting with him make you nervous?
69. ***II Kings 4:8*** *And it fell on a day, that Elisha passed to Shunem, where was a great woman; and she constrained him to eat bread. And so it was, that as oft as he passed by, he turned in thither to eat bread.* Delbert compared Beulah Thorpe to the Woman of Shunem. Do you think this was a good comparison? Do you know of someone in your experience who would compare?
70. In her emotional turmoil, Betty Jo found herself at the Baptist Church. How did Sister Tucker minister to her? How can we help those who are distraught?

Chapter 15

71. When Dottie Sue confronted Jimmy, what did he say that filled her with understanding? What was that understanding?
72. Why was it difficult for Beulah to accept Betty Jo's decision about school?
73. ***Proverbs 3:5-6*** *Trust in the LORD with all thine heart; and lean not unto thine own understanding. In all thy ways acknowledge him, and he shall direct thy paths.* Do you agree with Dottie's interpretation of this scripture? Why or why not?
74. What things might have come as a cultural shock to Philip? What threat do you think Philip posed to the sheriff?
75. In worship, Betty Jo knew her response to God should be of complete surrender. What was the nature of her struggle to obey? Tell about a time when you were challenged with doing the right thing.

Chapter 16

76. At the baptism, Brother Tucker was in a difficult position. Did he handle it correctly? Why or why not?
77. What do you think the text meant when it said that Beulah May and Maisie Davis *fellowshipped in the sorrow of the unspeakable?*
78. Betty Jo came to understand that her family was *imperfectly beautiful* and that she would have kin of her *own choosing*. What makes family a family?
79. ***Ephesians 6:10-11*** *Finally, my brethren, be strong in the Lord, and in the power of his might. Put on the whole armour of God, that ye may be able to stand against the wiles of the devil.* Tell about a time in your life where a struggle you faced was clearly a spiritual battle.
80. *Love, Himself, was all that could help.* Do you think there are situations and problems where it is beyond the ability of people to help?

Conclusion

81. How did each of the characters change throughout the course of this story? Which character/s truly *fell?*
82. Which character did you identify most with and why?
83. ***Psalm 68:5-6*** *A father of the fatherless, and a judge of the widows, is God in his holy habitation. God setteth the solitary in families: he bringeth out those which are bound with chains: but the rebellious dwell in a dry land.* Reflect on the story of <u>The Fall and the Lift of Love</u>. In what way was this scripture fulfilled in the various characters?

Scriptures
*All Holy Bible scripture quotations, references, and paraphrases
from the King James Version, Public Domain*

Part I

Chapter 1
Proverbs 15:1 A soft answer turneth away wrath: but grievous words stir up anger.
Chapter 2
Hebrews 9:27 And as it is appointed unto men once to die, but after this the judgment:
Chapter 3
Psalm 122:1 I was glad when they said unto me, Let us go into the house of the LORD.

I John 4:7 Beloved, let us love one another: for love is of God; and every one that loveth is born of God, and knoweth God.

Ephesians 3:20 Now unto him that is able to do exceeding abundantly above all that we ask or think, according to the power that worketh in us,
Chapter 4
I Kings 17:9-16 Elijah and the Widow of Zarephath

II Corinthians 6:2 (For he saith, I have heard thee in a time accepted, and in the day of salvation have I succoured thee: behold, now is the accepted time; behold, now is the day of salvation.)

Philippians 4:19 But my God shall supply all your need according to his riches in glory by Christ Jesus.
Chapter 5
Galatians 6:2 Bear ye one another's burdens, and so fulfil the law of Christ.

Matthew 5:45 That ye may be the children of your Father which is in heaven: for he maketh his sun to rise on the evil and on the good, and sendeth rain on the just and on the unjust.

Numbers 6:24-26 The LORD bless thee, and keep thee: The LORD make his face shine upon thee, and be gracious unto thee: The LORD lift up his countenance upon thee, and give thee peace.

Matthew 7: 3 And why beholdest thou the mote that is in thy brother's eye, but considerest not the beam that is in thine own eye?
Chapter 6
Ephesians 5:6 Redeeming the time, because the days are evil.

Colossians 4:5 Walk in wisdom toward them that are without, redeeming the time.

John 8:32 And ye shall know the truth, and the truth shall make you free.

Part II

Chapter 7
Matthew 11:28-30 Come unto me, all ye that labour and are heavy laden, and I will give you rest.
Ecclesiastes 4:12 And if one prevail against him, two shall withstand him; and a threefold cord is not quickly broken.
Matthew 6:9-13 The Lord's Prayer

Chapter 8
John 14:1 Let not your heart be troubled: ye believe in God, believe also in me.

Chapter 9
Psalm 107
Esther 4:14 For if thou altogether holdest thy peace at this time, then shall there enlargement and deliverance arise to the Jews from another place; but thou and thy father's house shall be destroyed: and who knoweth whether thou art come to the kingdom for such a time as this?
Luke 22:42 Saying, Father, if thou be willing, remove this cup from me: nevertheless not my will, but thine, be done
Jeremiah 8:22 Is there no balm in Gilead; is there no physician there? why then is not the health of the daughter of my people recovered?
II Corinthians 5:7 (For we walk by faith, not by sight:)
Psalm 40:1-4 I waited patiently for the LORD; and he inclined unto me, and heard my cry. He brought me up also out of an horrible pit, out of the miry clay, and set my feet upon a rock, and established my goings. And he hath put a new song in my mouth, even praise unto our God: many shall see it, and fear, and shall trust in the LORD. Blessed is that man that maketh the LORD his trust, and respecteth not the proud, nor such as turn aside to lies.

Chapter 10
Philippians 1:6 Being confident of this very thing, that he which hath begun a good work in you will perform it until the day of Jesus Christ:
Revelation 22:1 And he shewed me a pure river of water of life, clear as crystal, proceeding out of the throne of God and of the Lamb.

Part III

Chapter 11
I Peter 5:7 Casting all your care upon him; for he careth for you.
I Corinthians 4:5 Therefore judge nothing before the time, until the Lord come, who both will bring to light the hidden things of darkness, and will make manifest the counsels of the hearts: and then shall every man have praise of God.
John 8:12 Then spake Jesus again unto them, saying, I am the light of the world: he that followeth me shall not walk in darkness, but shall have the light of life.
Matthew 6:34 Take therefore no thought for the morrow: for the morrow shall take thought for the things of itself. Sufficient unto the day is the evil thereof.

Isaiah 40:31 But they that wait upon the LORD shall renew their strength; they shall mount up with wings as eagles; they shall run, and not be weary; and they shall walk, and not faint.

Chapter 13

Psalm 34:8 O taste and see that the LORD is good: blessed is the man that trusteth in him.

Romans 8:28 And we know that all things work together for good to them that love God, to them who are the called according to his purpose.

Mark 2:28 Therefore the Son of man is Lord also of the sabbath.

Chapter 14

II Corinthians 1:3 Blessed be God, even the Father of our Lord Jesus Christ, the Father of mercies, and the God of all comfort;

Esther 4:14 For if thou altogether holdest thy peace at this time, then shall there enlargement and deliverance arise to the Jews from another place; but thou and thy father's house shall be destroyed: and who knoweth whether thou art come to the kingdom for such a time as this?

II Kings 4:8 The Woman of Shunem

11 Corinthians 5:17 Therefore if any man be in Christ, he is a new creature: old things are passed away; behold, all things are become new.

Chapter 15

Luke 19:13 And he called his ten servants, and delivered them ten pounds, and said unto them, Occupy till I come.

Proverbs 3:5-6 Trust in the LORD with all thine heart; and lean not unto thine own understanding. In all thy ways acknowledge him, and he shall direct thy paths.

James 3:1 My brethren, be not many masters, knowing that we shall receive the greater condemnation.

Isaiah 54:12 No weapon that is formed against thee shall prosper; and every tongue that shall rise against thee in judgment thou shalt condemn. This is the heritage of the servants of the LORD, and their righteousness is of me, saith the LORD.

Ephesians 6:12 For we wrestle not against flesh and blood, but against principalities, against powers, against the rulers of the darkness of this world, against spiritual wickedness in high places.

Matthew 19:26 But Jesus beheld them, and said unto them, With men this is impossible; but with God all things are possible.

Chapter 16

Matthew 28:19 Go ye therefore, and teach all nations, baptizing them in the name of the Father, and of the Son, and of the Holy Ghost:

Nehemiah 8:10 ...for the joy of the LORD is your strength.

Galatians 5:22-23 But the fruit of the Spirit is love, joy, peace, longsuffering, gentleness, goodness, faith, meekness, temperance: against such there is no law.

The Book of Job

Ephesians 6:10-11 Finally, my brethren, be strong in the Lord, and in the power of his might. Put on the whole armour of God, that ye may be able to stand against the wiles of the devil.

Songs
All Songs quoted or referenced are from the Public Domain

Part I
Chapter 1: "Down in the Valley." Traditional American Folk Song.
"Love Lifted Me." James Rowe, Howard E Smith. 1912.

Chapter 2 "Dors, Dors P'tit Bébé" (Sleep, Sleep My Little One).
Traditional Cajun Lullaby.

Chapter 3 "Love Lifted Me." James Rowe, Howard E Smith. 1912.

Chapter 4 "The Hallelujah Side." Johnson Oatman, Jr.,
J. Howard Entwisle. 1898

Chapter 5 "Polly Wolly Doodle." Traditional American Folk Song.

Chapter 6 "This World is Not my Home." Anonymous/Unknown.
Arr. Albert E Brumley. 1919

Part II
Chapter 7 "Blessed Assurance." Fanny J. Crosby, Phoebe Knapp. 1873.

Chapter 8 "When We all Get to Heaven." Eliza Hewitt, Emily Wilson.
1898.
"Dors, Dors P'tit Bébé" (Sleep, Sleep My Little One).
Traditional Cajun Lullaby.

Chapter 9 "Blessed Assurance." Fanny J. Crosby, Phoebe Knapp. 1873.
"Love Lifted Me." James Rowe, Howard E Smith. 1912.

Chapter 10 "Down in the Valley." American Folk Song.

Chapter 11 "Joy to the World." Isaac Watts, George F Handel.
"Dors, Dors P'tit Bébé" (Sleep, Sleep My Little One).
Traditional Cajun Lullaby.

Part III
Chapter 13 "Joy to the World." Isaac Watts, George F Handel.

Chapter 15 "We'll Understand It Better." Charles A. Tindley. 1905.
"Doxology" (Praise God from Whom All Blessings Flow).
Thomas Ken. 1674.
"Dixie Land." Dan Emmett. 1859.
"Everybody Ought to Know." Verses: Herbert Buffum.
American Spiritual.

Chapter 16 "Love Lifted Me." James Rowe, Howard E Smith. 1912.

ABOUT THE AUTHOR

Upon completion of a teaching career and after
a ministry of performing southern gospel music,
Debby L Wynkoop
is now weaving stories and crafting poetry.
The Fall and the Lift of Love
is the author's first historical fiction book
for an audience of mature youth and adults.
She is a native of Idaho, who is proud to be the
granddaughter and daughter
of fine East Texan gals.
She lives with her husband, Dave Johnson,
and their cat, Sugar, in Southwest Idaho.

Books by Debby L Wynkoop
Available on Amazon Books

Images About Town from the Poet's View

Children's Books
Blossoms in the Desert
Poetry for Idaho Kids
ABCs of My Faith
Seasonal Adventures

www.ingramcontent.com/pod-product-compliance
Lightning Source LLC
Chambersburg PA
CBHW030157200626
46812CB00017B/2271